That Was a Shiver,
and Other Stories

That Was a Shiver

and Other Stories

James Kelman

CANONGATE

Published in Great Britain in 2017 by Canongate Books Ltd,
14 High Street, Edinburgh EH1 1TE

www.canongate.co.uk

1

British Library Cataloguing-in-Publication Data
A catalogue record for this book is available on
request from the British Library

ISBN 978 1 78689 090 0

Typeset in Bembo by Palimpsest Book Production Ltd,
Falkirk, Stirlingshire

Printed and bound in Great Britain by Clays Ltd, St Ives plc.

for
Gill Coleridge

CONTENTS

OH THE DAYS AHEAD

Andy's hand was on her shoulder and maybe he squeezed a little, but the lower part of his body was against her and he was still hard. He had the boxers on and she wore pants but she still must have felt it, of course she would have and shifted from him. She seemed asleep but maybe not. But her breathing. She was awake. He raised the quilt and settled on his back, arms by his side. He was happy to lie there. Yes he was tired but he would hardly sleep now. That was that, and he had to go to work, sooner or later.

What did it matter? She shifted position, turning into him. Are you awake? she whispered.

Yeah.

Your eyes were closed. I thought you were sleeping

I was concentrating on your face.

Remembering what I looked like?

He turned to her, reached to brush her cheek with his index finger, tracing the cheekbone. The light glinted on her eyes. He leaned to kiss her cheek, his hand on her arm, but she was resistant. He withdrew and settled on his back. You're not good at relaxing, she said.

He didnt reply, then was stretching as far as he could, pushing down as far as he could, feeling a reaction to this at the ankles and over the tops of his feet and lower limbs, stretching out his toes, pushing up his hips. A couple of moments later he changed position, changed it again, then moved onto his side away from her. He was wishing away the erection. His feet had come out from under the duvet so that would help. How could she even think he was sleeping! It was just ludicrous. Did she not bloody

who cares. He was tired; tired and weary and needing to sleep, he really did need to sleep. He had an early start. Why could he not sleep? Surely he was past this stage in physicality for christ sake! Maybe it wasnt a stage. Eternal erections. All these years and still governed by that bloody drive to wherever, who cares. The gap between their bodies was less than ten inches – ten centimetres. That was a reasonable estimate. Definitely not ten inches, but the warmth, her very presence. Did she expect him to ignore that she was there lying beside him? It was stupid.

She really did not want sex.

That is how it was and he had to accept it. He had accepted it. She didnt ask him to keep on the boxers but she kept on her bra and her pants so that was that. By invitation only. He had to keep them on. Although it was his bed!

Mind and body. His mind was willing but his flesh was weak. In principle he did understand. He did. It was just this damn body of his, it seemed unwilling to accept reality. He grinned.

There was a twitch from her side as if she had felt his facial muscles move. Very interesting that she should 'feel' the face muscle but not a full-blown hardon. Life, who cares. But why had she come to bed with him? It was difficult to believe she would, unless – unless what? He had to get used to the idea. And sleep, if he could sleep, he just couldnt sleep. How could he with her there! My god. But would he scream? Do males scream? Of course they do. If not the precedent was his, to be his his his, all his.

The unmachoness. So what, bloody nonsense.

Wearing his shirt too! Ah well. An old one. Did he have new

ones? She chose it. He offered his entire wardrobe! She chose the old shirt, a comfy old effort he should have dumped years ago – although he did like it, a good old shirt, and she chose it! He grinned again. That was typical. How like a woman! Just like so amazing at times how they seem to know certain things!

His bloody neck was sore. She had the big pillow. He only had two on this bed, the good one and the bad one; the bad one was like a handkerchief or something, he would have been as well with nothing at all, but it made it difficult lying on his side. The best way was on his back but he didnt sleep on his back. On his front was difficult because of his nose getting in the way and most of all the lower regions. But even the nose. How could ye forget the nose. The nose aye gets in the way. Lie on yer front and forget about it. Yes but how can one, one cannot fucking forget it, then it pops and blood everywhere. His was a bleeder. Forget noses.

He thought the erection had gone but it hadnt.

Do erections 'go'? Where do they go to? What happens to the unused physicality, unused energy? Is something absorbed? What about the sperm that does not ejaculate, does it just get sort of submerged or kind of thinned out and then

Shut up ya fucking fool.

But it is true that we cannot survive without them but for 99.999% of the time they get in the way, they just get in the way. One might be glad to do without them. Except do what without them?

He was not bothered about not having sex but there was a physical reaction against it. Nor could he ignore her body. He stroked the curve of her shoulder. He wished for a pencil for a go at drawing her shoulders and neck, the hair straggling at the nape. She shifted onto her back and he withdrew his hand. Do you never sleep? she asked.

Her name was Fiona and she was powerful. This had not occurred to him. She came to his bed on the understanding there would be no sex but how could ye take such nonsense at face value? Can women do this? It was just crazy. He was to keep on the boxers. Utter madness. Maybe she regarded them as a kind of chastity belt. Of course these boxers were more like whatever. Where the hell had he bought them anyway? The January sales at Lidl.

How could he go to bed with a woman in the expectation of not having sex? In the name of god. This was not like going to bed with a long-term girlfriend for christ sake they had only met!

Exactly. So why would she have come to bed with him if not on a certain understanding? Jesus christ what time was it anyway!

He must have left his damn watch on the kitchen table or someplace. Usually it was next to the bedside lamp. Probably it was about three o'clock. But it could have been later. There was light but this was early June.

He heard the sound of her breathing; a murmur. Was she sleeping? Maybe she was. Maybe she truly was. He raised himself up onto his elbow to see her, and he could in this particular light and she looked good. Man, she did. She just looked good really, the shape of her shoulders and neck and just her body, her hair and so on, just everything. He kissed her on the nose, softly, his hand to the side of her face, cupping her cheek. Was she beautiful? Actually she was. She seemed to be. He tried to remember her completely. He couldnt: not completely. He entwined her hair with his fingers, twisting it and turning it.

Definitely she was awake. And cleared her throat as if to speak. He whispered, Shh, and started massaging her scalp. He wondered if she was smiling. It felt like she was, but maybe not. She might have been strained. Her eyes were shut. Then they were open again, and maybe she smiled. He stopped the massaging.

I wonder if they all got their taxis, she said. Sometimes they're hard to get at this time of night. Although there's usually plenty around here. How long has yer phone not been working?

He had moved from her and was lying on his back again.

Eh? she said. Has it not been working for a while?

Yeah. He shrugged. No I mean.

Why dont ye get it sorted?

Get what sorted?

Your phone.

I need a new one.

Why dont ye get one then?

I'm waiting for my stocks and shares to come in.

She paused a moment then slapped him on the shoulder. It took him by surprise. Hey, he said, that was sore.

I dont like it when you're sarcastic. She slapped him again, and again it took him by surprise. He was taken aback and it must have shown. But he could see her smile, and whatever it was – maybe that combination, hitting him with a smile on her face – the reaction was immediate god almighty, the proverbial knee getting hit by the proverbial fucking hammer, doi oi oing. From nothing to full, raging bloody hardon. She didnt realise the effect she had, she didnt realise, effect she was having! Christ! He moved suddenly to grip her by the shoulders in a sort of pretend-manner moving onto her as though to pin her down. He leaned to kiss her on the lips his body against her not pressing in but touching the length and she would have noticed how hard he was. She must have. She couldnay not have. That was impossible. His eyes had closed. When he opened them he saw she was studying him. He was a specimen.

She knew the state he was in. He rested back from her, on

7

his elbows. His breathing was harsh and he needed to calm down; he was sick of this, it was like a stupid game. How stupid could it get? The duvet was mainly on her side so he could let his right leg lie outside; help the calming-down process. But this was ridiculous. He felt like saying it to her I mean for fuck sake what age are we at all it's not like we're bloody eighteen years of age! Christ almighty!

Yet maybe she didnt know. Maybe she lacked experience. She had been married to the one guy for years and from what he could gather he was not the most physical of chaps.

What did that mean? Did he not like sex? Did he not notice sex? Was he – what? What on earth did that mean? Not the most physical of chaps? But it wasnt her said that it was him, he thought the words, picking up from her. He had just picked up that her husband wasnt really bothered.

Even how she smiled, there was an uncertainty about her. So apart from him, her ex-husband, apart from him, what males did she know? Some women just married guys that asked them. Maybe she was one. So she didnt really know other guys. She didnt realise they wanted bloody sex all the fucking time jesus christ not all the time but just like these times when they were geared up for it and just like my god lying in bed with a woman ye had just met and was damn beautiful and sexy for christ sake.

Oh god. He really needed to calm down. I'm sorry, he said, I'm just tired.

When d'ye start work?

The back of eight.

I dont work Saturdays, she said.

Lucky you.

She said nothing. Then she yawned.

Want a coffee? he asked.

She looked at him as if he was daft.

8

Or tea?

Do you have any hot chocolate?

Hot chocolate. He laughed.

What's so funny?

Nothing. He grinned. Are ye serious but?

What do ye mean?

Hot chocolate? Ye think I would have hot chocolate?

Pardon?

I did used to have some.

It doesnt matter, she said.

I've got peppermint tea and like eh green tea.

Fiona smiled. Your friends go on nonstop, she said, everybody talking and talking and talking. I thought they would never be quiet. That what-dye-call-him? Him with the ponytail.

Tony.

He plays in a band?

He does, aye . . .

She was looking to hear more but he could not be bothered. Tony was Tony and not really a friend. Well he was a friend, he wasnt a pal. Pals are friends but friends might not be pals.

Andy, she said.

Yeah?

She didnt answer.

What? he said.

Nothing.

So if it was nothing why mention the guy? Tony in some ways was a shit but fair enough; who cares, who cares. She didnt know that. But he was a shit. Especially with women he was a shit, just like women didnt seem to know until it was too bloody late, the guy was just a fucking — whatever, not a friend, well he was a friend, just not a pal. Who cares anyway. Andy was tired. She surely appreciated that. He had stretched out on his back again. What the hell time was it? Maybe there would be no sleep either. He closed his eyes. Maybe he could doze.

She was talking again. He was awful high though wasnt he? Ye would've thought he was on something. He acted like he was.

Andy closed his eyes.

You were high as well, she said.

Pardon?

Ye seemed to be.

I'm no sure what ye mean by 'high'?

Do you play in a band? You yourself, do you play in a band?

No.

You've got that guitar.

Aye well I've got a fishing rod too. Actually I've got two fishing rods. What I mean by that, I dont do any fishing.

She shifted onto her back now and seemed fully awake. He wondered whether to switch on the light. She was gazing at him. Why not? she asked.

He looked at her.

If ye've got two fishing rods?

I only mean I've got two fishing rods and dont go fishing and it's the same with guitars. I've actually got three of the buggers, if ye go in the other room. Plus a keyboard plus a fiddle. I sold my sax.

God . . .

Only kidding. What I mean is because I've got something doesnay mean I am something. I've got guitars but I dont – whatever, I'm not in a band. So to answer yer question: no, I dont play in a band.

Ye dont have to be nasty.

Nasty? I'm not being nasty.

I only asked a question.

I know ye did, sorry.

I thought ye played in a band because of how the blonde woman asked if ye would play when she sang.

Andy stared at her.

I know she asked ye and ye wouldnt, however ye said it, I saw ye shaking yer head. And then she asked him with the ponytail, the old guy.

He wouldnt like ye calling him 'old'.

Well he is. When you wouldnt play she asked him. It would've been nice if ye had played.

Andy nodded.

I thought ye were going to. I've seen her in there before, the blonde woman. I would like to have heard ye. I thought ye would have and ye didnt. It would've been nice. Why didnt ye?

The thing is she was wanting to sing and it didnay matter who played. Well it did, but only in a wee way. She doesnay really care. It's her thing and that's that, whether it was me or somebody else. Anyway, I didnay have my guitar.

He offered ye his. Him with the ponytail. I saw him offering.

Andy sighed.

I saw him.

Yeah well.

Dont be so jaggy.

I'm not.

Yes ye are, ye're edgy. It's hard even to talk to you. Ye just seem to get stressed. I would like to have heard ye play, that's all. I would just like to have heard ye play.

Sorry.

It's not sorry. Ye dont have to say sorry. I dont need to know yer business. Obviously there's something. But I dont care.

There isnt anything.

The way ye're acting.

I didnt know I was acting. It's Barbara ye're talking about.

Fiona lay still. After a moment she said, I dont care. Just obviously there was something the way ye were acting. What about him with the funny hat, the man with the whistle? Is that a real instrument or what? I mean like a real musical instrument?

Of course.

He doesnt play in a band though does he? in a real band, I mean like playing a whistle!

Andy chuckled.

Seriously? It's a real instrument?

Are you kidding?

No.

That's Joe Wylie. Joe Wylie. He plays everything, the pipes, the flute, sax, clarinet, pibroch, the bloody bassoon. Everything.

What he plays them all?

Andy grinned. He carries the whistle in his pocket.

So he can just come out and play?

Exactly.

He sounds like a busker.

Huh! Joe Wylie! Probably he has busked anyway. He's done just about everything else. Some buskers are good ye know.

Have you ever?

What?

Been a busker or been busking? however ye say it, have ye? Have you ever done it?

What?

Been a busker on the street?

Yeah, well.

Have ye!

Once or twice.

Did ye make any money?

Eh . . .

Ye would if it was New York or Paris or someplace. London, there's buskers play down the tube. Imagine it happened here! Fiona chuckled.

It couldnt.

Of course it could.

No it couldnt, not down the subway, they'd get like arrested. The cops would move in. Music's barred in this town.

Dont be silly.

I'm not being silly. It's only in controlled areas. Like everything else. Subways are for going to work and other places of confine-ment. Everything's controlled. The cops and politicians have it sewn up. Just like the rest of society.

But that's everywhere!

I know it's everywhere that's what I'm saying, society, the whole of bloody society, that's Scotland, it's just like . . .

Dont get angry.

I'm no getting angry. We dont have to like it but because it's the same everywhere. I mean god sake.

Dont get so upset.

I'm not.

Yes ye are. I think ye worry too much.

 . . .

Ye shouldnt, she said.

I dont. I just . . . He sighed again. Ye know the song, 'Go Lie Down'?

No.

Andy sang:

> If you dont get angry lie down
> go lie down
> go lie down
> If you dont get angry lie down

yeah just lie down, lie down
you better lie down,
you dont get angry, you lie down

That's nice.

Yeah.

What it means is go away and die. Lying down is the same as dying. If ye dont get angry ye would be as well dead. Least that's how I see it.

You wrote it?

No, god. It's an old blues, a great kind of . . . He paused.

I wish ye had played tonight. Why didnt ye? Eh? They were waiting to see. I saw them. They thought ye were going to. When she asked ye, the blonde woman, they were looking to see, him with the ponytail.

Andy was silent. Eventually he said, Look it's not a big deal. I just didnt want to play, I wasnay like . . . He paused. I just didnt want to.

You write songs as well dont ye?

He shrugged.

So are they all musicians? Your friends? The ones that were there last night? Ye seemed to know them all.

Well not them all.

I just thought it was a bit strange. It looked like ye were going to play and then ye didnt.

He had his eyes open and could see by the shapes that she was looking towards him although she lay on her back. It was too dark to gauge the expression on her face.

I wasnt watching ye, she said, I was at the next table remember. I couldnt help seeing ye.

He shifted side on to her now, raised himself up to rest on his left elbow. I did notice ye, he said.

Eventually.

His chin was resting on his left hand now, he was gazing down at her. Ye were squeezed in at the side – you and yer pal.

Well I wouldnt have gone in by myself. She turned to him. I wouldnt have gone in myself.

Why because ye're a woman?

Of course.

Ye dont get hassle in there but surely?

Dont be silly.

Seriously?

Women always get hassle.

Yeah but no the Scotia I mean I didnay think in there, it's got the reputation for being good like I mean a place where women can go.

Huh.

People say that anyway.

Do they?

So I'm being stupid . . .

Ye're not being stupid it's just there's no such thing as a hassle-free bar. There isnt. Ye're wrong if ye think there is. Ye're wrong. Ye are.

Well . . .

What?

Sorry, it's just the usual like I mean if ye're young and good looking yeah, people – guys – guys will talk to ye and whatever I mean surely?

If I was an old woman I wouldnt get bothered by men?

No what I mean

I think I know what ye mean Andy, so about tonight of course I was with a pal. I wouldnt go into a bar on my own unless I was meeting people. I mean any bar, unless it was same-sex; gay, lesbian.

Andy turned from her and lay on his back, he clasped his

hands behind his head. I know that's most pubs but I didnt know this one as well. Sorry.

Sorry?

Yeah.

Why are you sorry?

No, just . . . I was just I mean it's supposed to have a good reputation for that I mean like just a place where women dont get hassle.

Is that a fact . . . !

. . .

Fiona said, I see ye smiling.

No ye dont.

I do.

Andy kept his hands clasped behind his head but turned a fraction towards her. Fiona had raised herself up on her shoulder, enough to be looking down on him. The light's on yer face, she said.

I was only smiling because of yer cheek: the way ye said, Is that a fact. It's funny. Sarcastic but funny. I'm not being critical. I know I had a few beers tonight.

More than a few.

He smiled.

Honestly.

Well I wasnay that bad!

I didnt think they were going to serve ye. Then yer pal too eyeing me up. Like trying to get off with anybody in that state – God! Come on back to our place we're having a party!

Andy looked at her,

That was what he said, as soon as ye went to the toilet.

Tony?

Him with the ponytail.

Andy shook his head. Sorry.

There's no need you saying sorry. It was him. He wanted me to go outside for a smoke with him.

Huh!

It was like hash he was talking about wasnt it? Was it?

Maybe, I suppose.

Fiona was silent for a time. She had watched for his reaction, then she smiled. That made him smile. It was a certain kind of smile and reminded him of somebody – an old-time film star maybe, whoever that was. But interesting, an interesting smile. Smiles can be interesting. Some anyway. Hers was. People seeing ye in a certain way. That was her, like she knew him. Or thought she did. Really. Kind of comical. His bad points too, as though she knew them and wasnay caring about them either. She had no idea.

Christ. He touched her shoulder and she moved slightly, but away from him, as a reaction, she wasnt stopping him. He traced a line along her upper arm; the outline of her right breast, shadowed. He could have touched it but couldnt. He could have touched as within easy distance easy easy distance, but he couldnt.

Really, she had no idea. If she thought she knew him! What a laugh. Fiona. Christ – but really, she didnt know anything, not a single damn thing.

That bastard Tony. It made ye laugh. A pal? Some pal. As soon as yer back was turned. He was known for it. Guys laughed. Except when it happened to you. A fucking sleaze-bag more like.

What is it? Fiona asked.

Nothing. But he had taken his hand from her shoulder. When? he couldnt remember, the thought of Tony, just so bloody stupid, but dangerous. Tony was a dangerous guy, dangerous because of how he made ye feel, like fucking battering him! Doing time for a guy like that, ye could, it was just stupid. The arrogance!

Then how he saw you. That was the thing too, it was like you were a total fool and didnt see what was happening! Jesus christ!

Yer head's twitching away! said Fiona.

Sorry.

Ye're away thinking.

Yeah. He put his hand to her shoulder again, massaging, gently, then stroking, stroking lightly, was aware of his breathing, now lying on his side in to her: she had turned her back to him but was not resisting his touch and he was aware too of her body, just her bum, the curve of her, the heat! coming from him too, and if he had closed in to her, only centimetres, god. He swallowed saliva.

Fiona murmured, You're thinking about the blonde woman.

What? No I'm not . . . He had stopped stroking but kept his hand on her shoulder. I'm not, he whispered.

It was her you were looking at.

Andy kept his eyes shut. He needed not to be as hard, not to be as hard as this. He put his hand to her shoulder again. I'm not thinking of her at all.

Ye were looking at her. Ye were.

Well

I knew ye were.

I've known her a long time.

I know. Barbara Peters.

Barbara Morrison. Peters is her married name . . . Andy shifted onto his back now but returned his hand onto her shoulder.

Fiona said: I knew the way she asked ye and ye said no, when she asked ye to play, I knew ye knew her, the two of ye, ye knew each other . . . Fiona was still lying on her side facing away from him, but lying very still. Ye dont get many Barbaras nowadays; it's an older name. I had an aunt called it; she was actually my mum's aunt.

Andy's hand rested on her shoulder. She made no attempt to shrug it off. He was not sure what to do but it was uncomfortable lying like this and he shifted back onto his side again and very gently massaged her shoulder.

He couldnt see her face but she could see his. He closed his eyes. After a moment he chuckled.

What? she said.

Sorry, I'm making myself laugh.

What? she said again, and she chuckled.

The way ye said 'the blonde woman', it was like how my granny would have said it. In a very disapproving voice, the blonde woman, as though being blonde was grounds for suspicion.

So I sound like yer granny?

Not at all, I dont mean that.

If ye think I sound like yer granny!

I dont. Of course I dont. It's just like how she used to say things, like how she injected meaning into ordinary words: The blonde woman – dan, di ran dan, my granny would have made it sound like the title of a haunted house horror story. Andy grinned, massaging gently.

Fiona was silent for a while, and she said, I just noticed ye were looking at her.

Well I might have been, I might have been, but I can assure ye of one thing anyway, one thing about Barbara

Dont, dont assure me of anything.

No but

No.

Yeah but

Dont; there's no need.

No I was just

Honestly, I would prefer ye didnt. Really. I dont care. It was only a thing I noticed. Fiona now shifted onto her back, and turned her head to look up at him: Who was it she came with? Him with the ponytail?

No.

Did she come with somebody?

Eh . . .

See!

See what? What do ye mean?

Ye dont even know who she came with!

Who Barbara came with – Ronnie probably. Ronnie was there. Ronnie Craig. Keyboard.

That's what I mean, she comes with a guy but nobody cares.

She's a singer but Fiona.

She wasnt singing when you were watching her.

I've known her a long time.

That was obvious.

But the same with most of the ones there. They're good acquaintances.

Acquaintances and not friends?

Andy sighed. He was now lying on his back, he clasped his hands behind his head. Some are friends, he said, some arent.

She grunted, amused. He glanced at her. She said: You are so predictable, if ye dont mind me saying.

Thanks.

It's because ye're predictable we find ye so funny, so stupid. She raised her hand and patted him on the chest. How many times have ye noticed me? How many times? I'm serious.

What?

How many times have you noticed me? Fiona was staring down at him but he still could not distinguish her face. Maybe she was smiling, he couldnt tell. Her hand was on his chest. He closed his eyes, hardly breathing. She sighed.

Sorry, he said.

You are way out. You really are. Way way out. You think we've only met this one time but ye're wrong. You remember my name, but how long did that take ye?

Her hair was sticking up next to her ear. He wanted to smooth it down, he unclasped his hands and reached to do it, and she allowed it.

How long did it take ye? she said. To remember? Fiona chuckled. She patted him again, her fingers in the hair there on his chest. She continued to look down at him, then turned onto her side facing out, but did not move away. Was she going to sleep? She made some sort of noise in her throat but it was peaceful sounding. Maybe she was going to sleep. Fine if she did. He had his work to go to!

His work.

Strange strange life. He touched her shoulder again then he moved to her and kissed very very slightly the side of her neck almost just like his lips nudging her skin. And she stayed so still he wasnt sure if she had noticed. He edged himself back a little. There was no movement from her but he couldnt stop it now and moved forwards onto her, settling against her, her pants, tight smooth, his cock upright: no, and he parted from her again, his right arm round her, brushing her right nipple with his fingers, through the bra material, he felt it, that kind of beautiful just how . . . christ. He tightened his arm round her, kissed the nape of her neck.

Nothing came from her; not in response. He waited moments. Nothing. He returned onto his back; and one of these trapped situations, having to unfankle the boxers and free his bolls, and that summed it up. That summed his life up. In a way it did. He figured she was angry.

So was he!

Well he wasnt.

But nearly! He nearly was. How come? Yet he felt it. Was he clenching his fists! Maybe he was. He pushed down with his arms, straining, feeling it in his upper arm muscles. He turned onto his side again, facing into her back, just the damn erection. Mind and body, just so so stupid. What happens to the flesh? Flesh is not weak, it just operates at a different remove. Cocks dont relate to minds but to flesh, and it doesnt matter whose. It was like the comedian giving his routine about ordering his dick to lie down. It just doesnt happen. Fiona with her bra and her pants. Yet he was glad, he was glad. So much worse if he had been nude. How the hell would he have coped! Never! Bloody never. She would have been the boss. The total boss! Nude hardons reduced to nothing, fuck all. That wasnay a nightmare, that was like an amazing control game. Thinking 'facial muscles', oh I can feel you smiling. Can ye not feel the hardon then? No. Oh well, strange. Not think so? Not think it is strange? Even just a wee bit! Jesus christ, all he wanted was a sleep, then to get up and go to work.

You are way out, she said, you really are. She waited for him to reply but he was not sure what she was meaning, being way out, but what about, way out about what?

Fiona said, You were surprised I came home with ye. When ye asked me and I said yes, ye were surprised.

Ye didnt say yes. Ye didnt say yes. Andy turned onto his side, and repeated it: Ye didnt say yes.

I said alright.

That's different from yes.

The thing is ye were surprised. You think we've only met this one time but ye're way out; you are way way out. Fiona turned onto her back now and her head inclined towards him. You remembered my name, but how long did it take ye?

What d'ye mean?

Ye didnt remember my name, at first. At first ye didnt.

Well

We met before but ye didnt remember. Ye dont remember now. She chuckled, then added, Ye're better not telling lies.

Telling lies? What about? Why was she saying that. What the hell was she talking about? He didnt know. He truly truly did not know what the hell she was talking about. He said nothing. Because there was nothing to say. He didnt have anything to say. He was not telling any lies. What about? What would he have lied about? There was nothing to lie about so why would he have lied? It was nonsense. This was bloody nonsense. Proverbial stuff, gender stuff, men and women, women and men, christ almighty, just bloody gender and he was sick of it, sometimes, really, he really really was, just go to bed and go to sleep and go to yer fucking work, that was all he wanted, nothing more, nothing nothing more.

Bloody blues, he could sing blues alright, fuck that! It could even make ye smile. Coming to bed in her bra and pants, why not a coat and a pair of shoes, it was just bloody stupid. But thank god he wasnay nude, just thinking about that, if he had been, christ!

Andy shook his head and settled on his back again. Just because ye get sick of it. Ye think of Barbara too, how Barbara used to just like how she played people. It was Fiona too.

Ye were just fucking laughable. Mind and body! Yer body isnt even yours. Stand at attention. She touches you and that is that. You tell yer body, Dont move at all costs! Just stupid. A-ten-shun! Flesh flesh flesh.

Lies! Why did she say that.

That is women. That for him was women. He had no idea. All the stuff behind him – he hadnt told her about that – his life, all the previous crap. He hadnt told her about a damn thing.

Nothing. For all she knew he had a score weans and five bloody ex-wives. And why should he have told her? They had only just met for christ sake.

He listened for her breathing. Obviously she was awake.

I'm not telling any lies, he said. He swallowed saliva. Not because he was lying; he wasnt. It is simply that is what he was doing, swallowing saliva. He didnt have to justify himself. He stared at the hair at the back of her neck, his head now balanced on the palm of his left hand and he raised his other hand, lifted the hair free from her shoulder. But she edged away: only a little but enough, enough.

He lay on his back again. That was him now, that was him now for sure. No more no more, no more McCrimmon. No he didnt play for Barbara, of course he didnt play for Barbara. They could all go and fuck themself. It was the superficiality, he hated that above all. Ye wanted to be honest and straight with people and it didnt work. That bastard Tony who was his pal, supposed to be.

What did it matter, women or whoever? He was out of bed, had swung his legs out and over the edge without thinking, and he stood. It was quite cold and he shoved on his T-shirt. Fiona raised herself up on the bed. A cup of tea, he said, ye fancy?

Ye dont have hot chocolate? I'm joking.

He smiled. Sorry.

You say sorry a lot.

Actually I used to have some ye know, in the cupboard some-place.

Oh you've got a cupboard?

He scratched his head.

Tea's fine, she added.

Ye sure?

Yes.

I definitely did have a tin of hot chocolate. I had Horlicks too. Things vanish in this house. Sometimes they turn up again, sometimes they dont.

Are you cold? she asked.

Me?

Ye're hopping about.

Well it is cold.

Ye look like ye're freezing!

Okay, he said and walked ben the kitchen. He did have central heating but it had the habit of switching itself off. What a facility! It only worked when it wanted to work which was hardly at all nowadays. Past tense, like most everything else.

It was true about things vanishing. It happened with a particular mug he liked. It disappeared then turned up out the blue. He thought of it as an independent wee soul who liked to visit other pieces of crockery. He told his daughter that story. It turned out the only mug was the one telling the tale. He hadnt seen her for a couple of weeks. She was a polite wee girl. He wished she wasnay. He wished she was a harum-scarum, a proper wee kid, one that didnt worry. She worried. At seven years of age. If she wasnay polite he might disappear altogether.

Ach, enough; enough enough.

He made a slice of toast and ate it while making one for Fiona who was delighted when he returned; amazed and delighted. He switched on the light. She was sitting up in bed, had pulled a cardigan over herself. What a smile. A beamer! The way to a woman's heart, he said. He passed her the toast and placed the tea on the floor at the side of the bed.

Thank you!

It's only toast!

The smell alone! When ye were making it, I wondered if it

came from next door! I didnt even think I was hungry! Oh but where's yours?

Mine, I scoffed it, while I was making yours. It's just a wee toaster. It only makes one at a time.

It must be the last of its kind, she said, reaching for her tea.

Yeah, well. He shrugged.

She sipped at the tea, munched on the toast. He grinned. What? she said.

Nothing.

She lifted the last of the toast and put it into her mouth but noticed he was still watching her. What's wrong? she said.

Nothing.

Ye're just standing there watching me. Why arent ye coming into bed?

I'm waiting to put the light out.

You should have a bedside cabinet. It would be useful for putting things on, including a lamp.

I used to have one.

Yer books too, ye could put yer books on it. I know ye're a reader.

Yeah. He smiled again, to which she noticed but made no reference. Another reason why he was standing there! He was waiting for an invitation! How come? It was his bed but he was the guest. Weird. It was an old pair of boxers too. Tried and trusteds; the kind ye wear to yer work, if ye are unlucky enough to have work to go to.

She had finished her toast now.

Ready? he said.

I'm fine, she said. He turned and switched off the light. In bed he faced out the way, away from her. She dropped her cardigan to the floor.

But it was weird. He hadnt been expecting to be in this

situation. Which said much about him and where his head was. At one time he would have dressed for every occasion merely in the off-chance of bumping into a woman. Footloose and fancy-free. He was neither and this was neither.

But what exactly was it? There was nothing between them. She was in his bed but they hadnay slept the gether in the accepted sense: in other words sex, there wasnay any! They were in bed for sleeping purposes only. So that degree of familiarity did not exist between them. Nowhere near it. Not even a prolonged kiss like from her as well as him. She maybe pecked him at one point but not an actual kiss, not a proper one.

But she didnt appear to grasp any of this. She was acting as if they knew each other really well. Christ almighty he had only seen her twice in his life and the time before tonight was only hazy, very hazy, although she had a clearer vision. The truth is he couldnay remember a single damn thing about it. What could he remember? Nothing. He had been drunk. Another fucking night of nothing.

That was him, that was his life. Tonight too. The beautiful Barbara. Bla bla. Just shit, all shit. Humbug and crap nonsense. In three hours' time he would have to go to work. That was the reality. Wage-slavery. All of his hopes and dreams. What was he doing with his life? It was just fucking shit and he was just utterly daft, a mental kind of lunatic, and he would never sleep anyway, what was the damn point of it all? He turned onto his back; it was like nowhere to go; he didnt have any place, and Fiona there. She was looking at him. Why are ye sighing? she said.

I'm not sighing.

Yes ye are. What's wrong?

Nothing's wrong.

She kept looking at him.

You have an inquiring gaze, he said.

She kept looking at him.

But I dont criticise ye for that. Which reminds me. Am I right in saying this, or have I got a faulty memory: before we left the pub – am I dreaming, did you accuse me of having a shocking sense of humour? If so it is a most interesting phenomenon because at one time I fancied myself a comedian. Honest.

I dont like comedians, they think they're smart and they arent. They act like schoolboys most of them. That's what they remind me of, boys from the third year acting big.

Does that include the females? he said and added quickly, But how can ye not like comedians? Although there again . . .

She muttered, Oh God.

Okay?

She sighed.

Now it's you sighing, he said.

Your feet are cold.

Because I was making the tea.

Do ye not have a pair of slippers?

He chuckled.

What's so funny?

The very word itself! Slippers, how it represents an entire way of life, like a whole world. So a whole world of meaning. What it all signifies. Just the word itself; that's what I'm talking about. The way I see it, being a comedian in periods of social abjection is the pinnacle of public achievement. Either a comedian or a sports star. It's only temporary. Once ye pass through this what-dye-call-it doldrumistic phase ye need them, comedians and athletes, football players, then ye start to get musicians after that, artists and writers; then a few years later everybody's fighting for independence. So it's a form of liberation.

You're not a comedian you're a musician.

No I'm not.

Yes you are.

I play music but I'm not a musician. I know musicians, I'm not one.

Yes you are.

No I'm not. He raised his head to see her and their hips touched, their hip bones.

So him with the ponytail, is he one?

Eh . . .

Yer duvet's too wee. Look, she said, clutching the duvet up to her chin, waggling her feet at the bottom. He pushed his arm beneath her shoulders and neck. She allowed it. He let his other hand lie there on the bed. So is he? she said. Tony whatever ye call him. Is she with him now?

Who?

Her, the blonde woman.

I dont know. Maybe. Barbara, yeah, probably she is, I would say, probably.

Mm.

If he had allowed his arm to come right the way round her it would have been touching over her breasts, just below, but nudging them. Maybe she was thinking the same, she shivered. Did she? Slightly. She did. Her head came onto his chest and the twinges again immediate but a great feeling and he wished he was naked, he just felt like that, to do with just being free or something, his body being free, even if he fucking wasnay – stupid thing to say of course he was, of course. Just stupid. He was aye guilty of that, stupidity.

But if she was naked, her tits – boobs, softly, he felt them; she was turned into him slightly and he did. Her hair tickling his face. It tickled very much and affected his nose and his eyes. He didnt mention this in case it went against him. It would not have been a criticism but people take things differently. He had to move. Are ye cold? he said.

No.

Shivering is a reflex action anyway and we cannay be responsible for reflexes. It's not like intentional, like it's an intentional thing. There's all these different parts of the body and if some outside thing happens it just reacts, the body.

Fiona was silent.

Anyway, you will be glad to know I gave up the idea of being a comedian.

You're a musician.

I was too droll. Droll's good but no in Glasgow. Ye get compared to the greats.

The who?

The greats. Chic Murray, if ye've heard of him. Have ye heard of him?

No. Maybe. I dont think so.

Andy shrugged. Ye find it in countries going through a bad patch of inferiority, a kind of mass infantile behaviour. We all suffer from it, like in primary school we're all sitting there and the teacher has to leave the room, so everybody starts farting and burping. The boys do anyway. Maybe girls dont.

I'm not sure what ye're talking about.

Dont they?

What?

Doesnt matter. It's just like a theory I have. Or used to have! You've just shot it down in flames.

Fiona chuckled.

I felt that! Your facial muscles twitched.

I was only wanting to say about countries going through a bad patch, did ye mean the whole country?

Eh . . .

Ye said countries going through a bad patch.

Yeah.

Do ye mean countries?

Sorry, what?

Fiona said, Is it the whole country ye mean or is it like working-class people?

Eh, working-class people, I suppose. Yeah. He raised his head a little to see her face but could only see her hair, until she turned her head and settled her hand on his stomach and nestled into him side on. And she yawned. He was aware of her boobs almost like squashed on the side of his chest, they were squashed and just – fleshy. The shirt she wore was open and her boobs bare against him, she was not wearing a bra. She had taken off her bra and he was hard. He was going to say something, what-ever, whatever it was. She had taken off her bra. Her breasts were squashed in against his chest and felt just – he drew his arm round her more tightly. She eased herself away. Who's the wee girl in the photograph? she said. The one on the wall, standing next to you.

My daughter.

After a moment Fiona said, I knew ye were married. I knew ye were.

Well, divorced. How about you? Do you have any kids?

I knew ye were going to ask that.

Well because . . .

Because ye're nosy.

Andy smiled.

Ye are, she said, ye pretend not to be. She removed from his chest but raised herself, closing her shirt; she sat up with her back to the bed-end, leaving an absence, he was so aware of the absence, of her absence. The warmth of her, from her. Why are ye smiling? she said.

I'm not smiling.

What are ye doing?

Not smiling. A gentleman doesnt smile at a lady.

Fiona reached her hand to the centre of his chest, twirling the hair in her fingers, then pulled out a hair. He reacted with a shriek: Jesus christ what was that! Jesus! That's sore! That's actually sore! It's a sore thing to do.

I know!

I mean really.

Yes.

God.

Coward!

Coward? What do you mean coward? Andy shook his head.

I warned ye about smiling before.

Christ almighty! Pulling a hair out my chest! It was probably the only one I had too! Andy chuckled.

I dont like ye swearing.

Huh.

I dont. Sorry.

Christ almighty isnt swearing.

It's worse than swearing.

What?

It's a lack of respect for people's religion. Fiona glanced at the window. Daylight now, unmistakably. She shivered.

Okay? he said.

Do ye have another duvet?

Duvet, eh, no, sorry, I dont, sorry.

Have ye a spare blanket?

No . . . what are ye cold?

Not so much cold but it's uncomfortable with this one ye have, when it gets dragged over yer legs, the way ye're moving about all the time.

Aw sorry I mean yeah . . . Andy got out of bed and in the lobby he found his big coat then a spare cushion from a chair. She watched his return. He passed her the coat but held onto the cushion and proceeded to plump it up for her. This is an activity known as pummelling, he said, the experts call it 'plumping'. People plump up pillows. Nurses do it. Let him plump up your pillow, they say; plump plump.

Fiona smiled.

If it was a male nurse he would say 'pummel'; let me pummel yer pillow. Know why? Because plump sounds gay and they wouldnt want to sound gay. I'm talking about some.

Fiona was silent.

Only some. Some dont mind at all. Male nurses I mean. Because they are nurses doesnt mean they are gay. Andy frowned. Sorry, he said. Where did all that come from! I'm not anti-gay at all, not even like the slightest slightest. Just some words are amusing. Plumping. It just sounds — I dont know — vulgar. It makes me think of fat people. Plump equals fat.

I'm plump.

Nonsense.

I am.

Nonsense.

I dont care and dont know why ye're going on and on; fat and gay and . . . Fiona shook her head. It's just stupid and prejudiced — fat. It's horrible, just a horrible word.

I didnay mean it like in any sort of . . . I'm not anti-anything. I'm not.

Yer jokes dont work anyway. They dont. I'm sorry, they just dont.

Well, I'm not a comedian, that's for sure.

Ye're a musician. Ye're a musician.

Whatever.

Ye are.

I'm not prejudiced anyway so just I mean like if any of my mates heard this conversation they'd be like who are we talking about here because it wouldnt be me.

Bla bla.

Andy waited by the side of the bed, aware of the cup of tea he had left there. No doubt he would kick it over before the night was over, before the morning was through, before dawn had broken, whatever time it was. But it had broken, the daylight through the window, oh god and work, work work.

The teacher returns to the room and everybody is silent and sitting with their arms folded. But it's all a lie and the teacher knows the teacher knows the teacher always knows.

She was on her side facing away. He needed to say something. He didnt want her thinking anything bad. How come she did because he wasnt like never ever anti-fat, anti-gay, he was not anything like that, racist, that horrible bigotry horrible horrible shit. None of that. Never. He told bad jokes. He told them bad; maybe they were good till he told them, it was him, he made them bad. What else? He talked too much. That was normal he was just normal. She just

something

He needed back to bed; maybe he didnt.

THE
CARTWHEELS
OF LIFE

Kids come stoating in the door like ye werenay there. Oh fuck maybe I've disappeared! That was how ye felt. Ye dont know whether to laugh or get annoyed like how in my day there was a bit of respect for folk about to hit the eternity trail. Us auld-timers I'm talking about. Okay boy meets girl: I know all that, the cartwheels, jigging about in their shorts and skirts; I understand the scenario, sex everywhere and high spirits, great. One allows for that, growing up nowadays: different to the likes of us. Me I should say. I'm speaking for myself. I dont want to use the plural in that way. I'm no trying to talk for everybody and that's how it makes it seem. If it happens it isnay intended, and if I have done it I apologise, it wasnay deliberate. I hate that kind of thing. I'm no wanting to be one of these moaning-faced old bastards that hate weans. And I'm no one. Rest assured. I've got grandkids, and I love them. But I'm no goni keep my mouth shut if things are wrong and nowadays they are wrong. Ye could start with the 'us', using the plural in that sense. That is worse than a bad habit, it is a misguided confusion and it only spreads mental disarray. 'We' this and 'we' that. Everybody is at it, from top to bottom, all as bad as one another, all falling for the propaganda. My parents were the worst, and that's going back, my maw's been deid thirty years. My da? well, who knows. That's another story. But begin from them, and it's the education system. Which is obvious. Nothing new about that. Fine, so we all know where the blame lies but so what, if naybody does fuck all. And they dont. Onwards in ignorance. The cartwheels, the shorts and the short skirts: know what I'm talking about. Young folk aye, but they're no weans, aw flashing their kit. Who cares? And too easy to blame the system. As a kid myself I was a dunce. Inside anyway, if I wasnay one on the outside. The kind of boy that gets lost in the stream. I wasnay even the class clown. That was a pal of mine – Hughie Montgomery; Hughie died twenty years ago. It was a blow to us all. I miss him. It was something to do with community. That was it in the auld days. Weans nowadays know nothing about that. Ye feel sorry for them. Ye see them going about, ye just feel sorry for them, stoating in with all their stupidities. Ye think all sorts when ye see them. They dont seem to worry about stuff. No like how we worried. Ye see them dancing, just dancing; good-looking wee lasses. The boys too. They're all nice to look at; young folk doing their jigs and polkas, legs flashing; it cheers ye up on a dull day. Nay thoughts of changing the world. No like us, revolution here, revolution there. Nowadays they dont worry about that kind of thing. Only each other, they just go with each other. They dont care about adults. What about adults? Ye want to ask them. Fuck the adults. Reminding them they are going to be adults themselves, they just look at ye. Daft auld bastard. Although some of it could be left for the classroom. That is my opinion. No that we ever got cartwheels. No me anyway. I couldnay do a cartwheel for love nor money. I couldnay. I tried to try it and couldnay. I had this fear of banging my heid on the grun. A cartwheel but what is a cartwheel? Ye spin round in a tight circle, like a somersault. Maybe it is a 'somersault'. I'm no sure the difference. Did I ever? Maybe I didnay. I thought I did. What I do know is I couldnay do it. And either ye can or ye cannay. There is nay inbetween. Like standing on yer hands. Ye do it or ye dont. Naybody does

it for ye. Ye jump to it: allez oop. Nowadays they're all at it. Ye
score a goal and that's that; ower ye go. It makes life look simple
too and that's the problem. Because life isnay simple. Ye think it
is and it isnay. No matter what they tell ye. I'm talking the
propaganda. Ye make plans. I did. Same as everybody. All us
anyway. Talking my generation, people try to put ye down.

Stopped in my tracks. That's the song. Dont try to think what
we all say. It doesnay work anyway. People die, they drop off;
they fall away. One minute ye're all there, the next ye're gone.
Where did ye go? One day ye notice: Where's Hughie? I havenay
seen Hughie for a while. He's deid. Hughie? Aye. Hughie's deid?
Fuck sake. That was a blow but Hughie, drapping deid like that.
Standing outside the supermarket and ower he went. Talking
best mates me and him. The rest of us keep going. Me anyway.
The wife too. She liked Hughie. He made her laugh. He had
that knack.

Naybody can plan simplicity. It doesnay matter how hard ye
try. As hard as ye like. She feels the same, the wife. I telled her,
They're just young people I says. They're no that young says she,
with all their dancing and jiggling about, all shaking this and
that, breasts and bollocks, shouting and bawling. That's just physicalities I says. Their breathing too I says, that is a physicality,
listen a minute and ye'll hear. It's laboured; their breathing's
laboured. I noticed that. That was weird. I found it creepy. Jigs
and polkas. I used to like jigs and polkas, she said, the wife, and
she shook her head at me in that auld way she used to do,
looking to see who else was there, if anybody was and if they
were were they listening. People listen. She hated that, she was
a very private person, just honest privacy for honest stuff. Some
want privacy for shady stuff. That wasnay her. She just hated
nosy people. I didnay see anybody listening but that didnay mean
they werenay. They might have been. Maybe they were there,

maybe they were listening, and looking. People do that. People close to ye as well, wherever they are, ghosts flitting about. Ye keep quiet, thinking about other stuff, how it used to be when people were all there, like whoever, the wife, Hughie, my maw and da – except him, forget him, waste of fucking space my da, wherever he is, wherever he was: wherever he went; fuck knows where he went, cowardly bastard. Ye think of that 'life is plural' crap. It doesnay work for all ages, not like with generations. Ye are aye in a zoo. Folk like us. Other yins are invisible. If that suits them then fuck them, that is their choice. Zoos and invisibility. I prefer weans anyway, they dont see ye, too engrossed in their own physicalities – ye could even say spiritualities because of how they are in their own head, their own mind; in their own mind in their own body. And it makes ye shiver. Me anyway. The way they dont see anybody. Is that courage? Am I seeing courage? Or stupidity? Are they just deaf, dumb and blind, and without a brain? Ye could be standing there and they would barge their way past. They knock ye ower. I kept out the road. No the wife. Sterner stuff. Ye worried about her. She was never there. No when ye needed her. Where did she go? She disappeared. How come? It was creepy.

Plus the stuff needing to get done. Who did that? I didnay. She did, she just went away and that was that, she did it. Whatever. If it needed doing. I didnay notice. I should have but I didnay. It was like I had forgotten how. I just seemed to go about, and then what, mishaps. Shapes dotted about.

Ye try jigs and polkas. Not on yer tod; ye wouldnay manage that. We all need partners. Me too. Mates. Mine was Hughie Morrison. Hughie died. I miss him. All ye see is them stoating about, through the door in they come, breasts and bollocks, there ye are and ower ye go. Okay but keep it to yourself. Ye want to pretend. Dont. It cannay be helped so it doesnay matter. If it cannay be helped it cannay be helped. Ye keep it to yerself. Yourself, myself, us alone. Nay whispering. I hate that whispering. Whose are the voices, all the voices. Inside my mind it is like tattooed. I was doomed but naybody telled me. On I ploughed. In a golden glaze. I think of that. Golden glaze? What does it mean except it is good. We say these things. What are they? Do they have a meaning? Ye think of a nice malt. I do anyway. Slàinte mhath. People think we know but we dont. The weans understand that. They dont hear us mouthing. Yellow cocoon. What is that? In a yellow cocoon. Is that death? Golden glaze, yellow cocoon. Golden glaze good, yellow cocoon bad.

We dont need no intoxication, talking about my g g generation. The weans make their own, skipping to Maloo, wherever that is. They will dance and they will sing. Balls stoat. So do people. Some are doomed to fail. I saw young ones in the statuesque position. Eastern idols. They reminded me of that: one boy and one lassie. Two in one. So wrapped roundabout one another they were inside as well as out. Snakes and tails, a snake swallowing its own tail. The boy might be up the lassie, her wriggling and him pushing. She would know, the wife. She would look and say, Oh I know what he's meaning. He is meaning us, that is like me and him. That was us two. Talking me and him, me and him isnay plural, no a woman and a man; we are two separates coming the gether. Oh my, ye see them in shorts and short skirts. See their arms: folded stiffly. Why would that be? Balletic. That was them, that was their attitude. Boys and lassies the gether, that was them; that was them dancing, it was their dance.

I apologise. We are all individuals. An individual is a one and only. We do our handstands and cartwheels but this does not carry us, does not lift us o'er, soaring. We stay on the outside.

That was how they danced. They put on their show. They did that then disappeared. Weans do that. That is what they do.

Dont rely on weans. They leave too. Ye sit there and that is you; ye look for the wife, where is she? ye dont see her. Hughie? Where's Hughie? Next is the weans. In they come through the door, that is what they do, not knowing the ground is hallowed. It is ours. We make it hallowed. We put ourselves into it. Our spirits and all everything and the rest that goes between us. Everything that is and has gone, that went between us.

In seeing them we reach the courage and it is maybe our courage. We dont fool them so not wurselves either. Not anybody. We are not trying to fool anybody. Me too. I would never, not myself. There isnay a tomorrow, what ye mean by tomorrow, there isnay one. It might be high up and you looking down. If this is what ye believe. Gardens of Eden and garlands of leaves. Grapes. Where are the beautiful maidens? Hughie used to say that. Where are the beautiful maidens? There they are there, look at them dance look at them sing. The wife too, laughing, how she laughed, she had that laugh and I try to reach it, so if I find it, if I do, I think I will.

CLINGING ON

It occurred to me I was awake. From here was difficult. I had to remind myself that the 'that' was absent and its significance, its significance, the 'absence' or non-existence, or negation, and to piece together, or distinguish the several parts. In normal, or regular – I speak of the day-to-day – discourse or communication the sentence would have written as two part comprising two clauses: 'It occurred to me that I was awake.' A writer of prose might well have used a 'that' and therefore lost the meaning for the second clause 'that I was awake' slips into a past, or simply different, time zone. Whereas a poet might have written, or expressed the sentence separated by line-spacing, thus:

It occurred to me
I was awake.

Finer prose-writers are wary of making use of the poet's devices. They do so, but cautiously. What is clearer now is the separation between the two clauses is not just ambiguous but offers a minimum two meanings and these may be conjoined principal statements: 'It occurred to me' and 'I was awake'. And might be expressed, or written, 'It occurred to me (I was awake).' The difficulty is the use of brackets suggesting a banality which amounts not to tautology but, upon examination, of one statement the other may be found. Nought can occur if one is asleep. If the act of occurrence has occurred then certainly one is awake.

Following this I can express it thus: 'I was awake; this realisation had taken hold of me' and, the corollary, that I might be expressed as a sentence; if so the use of the term 'might' is the key to the evaporation of the space between us (me and reality). From here it follows that I may or may not be so expressed. I was aware of that. Oh God.

THIS HAS NO TITLE

What is escape is not so much escape as the unplanned. My life had reached a point, deteriorated to the point, been arrested prior to this, this point, utter disintegration. The desire for death is desire and desire is activity. I had avoided it in other words, where escape is not avoidance, and was looking for a why, why why why.

Get a grip of your emotions!

This was a scream. Sitting on a bus too, my god, a bus, I was on an actual bus journey. Other people dont have these problems. How do I know! Can I get inside their head, their brain, their fuck sake what

Everybody does. In one way or another they do. The whole of humanity. I was sitting there, returning home, on a bus, the bus, my bus, and the wife was waiting. Where had I been!

We can only return. I knew that. I had no desires, expected none, was over the worst, all of it. Equilibrium obtained, he said with relish. Having returned, returning. Before returning one has to have returned.

What did she think what would she say?

But what did I see was the real question. Okay, it was night-time; nighttime is the righttime. Were it daytime, oh god things would have been visible. As it was, no. Immaterial reality. God with a capital letter. Not even the moon. Fucking nothing. Inside the bus was different. I preferred inside. Persons are good. I watched the woman in front, the back of her head, neck, and shoulders; her hair straggling over her red coat. Long dark hairs, unbrushed, although she couldnt, couldnt have brushed them, had she wanted, she would not have been able to brush them, tidying them so to speak. I could have, could have straightened them, reached to her. But she would not have wanted me to do that. I would have done it for her. Women are, and we, we males

My wife sometimes

forget it.

Others avoid touching, personal data concerning 'the body'; bodies, bodily functionings, meat and blood and bones; one exercises the cleaver, the chopper, to do with bodies, I never minded that; others may. I was always good, having the liking, for people's bodies and could always touch them and would have been good in that type of job. Instead it wasnt, was not to be.

I hated stores most of all. Stores. I was always too cold, too cold. Or hot. I was hot too! I was. Discomfort, discomforted. Why was that? Discomfited. That was stores for you. And you didnt see persons you liked. Just persons you had to see and if women came down from the office they always went in to see the storesclerk. We used to smile and be friendly and they smiled back but they never stopped to say hullo: hullo. I envied them walking about, women from the office, and girls, their shapes; girls have shapes, taking their messages to people, I would have taken a message, in itself this would have been the message, its delivery; give it to me, I shall take it, execute the charge. I would have liked such a position.

The way of the world. Had I been female I would have found more suitable employment.

Women's positions suited me better. Women are good at touching. But I was born a male. We are born into the world and the few choices we have are determined by that.

The busdriver was angry. I would have driven the bus better. I dont think he was good. He pressed too easily on the brake pedal and people were hurled this way and that. Elderly people too, and their bodies, fragility, wrists and joints and so easily damaged, bruised limbs, the limbs of elderly people, bone diseases. This man was not simply pressing the pedal he was kicking and booting it. No wonder the passengers didnt like him. And they didnt, they certainly did not like this man. Perhaps too he was racist and was annoyed because persons foreign to him were on the bus; many foreign persons, and languages. Their homes were damaged.

I think of places and not countries. Countries are for rich people, their determination, the freedom to accumulate, building their moats and defence arsenals.

Then the man coming along the aisle, a big heavy fellow, he sat down next to me. I knew he would. I had made the space. He noticed I had and nearly smiled, just how he looked around the eyes like it was almost a smile and hoped I would notice it. A recognition of the other's humanity. There would be this between us. Otherwise he would not have smiled, not as an outer expression; but I was very conscious of his large body, a squeezing-in, squeezing-in. He was a plump man.

Had this been a revolutionary situation.

People dump their bags and their coats on the spare seat next to them to stop folk sitting down, in case their bodies 'touch'. I make space for them. I like to see them there and think alongside with them. They make thoughts go in a different way. So we are in the world together. But why are they so large, the fleshiness, so all fleshy? When our first child was a baby she had rolls of blubber on the upper thighs. I cleaned the diahorrea, sluicing between the rolls, how red the skin, how sore it must have been yet she bore it in wonder.

The big guy resembled a murdered victim. One knows the signs, one comes to recognise them. His profile was strange. He looked around when he sat down, almost timidly. He was used to being watched. Persons stared. He knew this also. Were he to glance without warning, rabbits in headlights, staring, transfixed. They would have been. Had he glanced round he would have seen such persons, had he been quick, these fellow travellers.

We journey not as one.

A human being who sits beside me, looks at the same things and sees them so that for one split second we might experience the same thoughts. Then if the whole bus, if everybody, all sitting there, if something happens outside to interrupt everybody in their own thoughts to suddenly look at the same thing, and see it, for that split second.

I was wrong to say he resembled a murdered victim. I jumped to conclusion. My wife rightly pilloried me for this.

There are times I believed myself on the wrong bus, as if it were the wrong country. Maybe I stepped on a bus in a different dimension. In this dimension no one arrives at a destination, round and round I go until then I am dumped back where I started, legs wobbly and my mind, wherever it has been.

At least I could look at them, listen to them, see their faces. Persons in their own dreams. Those dreams about one another.

Important issues arise from that. We have to consider them. We have to. Me too. Even though tired, I was tired, very very, so tired. A true and authentic exhaustion. Although I once believed this kind of exhaustion begins from the intellect and must begin from the intellect. But perhaps not, this one anyway; it doesnt.

We can have this case and that case and this one had laid me out. I didnt think I could rise from the seat. Perhaps the big heavy fellow would help. But was it my stop? Outside the night was a block of black paint without a single shard of light, not one. He could hold my arm and pull me up out my seat. But could I ask him. Yes. Of course I could. I would. He was staring away to the front of the bus, watching the driver. The driver was a sorry individual and all knew that he was. I was sorry for persons like him; typically I pitied them. But not this night; this was not a typical night. I wished the busdriver would stop behaving so badly. If

It applies to the mind, if the mind

conditional thoughts

Such is physical. I was unable to move. It wasnt the brain telling me something it was my body. Brains do not talk. Bodies do not listen. My brain was powerless. It was part of my body and could not be otherwise. I asked my daughter 'where does the thinking take place?' She said, 'Everywhere.'

Ethereality. In political or campaigning work the condition has a name, we call it burn-out. It is a good word for a bad condition. It stops us and we can no longer, can no longer

So that even people and persons of whom we may wish not

I can say we, and I am glad I said we. We call it burn-out. Ones who speak about burn-out with personal authority know more is meant than mind and body. This is because we embrace the emotional and what in older terminology is called 'the passions'. So it isnt just mind and body.

What are the passions? What else but the qualities of humanity. Who are we and what are we. We persons are human beings. Such are our qualities, we are the summation. Yet they may leave us. The qualities of humanity identify

This big guy, I mean, for example. It had become difficult for me to move. I considered moving. His left thigh jammed me down, to get out the seat how to get out the seat, if it was my stop I could not get out the seat and would be my stop, and to press the button, reaching the button, I would press the button.

The qualities of humanity identify us and one difficult truth is how those too might disappear. Not forever. Not necessarily. It is true that for some persons they do. They never return, they are wrecks. We see them beached.

The woman sitting in front of myself past her stop. I knew she was. This was an effect of the long dark hair that I so loved to brush, straggling the collar of her red coat. I would offer support. I would lean to her and whisper not to worry, come the terminus and I would be there for her. I would never abandon her. It is the expectation of humanity. I never would abandon her, nor indeed the big fellow.

Persons are vessels, having emptied, become washed-up. They are unable to lift themselves, raise themselves to dry out. The sap in the body evaporates, breath dying, their very breath.

Persons dragging themselves across the sand toward the river and that quick flow of water, getting themselves close enough that the pull of the current might operate on them too, and why not, why not. I saw them cross the sand. They attempt this and I was glad to see it. I call this 'activity'. We watch the healthy, fit and strong. We notice their limbs threshing, tongues lolling. That is not healthy. Persons gasping, indicative of what is to come, the want of oxygen, them requiring more, a wee bit more, a wee wee bit. Those within the current pull, pull. Ahead is the sea, if only they can drag themselves, moving, and so forward, moving forward, to drag themselves, if they can. But there is the lack, it is our lack, that weariness, overwhelming, it is, enveloping us, how can we move, be expected to move, we are always expected to move and we cannot cannot do it. We cannot move. Even us, if we are returning. And that was me, supposedly, on this bus and the bridge over the river. The woman in the red coat and the long dark hair. If this is returning. I dont think it is. I wouldnt think we can return. Perhaps never. Water is infinite and so are we. Only we become stranded. Fit and healthy, mind and body, missing something, for between these two is an absence and it is this absence which we cannot name, cannot name if I could but I could not and it was this, this is where it began. I was without it, and knew that I was, and without it there is nothing.

The big fellow was self-conscious. I was aware of his flesh. I smiled. Do you mind, I have something to say.

Pardon? he said.

Look around, look at the faces and bodies, the intelligences. I see elderly folk spin like tops.

I dont know what you're talking about, he said.

Are you sure about that?

The man frowned. I smiled. Listen to me, I said, individuals who suffer or grasp fully the nature of burn-out rarely commit murder and do you know why?

But that word 'rarely' is wrong, completely wrong. I mean never, never never never, never never ever ever ever do they commit murder for that understanding implies a unity of the qualities, and murder cannot surmount unity, it can never do that. For that is to end, that is inserting an end, that is putting an end to it and how can that be, it cannot be because unity because unity, including the end.

People must only be destroyed.

The big guy, the heavy fellow, the man sitting next to me; I smiled because I knew it already. He would rise from beside me and I would touch the coldness his absence would bring. I did. He struggled along the aisle. He did not look back. He must have wondered what I was doing, was I following? He may have been fearful. When I communicate thus the lieges are so.

I see faces in profile. I look at them. Human beings. I might shiver. Certainly one shivers. In their own dreams, uniquely singular dreams, inhuman dreams, as anything uniquely singular must be. They stagger along.

The bus stops. The big fellow. The busdriver allows him an extra five seconds: one, two, three, four, five. He alights safely.

This returning, to have returned, one more time, picking oneself up, up off the floor, a remnant of strength, continuing the struggle, enduring. That was him. Every day of his life, picking himself up and staggering along; lifting himself up, easing himself along. His wife at the door: 'You made it?' 'Yes.' 'Well done.'

Movement alone, ourselves alone. Support is rarely forthcoming. Those closest to us are ill-equipped. They know nothing of escape. Yet each of us has the need.

always returning, attempting to, dragging ourselves. What is our condition? We cannot recognise our condition.

First the understanding. Unplanned events relax us. Moments of calm are vital. The calm allows us to remain in the prime, the prime, and to recognise what it means, if this be a moment. We use the bus. We travel to a destination. A bus is community.

Persons escape to a destination. They hold out their hands. They do not smile. They cannot be distinguished easily. They were in and they were out. I could be amongst them. And our collective head! nodding, aware that we are.

I had to turn my own head, I was needing to cry out. It was a need I could not perform. Needs have a requirement, implementation. This need I could not implement, which to me was a sign, just like the head-nodding was a sign. I saw it in others. I say 'head', thinking of the back of the head but is it the chin? the effort in holding aloft the head, the skull. Skulls are heavy. We hold them aloft, we succeed for as long as we live. I saw the head of the woman in front, how it too nodded, it too. It disturbed the hairs on the back of her neck causing their collision.

Hairs that collide.

Life is a function of that, that success, that we can hold up our heads. And what we discover is banality.

The poor busdriver and his stupidity. Persons know it. Individuals do not hide from the truth. Some shield the truth. If it is not an easy truth. Persons have no desire to realise this truth. It is a difficult reality. They shield it from others. And those who recognise their condition for what it is they will not lead people toward an understanding lest they themselves suffer. This happens, it is their expectation. It is too late. Already it has happened. Already they have suffered. Understanding derives from that. We talk about truth being conditional, but more precisely, it derives from a condition.

I saw out the window now. I stopped it. I do not like staring. I looked around me, seeing persons in their various stages, and their agitation. The woman in the red coat whose lips moved. I looked and saw and I know that they moved, her eyelids flickering. Was she praying? What was in her mind? The words of a song? Part song of a song? She had heard me speak to the man. There is a phrase 'nineteen to the dozen'. Was she about to bite a fingernail? If so whose? Hands come reaching.

One fingernail. A hand reaches from below. It could have been mine.

Who could stop such a hand?

My jaw ached; I had been smiling. That sense of futility. We persons, and doing our best. I, therefore, was glad to be on this bus, to be returning alongside them,

and then

THE STATE OF ELIXIRISM

Near the hut where I slept that night there was a brick-built barn. A tap fixed into the wall supplied drinking water. I drank then washed, collected a certain bag of possessions and departed swiftly, hoofing it along a narrow winding road banked by thick bushes and occasional small woods designed that the mansions and castles of superior persons be concealed from the gaze of the yokelled minionry of whom I was one, yea yea yea; three times wit' the yea. A bird whistled. I answered the call. My answer went unheeded. Unheeded! Hey Mister Bird, why dont you fuck yourself! I looked to find this culprit with a view to killing it stone dead, and partaking of breakfast, instead discovering a lane. One cannot eat a lane and I was fucking hungry man I was fucking hungry. Pulling out the feathers, one pulls out the feathers. The hunger affects one. Such that pain, more of a discomfort, the stomach kind of – that like – what kind of pain is that? ach well who knows, one walks, though the road be weary. Down this lane and beyond a cluster of white-washed cottages a sudden flash signified a mirror, positioned that drivers might identify danger before exiting the blind-spot driveway. I was blinded a moment and blundered into a ditch

even blundering, what an act! I blundered. So human, so human. I am a human he screamed, prior to choking on his tongue, mistaking it for a slab of ox liver

where I spied a bottle of strong cider. A spectacular but by no means extraordinary turn of events: I once found two bottles of a not-inferior fortified wine.

But strong cider?

Nice.

I twisted open the cork and swigged, swigged and again swigged. Le cidre le cidre 'twas elixiric. I sat on the bank of the ditch. Whew. Man, but what a hit. Really, fuck, wow; the insides exalteth.

Prior to then my state had been somnambulistic, barely considering my life, not as a retrospective concern but as to how good it had become. It had become good. Really. This was incontrovertible, not given that one starves but as an effect of it.

I had to grin, sitting there on the grassy bank, the dampness a reminder. My bum is damp! ergo sum.

This area was devoid of lushgris which is my only name for these God-bestowed long stalks of grass that one tugs individually, and out each comes, the lower ends so so juicy.

I continued along the lane. Soon I found myself returned onto the narrow, winding road, pausing now and again for a swig of le stoof. How had that happened? This was magic man, fucking magic. The experience. Yea, and thrice yea.

Yet a gap existed somewhere or other at the back of my mind while also a developing anticipation of finding a place for a genuine sleep, one of lying-down proportions. I refer here, for sociological purposes, to the notion of *phased sleep*. We have singular sleeps, magical sleeps, natural sleeps and honest sleeps, fitful sleeps, and false sleeps. A genuine sleep is one of lying-down proportions, and I stand by that. And when one refers to 'finding a place' one, in general, refers to *the* place. There is only one. This is located, perhaps, on the grassy bank of a little fortified stream sited providentially for the weary wayfarer.

A strange land. Once upon a time I was familiar here, a

familiar, familiar here and within. I needed a seat, oh God, a seat is equal to, is equal

The hedge at the side of the road had become less big and less thick while the tarred surface of the road softened beneath the strong sun, the smell reminding me of childhood days in cramped city streets. My feet had become hot, hot, very very hot and I had to sit quickly, again by the ditch, unloosening the laces and taking off my boots. Bare feet. I massaged my toes, Oh God in Whose Existence I do so believe. All of this. Existence. In toto. Conveyed by a sigh. Serenity has a place here, finds its niche.

I walked a few paces and entered a bower. Here were trees but sun rays entered. I had by then taken off my T-shirt and brought out the bottle. I sat down on the good earth and swigged the last of le cidre.

Oh.

The sounds of the country, the silences too, and the fragrance. I became aware of one sound, similar to the slow movement of a stream and turning to peer through the near bush I saw its glint a hundred yards off in a gully, the sun on the ripples, mild ripples. I gathered the empty bottle and stuff into the bag, knotted the laces of the boots together round my neck, and walked towards the gully. On the bank of the stream I spread the contents of my bag on the grass, awarding each article its own space. I was pleased and made to do something, whatever it was, maybe just sit down beside them and examine them or something, I dont really know, my stomach seemed to have risen, the internal diaphanous bag, the cider gurgling, bubbles up further, the gullet. Oh dear. Now I lay me down to sleep.

I did indeed, I lay myself down closing my eyes but spun off someplace and quickly reopened them. The spinning resumed. I braved it out, clinging on

The sense of late summer, a peaceful quality, days yet to come. Raising myself up, lying on my front, staring into the water. It was deep in places. Clear brackeny water; pebbles and rocks on the bottom, weeds moving gently in the current. So there was a current; these waters were not stagnant. Obviously I had to go in. There was no question about that. I needed to move within the water, whether to swim or not was irrelevant, I just had to walk in it, stand still in it. I picked a dozen of the juiciest docken leaves and laid them along the bank. I could use them instead of soap because of course I needed to wash, and seeing my feet, my toes in sore need of a wash, not just the feet man I was a smelly bastard, the undersides of my arms — what my granny called 'tidemarks', Get rid of these tidemarks son, you will have to, sooner or later, later. Life's tidemarks, marks of the tide, of life itself. Life life life. Yet the undersides of these arms of mine! More than tidemarks. Dirty white streaks. Leftovers from my last job. What had that been? Jesus! What the hell was it? My last job! I had had to leave in a rush the day before yesterday, two days before yesterday, or was it three? Through no fault of my own it might be said, given one's temper can be frayed, frayed and these gaffers, managers and foremen. Farms may be factories, but I aint no fucking chicken.

Who cares.

I drapt the jeans and stepped to the edge, dipped in the right side toes. Freezing cold water. I submerged a foot. This foot, old pal of mine, I submerged it, seeing the hairs on my lower leg rise in protest. Old pal or not this gnarled extremity required the cold water treatment. I forced the foot down onto a flat rock amid the pebbly bottom then stepped in the other. The water rose to that knuckly bone beneath the knee. Cold, yes; freezing? I do not know except there was little feeling in these lower limbs of mine and the feet could have been cut and leaking blood, for all I knew, piranha too, plentiful in the land of Angles. These feet were numb and deadly white in colour. Too cold for comfort this water. I returned to the grassy bank, pulled on the jeans and sat, using the docken leaves on my feet, pressing the sap into them. I stretched out on the grass. I am a vegetable. Sap or blood. The sun had been hidden by a cloud of many layers but the last of these evaporated. I watched the sun revealed. The heat from it was quite amazing. I got an erection immediately in a most natural manner. The vegetable aspect of one's body. I sat up. This was no time for erections. Yet it maintained itself in spite of certain mental efforts. 'Think of churches.' Who gave such advice? Unless I dreamt it.

Guzzy, is there a word 'guzzy'?

When I wakened

Thus had I dozed.

Was the heat greater now? Yes. Past midday too, and the sweat on my body! I slid down to the water's edge and onto my hunkers, resting there. I submerged my hands, my arms, ohhhh breathe in breathe in. I could sluice the water up under my oxters, over my shoulders, onto my chest, I cleansed my face and neck. My eyes closed; my eyes had closed. I was crouched there and motionless I was motionless I must have been motionless, but then gazing at the water, the lady's reflection, my eyes no longer closed. She was sitting on the other side of the stream, close by clumps of ferns, this lady. The bank rose higher here and the line of the stream slanted strangely that almost she lay out of my field of vision and may have assumed I did not see her. A stately and majestic country home or castle was located in the immediate vicinity. 'Twas her abode. 'Twas my conviction, wearing a summer dress of a kind favoured by all, having two little thin straps across the shoulders, Oh my Lady. Those straps may be thin but but for them the dress would collapse onto the ground, falling or crumpling in a heap at her feet and these feet might step out of such a garment. She was sitting with her knees raised, her elbows resting upon them, hands cupping her chin. And I did see her, truly I did and now of course pretending that I had not and again dropped my jeans, dipped both feet into the water until touching the pebbles, then I rose, pushing myself up from the bank. The water was cold and necessarily so, creeping over my knees, but not so cold as before; I stared into the water, concentrating on this, and waded a third of the way across. It was a little deeper now and I might have swam. Instead I returned to my own side and stepped out onto the grass maintaining the pretence that I was alone, leaving my jeans where they were and lying stretched out on my original place halfway up the grass slope, shielding my eyes from the sharp ray of sun. She perhaps would have thought my eyes closed but they were not and I could see her clearly enough, this beautiful beautiful lady, of indeterminate age. My legs had dried but the chopper was rigid and it would not go down and I thought to cover it with my T-shirt, yet seeing her shift position, her legs now outstretched and her hands underneath her thighs. I shifted my own position, laying my arms alongside the length of my body, closing my eyelids. I was waiting, I waited. A rustling movement, as of her rising and entering the stream, lifting her dress clear of the water, carefully stepping her way across, focused on the water alone as though in ignorance of me, then approaching from the stream, passing where my jeans were lying. She lowered herself down to kneel on the grass oh so carefully, lifting her dress that it flopped to cover her legs entirely, her hands lightly on my ankles, rustling the hairs over my knees and upwards to where the hair stopped on my upper thighs and they moved to each other, her hands, meeting together round my chopper, gently, but increasing the pressure until I had to flex strongly to withstand the firmness of her grip. When she released it imprints of her hands would remain on the skin. I stopped flexing. A mild draught, the wafting of her dress; she had risen and was standing, or had moved, kneeling closer to me. I needed to look at her, needed to see her, and if she had arisen her knees would have crisscross marks from the grass. Had she settled back, sitting on her heels? Perhaps I think perhaps, the unzip of her dress, it falling from her onto my feet, and her hands returned to my legs, moving upwards again but where they had come together previously they now parted, off from my body and onto the grass on either side of me, her wrists set firmly against the sides of my chest. She lowered her body until the top of my chopper touched the insides of her thighs, she moving forwards again until her face rested against my cheek, her tongue touching my lips, now her hands propping herself, manoeuvring herself, enclosing me, taking the weight of her body on her hands and moving slowly upwards, and down and now I thrusted and thrusted again but then was able to stop. Neither of us moved for several moments and when eventually we did we did together. I had raised my arms and placed them round her. We were moving together, we were. I marvelled at this. On it went and I knew I was smiling a true and honest smile. There are many types of smile and this was one such, there by the stream, my bag of possessions, thoughts of food.

(TZEKOVITZ
WAS ANOTHER)

Mind you, I said, some writers can write a story about any damn thing in the world. Choose an object and tell me what that object is, I shall write you a story about it, I shall hand you that story as a finished piece by tomorrow morning. This is what they tell ye. Tzekovitz was one such writer and John Harvey was another. You too, I said. Dan . . . ?

Dan.

Dan Driscoll?

That's right son.

Dan Driscoll; how could I have forgotten? I was chairing this Writers' Group. Dan was wee and skinny and who knows what age; deaf when necessary, wore a bunnet and specs with thick round lenses. National Health specs they used to call them, granny specs. The auld bugger sat to my left side with his chair pushed back. He could see me clearly but I could not see him without shifting my own chair. What a tactic!

Dan had no interest in what I described as the practicalities, none at all. He did not disrespect them, just had no interest in them. Nevertheless he listened politely when I was advocating precision, exactitude and the miracles of meticulousnessnous, such that draft after draft after draft should be produced toward that end. He waited to ensure that I was finished talking then handed me two stories he had written earlier that same day.

The other people in the group smiled and watched for my

reaction. They accepted Dan as a phenomenon and appeared to equate it with his North Bringlish origins. But how seriously should he be taken was the key question. Very seriously. Somebody who could write this number of stories? How else should he be taken but seriously?

Dan had been privy to some exciting military events and incidents during his lifetime, had survived serious wars and violent interventions, been stationed in some of the more devilish outposts of Empire. When Britain was not at war with other business rivals, and Dan was not in the army, he generally was unemployed, along with the usual countless millions. I dont know if he wore a poppy every November. He maybe had one pinned in the dark interior of his bunnet. During one bout of unemployment the Bringlish Government had him interned in a work camp in the Renfrewshire area. His family fended for themselves while he was locked up. The politics of this seemed not to bother him but he was watching me when he let slip the information. I said, Where did it happen?

I had a feeling ye would ask that son, he said, nudging the specs up his nose, and off he went with an incredible yarn about the time he

Dan, I said, ssh. Ye've got to stop this. If ye talk it out yer system you will never write it.

Write what?

Yer story.

My story? He squinted at me and sniffed, took off his bunnet and pulled out another two manuscripts from inside the lining. These two had that same tiny blue-ink scrawl, handwritten on the kids' lined exercise pages. That made four this evening. I wasnay goni give ye these till next week, he said.

Next week? Am I here next week?

Take them now son in case ye arent.

Ye keep calling me son. I'm sixty-four years of age.

Dan blinked, pushing the specs back over the bridge of his nose. The woman who sat opposite smiled. Dan smiled back. Edith, he said, did I ever tell ye how come my nose got broke?

No, said Edith and leaned forwards a little to hear the yarn.

My attention was diverted by the extra two stories Dan had passed me. I held them up to the light to examine them.

Is that a trick? he said.

It is Dan aye. I can tell a lot from the paper a writer uses.

He fixed the bunnet back on his head and straightened it. I folded the pages carefully and put them in my folder. Thanks, I said.

Nay bother son. I'm one of these people who are aye on the spot when momentous occasions are unfolding. That's why I write so many stories.

Aw. I grinned.

I wouldnt scoff, said a young fellow.

I'm not scoffing, I said.

Edith was smiling. Dan nudged the glasses up his nose a little. His eyes seemed particularly large whenever she was speaking. She addressed me directly: The genesis of this goes back centuries, she said, and is referred to by an early Roman chronicler; Heraclitus I believe. It may have been Oxon. In those days soothsayers were commonplace. They not only perceived but derived patterns from major human tragedies, horrific calamities; earthquakes, tsunamis, erupting volcanoes. They had noted that among the multitudinous crowds of people who chanced upon these scenes of devastation, were clusters of individuals whose faces were familiar. These people appeared at the scene of these tragic events. Edith continued: There was the girl and the boy; the elderly lady and the middle-aged bearded fellow; there were the two women, the young father with the baby in swaddling clothes, his wife and her lover. The same faces, always the same, spectators, passively there, registering no emotion.

The rest were enthralled. Me too. I was not so sure about Dan. I couldnay see behind the glasses. When she finished talking I said, Edith, have you handed in a story yet?

No.

No?

I cant write stories to save me. I write poetry, she said.

I chuckled.

Sorry, I didnt think to amuse you.

God sake Edith that was a story! What ye talking about ye dont write stories!

I have tried, I simply dont understand narrative.

Nonsense! I said.

She frowned, but this frown became a smile and light glinted on Dan's spectacles. It is entirely up to you, I said, but let there be no excuses here. Yours is the anecdote of a born storyteller. I recommend you write, write and write again.

I glanced at Dan, expecting support. He had begun rolling a cigarette. Extraordinary. We all watched. When I was a cheery smoker I preferred roll-ups, I said. Even as a sad smoker I preferred roll-ups.

A man laughed.

You too? I asked.

Yes.

Dan glanced at me. I still play football son. Ever hear of that league they have for the over-eighties?

Pardon?

It's in the mountains of Switzerland yodel odel oh. Dan rose from the chair and wandered out the room without waiting for an answer.

He's off to the Caretaker's bothy, said a woman. He smokes

too. They smoke out the bothy window. Which is against the law never mind anything else.

Dan is a law unto himself, said another.

I said, If it was up to me I would let him smoke out the window right here in the room.

I have to say I would resent you taking such a liberty, said a man.

I was shifting my chair near to the window when he said this and didnt answer immediately. Him and the other folk waited for me to settle down, they were also waiting for me to answer the question. The guy who had asked it sat with his arms folded.

I said, Ye would resent it? Oh well.

I dont mind making allowances but there has to be a limit.

You have to remember the guy is hitting eighty, or is it ninety? I glanced at Edith who did not react. He doesnt have decades of writing ahead. What would ye rather find in a dingy cupboard: forty unedited stories by Tzekovitz or two finely hewn efforts?

Do you think he has others tucked into his cap? asked a younger woman.

In his bunnet, I said, yes I do. It is my firm conviction Dan Driscoll is a capable exponent of the conjuring arts.

People smiled.

A man said, Tutors give him crits but he never does anything.

What does that matter?

The man shrugged. What does anything matter?

No, I said, that's a non sequitur. Dan does what he wants and writes what he wants and thank fuck for that excuse the language. It's got nothing to do with us and why the hell anybody thinks otherwise I do not know.

The members glanced at one another. They thought I was becoming agitated. I wasnt; irritated yes, not agitated.

Why write at all? said a woman.

I sighed.

If it is only for the sake of yourself, she said, why waste breath?

What I'm saying is paying too much regard to other people's advice can kill a story. After all, whose bloody story is it?

Somebody described your books as fuction, she said.

I grinned. Look, I'm a writer of fiction and writers of fiction enjoy stories. Otherwise we wouldnay write them. That applies to Dan, he likes stories as well. That is why he comes here at the age of a hundred and eight or whatever the hell he is, calling me son, god's teeth, it is a mistake to assume I take this as a compliment. Dan is a storyteller par excellons and he narrates them here to one and all, right here in this room under your very nose. It is for us he writes them. Us in this room. Dan doesnay care about anybody else. Only us. We are the audience. He doesnay care about any other audience and he couldnay care less what happens to them afterwards. Publishing and all that malarkey, he doesnay give two fucks about that. He just wants us to read them. Me too. I might be a published author but so what, the only important thing for Dan is me here this evening as a member of this writers' group. That is how he sees me. Nothing more.

He doesnt read other people's stories, said a young woman.

Well we can all get impatient, I said.

Ssh, whispered somebody.

Dan was returning from the Caretaker's office. No one commented until he sat down. Light reflected on his specs and Edith was smiling.

I used to smoke roll-ups, I said.

Ye told me that already son.

Did I?

Ye did son aye.

Mm. I nodded.

Silence followed. How come they were waiting, there was so much to do, just so much, depending on how ye define a story, I said in answer to a question that entered existence of its own accord. Does it even occur to her that ye write stories? I said.

What was that son?

Apparently ye dont have that kind of relationship.

What ye saying?

You and the Missis.

The Missis? I didnay say a word about the Missis.

Yeah but she knows ye write stories I mean she must do. Or is she the kind of person that doesnt suffer fools gladly? I expect ye're glad she doesnay read them in case they concern her.

Oh they never concern her son. Dan declared this with an air of amusement but the way the bugger managed it allowed me a glimpse of the woman herself, a dark-haired girl from Argyll. This beautiful smile she had too. She didnt smile often but my god when she did! A certain exasperation too about her, that wee intake of breath and turn of the head. Perhaps she did read stories. Just not his. Or did she? When Dan made reference to a personage entitled 'the Missis' people assumed it was her he was talking about. But no, and even then. Somebody coughed. I cleared my throat. Much depends on how you define a story, I said.

Dan shifted on his chair so that he could see me more clearly. My back was now to the window and this caused shadows such that visibility was no concern of mine.

People come to Creative Writing groups under a variety of misapprehensions, I said. Some believe that these groups are composed of charitable volunteers whose existence is conditional upon committing the personal history of elderly and other nincompoops to the page for the good of mankind. Wanted: literary encounters: no reciprocation. Your interest is our interest. Our gratification is your every whim. Some of them are easy to spot. They only turn up when their own work is under the microscope. So it becomes the case that a mug like me asks the question: who cares about stories? Maybe nobody at all. Even me, yer poor auld fucking tutor. And if I do does it justify why I waste time on such shite? No. Stories are stories and not that important.

Nobody spoke for several moments.

Sorry, I said, I'm just blethering.

Who is Tzekovitz? asked a young woman apropos of something.

An artist whose letters I studied once upon a time. I used to do that. I gave it up. I was a boy who had learned to distrust translation. No mean feat for an unbearded youth. I regarded Tzekovitz as a form of harassed uncle. Mind you I still do, nearly fifty years later. And he was only forty-five when he died.

Forty-four, said a young woman who frowned at me in a mild manner, nearly smiling, smiling at me. I almost looked twice at her.

Okay, I said. What does he think about stories but, what does he think about art. That sort of shite is what I wanted to find out when I was a boy; I wanted to unravel that. What lay behind is what I wanted to know. What is the nub? A fool's errand. Keep 'thinking' out it. Nowadays I dont think much about anything, being honest, it drives my wife nuts. I dont know what other writers think and I dont care. Stories are a wee thing and not for everybody. That is how I see it. We come here because it is a place for stories.

Dan moved his head in my direction.

What age are ye anyway Dan, eighty? Ninety? Never published a story either let alone earned a penny from writing one. Am I wrong in that?

Ye are son aye.

I'm wrong?

Ye are.

Huh! I scratched my head, catching the whiff of old tobacco. It must be these roll-up fags ye smoke. I was warned off them twenty years ago on pain of death!

Maybe it worked, he said. He nudged his specs up the bridge of his nose. They jammed here and he took them off a moment. He sniffed and said to Edith: The last time I broke my nose was a few years ago hen in a wee town on the eastern coast, one of these places where every second guy ye meet works on the herring fishers, every third guy – well, that is the subject of one of the stories I passed on to the teacher here earlier. He hasnay read it yet I dont think . . .

Ye only gave me it half an hour ago.

As long ago as that?

I smiled.

You're the teacher son.

Ha ha.

Oh but ye are.

I'm no a teacher I'm a writer. Anyway, I said, your anecdotal digressions are more labyrinthine than mine. More elegant too but I have to say.

Thanks son.

A man said, People enjoy them, they're droll.

They are droll, I said. Folk never know if they are being kidded. I have always noted this quality; it happens rarely and always in folk other than myself. They speak of things that are extremely weird in a vague, quizzical manner.

Yes, said Edith, and that disguises certainty, and one cannot easily respond because one has never encountered such fanciful phenomena theretofore and must accept what is being stated at face value. From this derives the sense of a peculiar freedom, that one may narrate anything about anything.

It's true, said a young woman who had spoken earlier and whose name was Marcia and reminded me of somebody. Two weeks ago he challenged us to provide the topic!

What happened? I said.

He won, said a man.

Naybody wins in that situation. Ye got telled a story. And I'll tell ye another yin if ye give me something to work on. Make it hard but. The harder the better.

A weird, lengthy silence followed. Not a single person in the room offered a topic in response. I say 'weird' but that is what I thought. It connects to a 17th Century notion of art and freedom, liberty and the curtailment of the soul. I thought Edith might raise it there and then but when she didnt I decided against raising it myself. I wasnt keen on the way things were going. I counted sixty. Eventually somebody muttered, Okay then, shoelaces.

Shoelaces? Dan said to me, cupping his right hand to his ear. I thought ye were made of sterner stuff than that son shoelaces.

It wasnay me that said it, I said.

Dan nodded. How much time ye giving me?

Me?

You're the teacher.

Take as long as you like.

I'll do it during the break.

Aw jesus christ.

I noticed that he had his tobacco tin out and was already licking the gummed edge of a cigarette paper. He stood away from the table. I'll away now, he said.

I watched him leave, and the door close behind him. No one spoke for a moment. A man said, He wont take long.

He can take as long as he likes.

A woman sighed. I looked at her. She smiled with that air of resignation.

What's wrong?

He'll have it finished by the time he returns. He does this each time a newcomer appears. Two weeks ago he offered to write one for me.

Dont let him, I said. Ye've got to write yer own stories in this life.

You make it sound easy, said Edith. I find that off-putting. I'm sure I'm not alone.

You arent, remarked a man.

I dont mean it to be off-putting. I just dont know what it means, to write a story for somebody. I would hate folk writing stories for me. I have enough to do with my own. When people at Writers' Groups say they will write a story for me it usually means – well, I dont know what it means. Ye need to write it for yerself but. No for somebody else. Keep me out it at all costs.

What about shoelaces? asked a young fellow with such enthusiasm, such enthusiasm.

Are you writing yerself son? I said.

He smiled and nodded.

What ye must remember is that somebody gave Dan the word 'shoelaces' and now he'll write a shoelaces story. We all know that. By the time he's finished his smoke, he'll produce it out his bunnet and we'll gawp. We will. All of us here. So I'm goni make it the second part of this session, speaking as the so-called teacher, and it'll be a good wee story too; and about himself, at least he will give us to understand it is about himself and he'll put himself dead centre to it, even in the damn third person, what a guy! he knows the tradition inside out. His Missis will appear in it too. How do we know that? Because we know *her*, we know her already. How come? Easy, we listen to his stories. That one about the dark-haired lassie from Argyll. What was her name at all? Her with the beautiful smile, the merest hint of exasperation; nay wonder, being married to him, even wee things, minor things, dental hygiene, smelly feet, change yer vest, ye need a new one, change yer socks, ye need a new pair, change yer shoes, that auld pair's letting in – how many times does she have to tell him! Go and buy a new pair! On and on and on she goes, even when Dan is on the settee relaxing, watching the horse-racing on television, his favourite sport next to Secondary Juvenile Football in the Renfrewshire region of north Bringland. One of these settees ye sink into and think ye will never get out again, but he manages it easy, he got up and strolled into the lobby looking for his boots. She didnay hear him leave. That was deliberate. He tried never to disturb her, not if he could help it, especially fulfilling a command or direct request. The truth is he wasnay looking to buy a new pair of shoes, but a different pair, different from the ones he had, a pair that worked properly is what he was wanting; and he found a pair in an Oxfam shop down High Street, right in the centre of the old town up one of these wee wynds that hardly exist outside the town of – is it Taunton? One of these towns anyway, maybe Bath or Whitby. Dan is an easy-oasy kind of fellow but it aye needs two to serve him. Usually female volunteers. This occasion was typical. As soon he entered the shop and nudged the specs up his nose they came forward to greet him. The first was snobby middle class and she found him a most aggravating character. Ye alright hen? said Dan.

Some look she gave him! Then she disappeared. He got along with the second woman. She also was middle class but neither snooty nor snobby. This good lady found him the boots. A very fine value purchase. She went as far as to suggest that these boots were the best bargain in this entire charitable outlet.

Dan did too. Outstanding boots, he said, the Missis will be pleased. If stuck they would do for a game of football. Sometimes he passed a green and a game was on. So now if one of the teams was a man short he could volunteer himself. He was so impressed by these boots that he pulled them on there and then, waggling his toes in supreme comfort. Not only did Dan buy the boots he donated an extra pound coin to Oxfam. The only snag was they had no laces. Why do you not use the laces from your old boots? suggested the helpful female voluntary worker.

Dan did exactly that. He was so pleased with the boots that when he stepped outside the shop he nearly flung the auld yins away. He changed his mind at the last minute and returned into the shop, intending to donate them to charity. Unfortunately he met the snobby woman first. She took one look at the auld boots and held her head aloft: Sniff sniff sniff. They are rather old do you not think! She turned her back on him. What a cheek! If the Missis had been there she would have smacked her one on the gub.

He kept the old boots and retreated from the charity shop. He was goni take them hame, thinking they might do for dry days but he couldnay be bothered carrying them about. Dan was one of these guys who hates carrying anything, even in his pockets. It was his conviction that pockets were for storing hands. He was also prone to forgetfulness, forever leaving bags on buses. The good thing about hands, as far as Dan was concerned, even if ye forget them, ye'll no leave them behind on a bus. He dumped the auld boots in a place unknown and set off hame. By the time he got there he was hirpling. It was a weird feeling, he said later. I thought my feet had grown two inches. At my age? But this is what it felt like. My toes were bunched up. I was in acute discomfort ye might call it. They hurt like Hell and were very painful. The Missis was annoyed but. Who selled ye these boots! she cried. Was it that snobby woman with the funny brooch!

Oh now hen I did not notice any brooch, Dan said, I was too busy admiring the boots. And now I'm in agony.

Serve ye right, said his Missis, ye've done nothing but complain since ye came home. On and on ye go. Even when I'm watching television it's moan moan moan, complain complain complain, especially during these gardening, holiday and home-improvement programmes that I love so dearly. And that special one about selling yer own home and buying another one which is my absolute all-time quintessential favourite programme whenever presented by that nice dandy fellow with the three-barrelled name and the fancy cravat. Missing this programme is the last straw.

Dan hardly heard, he was examining his bruised feet in such a way that she too might examine them if of a mind. What a state they were! Black, blue and purple toes. He waggled them in front of her, distracting her attention from the television. My God, she muttered.

Dan looked at the television. It was thon presenter guy who wears these fancy silk scarves and answers to the name Reginald Duvet-Pottsgirth. Is he cousin to one of the Majesties? asked Dan.

Oh away and get yer damn boots, she said.

Dan's Missis was an expert shopper in her own right, and a noted collector of ladies' footwear size 3 in and around the southeast and west of southern Bringland. Dan once challenged her to count her shoes. What a task! Some had never been worn, still wrapped in tissue paper. They dont fit her feet, he told a friend, that is why she doesnay wear them. But she will not dump them. Never, she says, they will come in handy.

It turned out Dan's Missis had eighty-seven pairs of footwear in the house of which four belonged to Dan, including a pair of sandals he hadnay seen since their honeymoon, a time he remembered oh so well, that was the week the sun was shining in a clear blue sky. So eighty-three pairs belonged to the Missis. I thought ye had more than that, he said.

I'm excluding slippers, sandals and slip-ons.

How come? asked Dan.

Use yer imagination, she said.

I will. I'll include them in a story.

That cut no ice with the Missis. She held out her hand and he passed her one by one the boots he had just bought out Oxfam. Her eyes flickered shut a moment as though to grasp the inner essence of said articles. Then she stared at each with such intensity that the answer to the riddle seemed set to reveal itself. She reached out her hand, and entered this hand into the cavernous inners of the upper and discovered a new shoelace tied into a lump at the toe of each boot. This is why his feets were sore. He had been walking about the town the whole day with these bunched-up shoelaces cutting into the flesh at the tops of the tips of his toes. Now they were blistered to Hell. His Missis was shocked. Who gave ye these boots? she queried. Was it her with the snooty voice?

Och it doesnay matter, said Dan.

Or was it her with the brooch who is snobby but not snooty?

Dan sniffed but said nothing.

Hell mend ye, she said but was distracted by Dan gesturing at the television. Look hen, he said, it's that upper-class young dandy fellow ye like, him with the fancy scarves and the three-barrelled name; Roger Pin-Cushion.

His Missis glared at him.

Fancy a cup of tea? he said, and off he went to the kitchen.

The End.

The problem for me was that I had to invent much of that story myself, and I had to do it from 'scratch'. Dan did write one about shoelaces but the only bit I remember clearly was how it began, then the shoelaces themselves, how come they were bunched-up like that and shoved into the toes of the boots? Maybe it was the snobby snooty woman to blame. Maybe she had a thing about auld guys in tackety boots bought out charity shops, and her deigning to serve behind the counter too it wasnay right so it wasnay. These were key elements in the story though in Dan's original, maybe not, now I come to think about it, there was a bus played a part. Dan began his story by taking a bus from where he stayed in an outer suburb. He took this bus down High Street just past the library at the top of the street where all these charity stores and secondhand shops are gathered. Ye never know who ye might bump into, he said, including yerself son on the look-out for all these pre-owned book bargains, is that what ye call them?

Naw, I said, the last time I tried it, I was halfway along the street when the shadows appeared to lengthen, of their own accord, and I met a Bus Inspector I knew from the olden days.

Did ye son?

Aye.

Dan pushed back his chair, peered at me over the top of his specs. I know what ye says to him, ye're going to the west end of town so which bus will ye take? Do not take any, says the Bus Inspector, we're a wee bit short of buses the now.

Och that's an auld yin; I would have expected better.

Hang on a minute and ye'll get one, said Dan, I'm just going along for a wee blether with the Caretaker.

Check if it is raining outside while ye're at it, I muttered, I need to hit the road soon. Unless there's any wardrobes around? I could jump into one and pull shut the door.

The tobacco tin was already out his pocket. Will do, he said.

PICK UP THE PIECES

He made himself laugh aloud. Here he was racing along the Centreal Way and cutting back through downtown, amazed to find it was still there but trying to restrict his smiling face and eyes to the ground in front of his tootsies lest he was adjudged mad, mad. He was not mad, he was just glad to have escaped and to be here, free and easy; and so so glad to be free.

Glad glad glad: simply that. He didnt care he was hungry. So what! lacking the whatever, so what. Matters were positive. He laughed again with an immediate self-reprimand. Stop that laughing. Cut it out! At once ya fool.

True but it was all in the head.

He needed not just a million euros, a veritable million euros, but grub too; or food as we humans call it, veritable clusters of it. There used to be a place for the likes of him. But it was not there. He went to look and no. He used to get into that place, he just walked in, passed by the guy on the door with a cheery wink then a plate of macaroni cheese and pomme frit. But the door wasnt there never mind the guy himself.

Och well cheer up. Even without grub. What is this grub all the time. To hell with grub. Grub is just food, who needs it. Veritable clusters, strawberries and grapes, wee new potatoes, the ones you just run under the tap and let the red soil drain away, ye could fucking eat the fuckers raw, as with turnips when one passes a field and el coasto eez clearo.

All these things in shops. That is the thing about this downtown area. He spied one of them amazing men's tailors, geared to the city gent, and with that darkbrown wood exterior – shabby to the undiscerning eye but to him the pinnacle, veritabilus-a-um. He knew it would be there and the fates didnt let him down.

Talking about the panels, that darkwood, it comes with old-fashioned counters and grumpy old-timers tugging back their double-cuffed white shirtsleeves in their bid to sell ye a harris tweedsuit with red satin waistcoat of the fanciest fancy, designed for princes. Tailors to royalty, ye could aye tell by the ombience. One pushes open the door of entry: Dingading. Out pops the grumpy old sales fellow. Sir? A jacket please. Of the finest quality. Of a type worn by nonchalant movie stars. Not football players whose sense of style – what sense of style! They dont fucking have any, football players man these cunts know fuck all.

A 37" chest nowadays, the no-grub diet and so on. And furlined inners a necessity. In case of blanketslack, the lack of blankets, the 'nay blankets' syndrome. Bodily warmth there was none. One's bodily regions lay unprotected.

The cold is the worst.

Seriously but with a couple of hundred smackers to spare he would splash out on proper suiting, inimitably so. He would buy and don it that same minute.

Plus three pairs of thick woollen hose of the type worn by Mount Everest climbers and ye maun wrap them if ye'll be huvvin a likin fur it ye ken.

In this part of the world they thought him Scottish. Fair enough.

A jaunty woollen cap of the type preferred by Rover Scouts. Naw laddie I'll be werrin it tae.

Nay linen underwear. Seelk. Slippery substances. He thought as much. Swimming trunks, as worn by all these steak-eating world record-breaking guys. Built-in-bulge unnecessary. My trunk may have shrunk but not the appendages. Parties of the female gender would hasten to allay any fears therein, if one might find such a one available for empirical verification.

Lastly a jacket of the finest black leather

Once he had the money, this million euros or was it dollars? The truth is he was past the stage of clothes. Fuck clothes, who needs them. They can join food, fuck them all, margarine and whatnot, yoghurts, he was just glad, glad glad glad. Often he got the urge for dessert spoonfuls of natural yoghurt. Heaps of these spoonfuls, dinner spoonfuls, fucking ladlefuls man what do ye call that? a fucking eh whatdyecallit, a freaky dependency? One of the many he would have had if if and only if

The truth is, if truth it be, he felt dandy. Yeah, dandy. Outlook beautiful and bright. And looking the part with the unshaven, weatherbeaten countenance. Once the hernisheid reached an appropriate length he would trim that son-of-a-gun fucker.

One's beard was patchy in places but women regard such as boyishly appealing. Once it had sprouted for five or six weeks mayhap it would look better. There is a certain facial sprout adopted by excessively rich personalities in search of street cred-ibility. They domicile themselves in backstreet hotel suites for twelve days without shaving then come out for a week to exhibit their tonsorial appurtenances in fulsome suavity, then shave and hideaway for anar twelve days.

The trouble with him, him himself – if there be any trouble with him himself – is simple, plain and obvious: one has frittered one's life. Talking fucking mega here! This guy used to be good at sports and English studies. Perhaps if he had stuck in at them. Even he was good at drawing as well, if we are talking classrooms, he was; and reasonably so at mathematical equations. The teacher was aye giving him these wee gold star things his mammy stuck up on the fridge door. Maybe if he had knuckled doon. Instead of frittering it all away. Talking talent blues. Folk fritter. He was one such – fritterer rather than fritter, given one's father used to dunk slices of spam in a floury liquid then fry them and serve them to the weans under the heading 'fritters'. Tasty as fuck man if we are talking grub, and how can we not, grub is grub and as to survival, if survival will enter the equation, as enter it must, grub is of the essence.

But he needed a slash. He looked for a bookie's. One of the last places in the world that offered pissholes free to the public. Except nowadays ye have to ask for a goddam key. Imagine that man ye couldnay get a piss without getting a key from behind the counter lest one purloin the damn cistern.

Banged up cludgés. One performs the ritual.

There was a lady behind the counter engrossed on her phone, her phone! Her attitude left much to be desired. This was a bookie! Bookies were exciting places! A million eurobelles on the first favourite!

The sign on said cludgé door: For Customers Only.

Oh so it wasnay free after all; one had to make a bet first, fucking miserable bastards.

She watched for his response. He allowed a smile to play about his bulbous lips. She proffered the key. Then she stared at his fingers for a prolonged period. How come? It aint like they were podgy. Never. His fingers were never fucking podgy. Nay cunt could accuse him of that, podgy fucking fingers.

A million eurobelles! The first favourite, go on my girl, yippee! yippee!

Ah but the piss, the piss was bliss. And soap for one's hands. Oh man, the little things in life. He soaped the beard. Fucking carry on. Beards. He hated beards. Why did he have a fucking beard. Well now of course it wasnt a beard it was a set of bristles mayhap a full set of the spiky buggers. Imagine shaving but. Imagine a bare neck. What is a bare neck. Imagine post shave

glug glug

The water through the hair on the head. Without the hair on the head one would be bald. Even women. Cold water into his eye sockets and cold water onto his scalp and dripping down the back of his neck.

He ripped a handful of toilet paper and shoved it in his jacket pocket for future reference. Free resources nowadays were a rare find. He was in a lav someplace recently and there was a halfful bottle of beer balanced on the window ledge. A halfful bottle of beer balanced on the window ledge? We are talking cludgés man know what I mean these dastardly middle-class cunts and their shitty jokes, take a sip of that ya down-and-out fucker.

The lady at the betting shop counter ignored him when he returned the key. This was a very positive action on her part and indicated to him, with neither fear nor favour, that he remained in the world as a man among men, in the outside world. Who better to remind one than a lady of the female persuasion. This returning-the-key lark was a gesture of what one might term solidarity: he too was a human fucking bean man and he didnt care if people ignored him as long as they did so in a studied manner, as a deliberate action because he, he would look right back although surely she could have glanced upwards, it wouldnt have taken much, just to look up and over, and take a wee keek at the man who

ach.

At the same time but once was good, that she should look at him twice was beyond expectation. The most one could have wished was this who gives a fuck.

He returned to Centreal Way via the bypass and out the other side spied a damsel at the upstairs window of a huge Estates Agency specialising in Luxury Lets in Penthouse Apartments for the down-at-heel 'county' set.

For some reason he started doing a jig. Why did he do that! Mind you it was more of a yelping twitch, albeit a full-body one. He tended towards such behaviour following jaunts to the lavvy and other acts of social inclusion.

But it was true, the damsel was looking down at one from the upstairs window with an expression on her face, an actual expression – he could see it! And not looking down at 'one' but at him, him! looking down at him.

> dow dee dow dee doh,
> dow di dow di dee,
> dee dow di dow dee dah,
> dee dah dee dah dee dah

She was. He touched his forelock and beamed up a smile. She looked away.

He too had a mind. Or rather a brain. He had to stop these fantasies. The million euro business. Penthouse apartments and lassies in the bookie shop.

He had nothing. A Have-not. Nothing new in that. He had done all this before. Of course money was essential but when int it? The old ho ho ho, the sarry heid, the breid, el casho. For what might we buy with money? A fucking chicken sandwich for christ sake chicken a la chips, thick batter, putrified fat and burgers, beer-battered fish, poor auld fish man battered by a pint of guinness, oh well, what's new.

He who has nothing. One who has nothing. But what does

nothing mean? If he has nothing, or had nothing. What had he when having had nothing?

Beg pardon?

Was there a thought? He seemed unable to think. Was he unable to think. His poor old head. There was a scene in some old television drama that took place in 19th Century England when the servants appeared with course after course of grub. All these upper-middle-class English actors all sitting down to chicken legs and roasted mutton, tankards of ale and hot pheasant. Oh sorry we've got to film that episode again. Waiter, bring the grub! Yes sir says the waiter. I hope you people arent too full of pheasant, we got to shoot the scene again!

But no, he was not coping. Although in a way he was, although in a way he wasnt, a different way. Beer-battered fish and chips, he needed out altogether, out of this damn everything, everything.

The country and everything else. Out of town.

Here he was returned and the only answer was escape.

One encounters personal difficulty in perambulating the high-ways and byways in a manner that suggests positivity.

The lack of heaving pit-a-pats, breathings, babies and mothers, fathers. He cannot have this promise-for-the-future. No ma'am your royal highness, he cannot have it. He whose future

Who are we talking about here?

One is haunted by thoughts of prison and the constabulary classes; lawyers and that ilk, folk who wear fancy red waistcoats and go bump in the night with their harris tweed fucking jaikets. Your Honour, I recommend life! Life!! Lock up the fucker, he's a rat, he'll find a way, these mob people always do. He says he cannot avoid behaving like a human bean and as such has attendant requirements.

He would look for a place outside town, head south maybe. He loved society, the richer the better, falling off the edge, scrabbling the chalk cliffs with the fingernails, aint England the truth, with all their traditions and so on, one has to love it. He always did. How far to Rostoff? can he fucking swim it?

A million and one euros would be vunderbar vunderbar vunderbar, sung to the tune of 'On We Go':

> On we go
> On we go
> On we go
> Vunderbar
> Vunderbar
> Vunderbarar.

Why was he not rich though? God-given talents are rewarded by society and he believed he had these self-same talents. He was a one in a million talent and might reap the rewards post haste. Plus he had the heavy stubble so beloved of Male Celebs, the streetwise gestures. I might be a fucking billionaire but dont mess with me. It was only the dough, he had the fucking lot man if not for the old ho ho ho. A chicken sandwich, washed down by a half bottle of some arsehole's fucking urine man that is what we are talking about here. Treating yer fellow human beans.

Mind you, a man of his calibre, sensibility, sense and physique of an overall manly deport.

All problems are surmountable according to a wise old Scottish poet whose work was wrocht in Gaelic. He fought for the Hanoverians too, German Geordie and all that anglo-saxon crap.

But what about Carer Agency work? The idea of Carer Agency work! Caring for those who required support from society.

Mind the gap.

A chap of unknown theological leanings, a background blighted by race, ethnicity and diverse bigotries.

The lack of a proper basis to one's existence. Besides all of that he was raised a genuflector to the hierarchical god-class.

Wearily wearily. Howsomever, one trudges.

The trouble with life is the lack of a soundtrack, even a cheery hollywood song about working-class chimney-sweeps in mufflers, bunnets and torn semmits,

> hi tiddly toe
> it's off to gaol we go,

then the weans up the fucking chimney. Ma'am Yer Honour can I present to you one's ankle-snappers, they will scale the bricks on behalf of you and your weans and grandweans to do as you please Your Royal Divineness.

Coffees and green tea. He would take water with a slice of lemon, two Abernethy biscuits and a comfy chair a comfy chair, watching the wheels go round.

What about gross brains. My brains are gross. The chap has a palpitating brain your Honour and that brain, that brain

has left him speechless; bereft, left bereft, nay million euros.

People look at one. He needed to sit, to be free of stares. He found himself limping towards a tiny green area where there was a bench: edging his way clear of the lieges in said direction your Honour, in most ungainly fashion.

How come?

He dont like leixester Square. Something aboot that place drives a man nuts. He is a man. He dont care for the effing polisconfuckingstabulary either man stab yer ayn fucking abulary.

The plates o meat required a break else kaputo kaputare. One's feet your Honour, one's flip-flops.

He needed socks. A man needs socks.

There was nay space on the benches. Older beans sat on the grass, scrolling scrolling ever scrolling.

He flapped out the flipflops, hitting them on the grun. All sorts of gravel and wee chuckie stanes came flying oot. The feets were fine apart from that. Nay reason for limping.

Why o why had he left his native shores? Our hero wrung his hands. Okay it was a shitty dump but is that just cause? And it is not a shitty dump at all. He was a vainglorious type of fellow in search of meaning.

A shop in the vicinity advertised sales of clothes by Union Railways of Britain Lost Property Department. He heard about these sales in a rooming house for the confined class. Upmarket claes for the down-at-heel chap who was reassembling hisself on life's weary belt-driven

och shut up.

Honest to gahd. One dire Monday morning after the night before he required breeks urgently and buyed a pair at a polis lost property office. Nay kidding ye man they only let him oot on condition he purchased a pair of strides then sent him along the corridor to buy them. He will not divulge the city.

Okay: errors. What has been his greatest error? talking life here, what has been the greatest error in all his entire life?

He once flung away a coat. God forgive him. True but. A genuine actual coat. He flung it away. Thinking about it even now, one was astounded; at himself, by himself, his absolute – that word integrity because the cold the cold the cold, the cold, when it enters one's very marrow, thinking about it now, to fling away a coat

speechless,

about to have become so,

honest.

Shut up.

But was it his gravest error? Gravitas, gravitatis, his actual gravest?

Grass is grass and ants is ants. He would fucking eat ants. They even look nutritious. Toty wee blackcurrant clusters. But ants are nutritious. He heard that. Some fucking Charity for poor African Countries advertised that. Rockstars and footballers, boyish Princes of the House of Whisper: all comrades the gether. They buyed up these African villages in the name of the next life. Brilliant people, all giving their time for fuck all, aint they the bees knees. All we need is 20 sense a day off the general population and we can feed an entire village. That is what they were shouting, these cheery billionaire fucking bastards. Something to do with ants, a hundred thousand volunteer workers coming from Birmingham, Manchester, Glasgow and Liverpool, we'll feed the fuckers is the cry! No surrender.

The awkward reality concerning ants is quantity, ye need a few thousand a time for every wean. So these weans have to catch them. How do ye catch a thousand ants? One lays a bit of grub on the ground. The African wean exercises patience till at last a scout-ant arrives then passes on the message, then the mother-horde swarms across, then the wean licks them all up. One then returns the last ant to the grun to ensnare the next batch of toty wee clusters of nutritiousity. That was the brilliant idea of the boyish young Prince, his cheery rockstar and foot-balling friends agreed wholeheartedly

Say what you will, the countryside makes one ill.

He needed to get fit and healthy. Of that there was no argument.

Weightlifting exercises, wrestling clubs, gymnasia; oneself as a fit and healthy being. Learning to play cards and gamble profit-ably with interesting strangers. He could hustle down dimly lit lanes and corridors and have prostitutes for girlfriends.

Could his life be over? Had he been a normal sort of wage-earning guy this question, without fear of contradiction, would have preoccupied him. It is true he had possessed said coat then discarded same willy of the nilly. 'Twas done in a fit of pique. He was going through a believe-in-the-next-world phase. Get thee behind me Immediate Reality! Henceforth I shall tread the paths of righteous obedience, rule brittanicus, brittanicus rules the waves.

He hoped for a chicken sandwich out the deal. Talk about hypocritical bastards! A fucking charlatan man nay wonder he flung away the coat. He should have punched himself on the mouth. He deserved nothing less. He loved that coat. But couldnay concentrate with the necessary oomph. Ever tried punching yersel in the mooth? The jawbone aye wiggles out of reach.

How do other folk manage it? Has anybody ever? Autonomous limbs, ignoring the penis. He cannay imagine it. He tried. He just could not get one's hand to disengage from its cog-in-the-machine-of-life role, so to speak, to just leave go and act as an individual member. Order order. This House demands Unity. Thus does the fist steady itself at that last moment and merely taps him on the cheek instead of a major whack, whack whack whack, a whack on the gub that might break the old jawbone.

Jawbone. He came upon a jawbone once. It was on the lower reaches of a mountain. One jaw bone. Nothing else.

The Mysteries of the Universe. He would love a book with that title. He used to have a book.

Now here he was.

A huge Estates Agency. What do we make of that? The damsel at the upstairs window. She must have been bored. Looking out the window at him. What a building! It was a natural development too. He didnay know Estates Agencies grew to that size.

But she was there. Was she just making fun at his expense? What do we mean by that? Hey lady he got no expense.

Is expense a possession? Possessions he hath none.

But she was staring down at him. Jesus man, really. He should have called out. Young lady ahoy! Male-damsel in distress!

What is a male-damsel? A damson! A fucking damson man he am a damson. Damson in distress.

Veritably.

She was an audience. Maybe she was humming a tune at the same time, thus providing the missing soundtrack to his ungainly twitch of a dance, the rhythm of that, for he had such a rhythm. This has been remarked upon. She might have been blowing an encouraging tune through her beautiful lips, a low whistle, watching him do that wee jig albeit the yelping twitch, be careful it is a very old way of being that brings one nearer the light, that shard of light, he cannot utter the name, he cannot utter the name, he cannot utter the name.

Why he was doing the wee jig. These are questings

in demonstration of one's existence

madness lieth

for too long having had nothing, far too long, shedding clothes and dispensing with food, all contact with the opposite sex.

It is true. He even threw away a coat. Now to throw away a coat!

But were the redoubtable former pockets of said coat empty when one discharged it from in short one's shoodirs? Entirely. Into a fucking skip man a manky and smelly one, full of diarrhoeic rubbish, stones and brickwork, shite and assorted toenails.

Never mind. It was a bygone slice of life. Nevermore would he embroil himself in useless activities, he had deactivised.

Futile questings. The troublesome aspect to eggseestons: one's involvement in same.

Now here he was set to embark on another. He required to

inform parties. Lest he fail to return. He needed somebody to know if he had become an absence.

Bontsha the Silent.

A wee breeze in the park. Heh, that breeze is him, it wouldnay exist but for his absence.

A guy was looking at him. Really, this guy, he was looking at him! He was.

Mercy him. This was exciting. Why was he looking at him? All manner of questions raised their ugly mugs.

The guy was eating a sandwich, and smiling. He smiled back. But was it to him he was smiling? Fuck! Was this a pick-up? Maybe it was. Christ almighty. Such luck was beyond, was beyond, like it was like

beyond.

Was it true. But he was a smelly fucker.

He felt like giving the guy a kiss there and then in gratitude, the very idea, a man among men, axiomatic: I am a man. This guy is looking at me.

He very nearly spoke, was having to hold himself back.

Maybe he was an office worker out for a breath of fresh air, eating his lunch out in the open. It was all offices roundabout here. Ye would suffocate. The stultification of collegial-phobics, i.e. one's fellow officeworkmates. Escaping out for a smoke, fresh air, a bit of exercise.

Had he finished the sandwich? He seemed to have because he was not eating. Maybe he had half eaten it and stuffed the rest away. Was that possible? Not eating a sandwich when one has the choice. Are there people for whom such is reality?

Maybe the guy had something to say. What might it be?

The guy's napper and what lay within; the concealed phantasmagoria. What was going through the guy's head? Here they were sharing a bench on life's weary journey.

Imagine a conversation: Hi, says the guy, my name is Dave. What's yours?

Bontcha Bill.

Bontcha Bill. Is that true?

Yes.

D'ye work in an office?

No. I work for Lambert and Price the furniture store.

Lambert and Price the furniture store?

Yes.

Never heard of them.

Neither have I, I just made it up! The truth is I'm a farm labourer, in the old days you would have said 'peasant', hardly a complimentary term but so what if it be truth required. I've escaped from the country but intend escaping once again tomorrow morning if one makes it through the night.

The guy was in his own world, a dreamworld too by the look of him. The lines on his forehead. Man oh man this guy was tired. Then of course eating only a mouthful of the sandwich and stuffing the rest away. Poor bastard. There was something pitiable about that. He was worn down by the vagaries.

An insight gained.

I beg your pardon, he found himself saying, I was just wondering if you were married?

The man frowned. Yes, he said.

I only mention it because it is possible you might have seen myself in the pick-up context. At the same time if you had, I wouldnt hold it against ye, people have to act. The state of passivity gets you nowhere, that is inaction, the state of do-nothing. So at least you broke the ice, and a guy like me ye know, when one is skint, when one has no food and considering food, clusters of same, vegetables and berries, ants, and then that sandwich you stuffed out of sight, the halfeaten sandwich. The truth is, I speak in hunger, in the throes. Is the sandwich a figment of the old imagination? Grub is grub and food is food, ne'er the two, et cetera ad nauseam or is it nauseum.

The guy

There was no guy. No halfeaten sandwich. Figment if figment it had been. The sandwich figment. Futile imaginings. What comes first, the sandwich or an owner, its owner, owner of the sandwich. Which the egg which the chicken? The egg must come first, according to science, but for us . . . godly fuckers – call a halt,

call a halt

or is it the chicken?

Imagine a man who has a sandwich to eat, takes one bite then stuffs the rest of it back into his pocket. Would he give the sandwich to a deserving stranger? Is there such a question? Can such a question be said to exist?

Never mind if it doesnay because he, he

Farewell to one and all. He was not mad and knew it to the very core, the very core. For he too

ach

A FRIEND

She was a friend. I knew by her absence. So much that was her, the imprint she left. Hers appeared a gap in space but was a movement. By virtue of that, courses of action, how these are performed.

I learned about music. She was younger than me when she died, younger than I am now. The way I see it she did die even though technically she did not. She was not killed. Imagine 'killed', a woman killed.

She was breathing beyond the accident so that she might have died. She would have smiled as she did so. She was special.

I was not present. In discussing her absence I was hearing music. This was a development. My own life, it too, it has developed.

Her absence and music there someplace, music, filling the absence.

A thought is not a finished entity if it is not one. A thought. Thoughts are more varied. Thoughts; entities in my head, inside it. So that was it too, thinking of her and her absence.

And I can not get to it, and to her, what of her? I can not reach her. It is too painful; memories, image, neither an image, not a thought. She was a friend. Her smile was to me.

ONE HAS ONE'S WEANS

I was just in the door from work and was tired tired tired. Things had been happening and I was irritated. Every fucking thing. Not the kids, they were sound asleep. Not Wilma either. How could I be irritated by her? If not for her I dont know what would have happened. The job was so bad it was just like

forget it,

ye felt like murdering cunts.

Better no talking about it. Certain it is that without her I wouldnay have lasted. How do people manage without a partner? I wouldnay have survived. She took me out the mood – moods; it was moods. I didnay hate the job but there were things about it drove me nuts. As soon as I got home, closed the door, saw the kids and had a cuddle with Wilma the world reverted to one in which a person could cope without contemplating the murder of one's fucking superiors. The officer-class I am talking about. This story by Heinrich Böll, the German army on the point of retreat, their officer-class and the ones here in this load of royalist shit known as britsin were exactly the same. But why in the name of god did we all put up with it! Fucking hell, curtseying to these upper-class cunts. We are talking here about my grandpa. I remember him. He was a tough Glasgow guy and yet there he was yessir nosir threebags full sir

forget it.

Here's yer toast and cheese, said Wilma.

I dont want any.

Well I've made it.

Well ye can just unmake it.

She smiled and put it down on the floor at the side of my chair.

Seriously, I said, you'll have to eat it yerself because I'm not. I dont have any stomach left ye see.

D'ye want tea or coffee?

I'm not bothered.

Horlicks?

Horlicks!

Wilma laughed. I gave her a cuddle. Seriously, she said, there's been some lying in the cupboard for months.

That charred lump? Is that what ye're talking about? a lump of meteorite dust. Fuck knows where it's come frae, Saturn or someplace. I mind buying that stuff. Months ago. It was for you I bought it.

It wasnt for me.

It was.

I dont drink it.

Ye used to.

No I didnt. Not Ovaltine either, and not hot chocolate.

Hot chocolate. One drools at the words alone.

Shut up.

So ye mean I should dispose of the charred dust?

Do what ye want with it.

Jesus christ there's nothing I want with it, you're the woman. Women and Horlicks. Know what I mean. I laughed for some reason.

Ssh. Wilma frowned at me.

Sorry, I said.

Are you having a breakdown?

Pardon?

Sometimes ye act like ye are.

People are starving in nine tenths of the world Wilma, know what I mean, and the other tenth are like wohhh throw it all away. I'm talking about natural resources.

Ssh.

Sorry.

Wilma sighed. Ye banged the chair.

Did I? Jees.

It just makes a noise.

Sorry, oh god.

There's something about men, she said.

Sorry.

No but there is.

Because we tell the truth?

No because yez are so noisy.

I smiled.

Do you think I actually fall for that nonsense? she asked.

What nonsense?

Natural resources and the starving hordes. Eh, do ye think I fall for it?

Sorry. Did I say that! Jesus christ!

Ssh.

Sorry.

Ye'll waken the kids.

Sorry. I whispered, Fancy a coffee?

I wouldnt mind a cup of tea.

Is that a new skirt by the way?

Shut up.

Naw I'm being serious.

My Mum bought it for me. Remember Sunday, me and her went out? I've just been trying it on. Wilma turned with it, swirling the skirt. Do ye think it's okay?

Yeah. I shrugged.

Wilma stared at me a moment then turned away. To end the conversation. She knew where it was headed and wanted to end it. The new job. She had a new job. Her Mum would take the kids, nurseries and whatever, whatever. Because we couldnt manage on our own. We needed help. Help! Her family. Ha ha. Oh well. Fuck it anyway. The only reason the guy gave her the job was because she was wearing this skirt. It is the kind of skirt one notices. One cannot help fucking noticing. This is a truism about the sexes. It is why he gave her the job and it was pointless her denying it because the reality is she did not know because she did not understand. What went on in the male cranium, she just did not understand.

Fuck all went on. A short skirt: that is what went on. A skirt like hers and the best legs in Scotland man that is what went on with these fucking bastards. The job is yours. Start on Monday. Wear the same skirt and bend down a lot.

Women dont get it. It is just crazy and silly; mad mental shite and I would have resigned from it altogether, the whole fucking shebang, fucking he-bang.

Unfortunately I should have said Monday instead of Sunday. Sunday she went out with Mummy. Monday she went for the effin job. Thus I destroyed my argument. If I had had an argument. Did I? Fuck knows.

There was a serious side to it but what was it? One has one's weans and one's life to live, one needs to survive survive survive. Oh children, my children.

I shook my head and discovered the plate with the toast and cheese in my left hand. This was a reflex action. Her Mother was a nice sod. Obviously it was her bought the skirt. Of course it was. *We* could not afford a skirt. A skirt for the Mother of one's weans. Of course I couldnt afford that. Late capitalism.

I couldnt afford another fight, that is for sure. My world was composed of fights; battles, quarrels, rows and arguments: wars. Aw man. One wearied, one wearied.

This was me now until tomorrow at 10 a.m. These were the shifts I was doing; 10 in the ay ems until 10 in the pee ems. Four 12-hour shifts, and sometimes five if I was lucky enough to be looked upon favourably by the whitecoat managerials. The men killed one another for the extra day's work. I was no different. I was the same. I did not lead any struggle. I did not take part in any struggle. I allowed the fucking system to steam-roller me into oblivion oblivion oblivion.

Oh god Wilma of course we could have afforded the skirt. Of course we could have afforded the fucking thing. She had looked at me. That was the problem. I didnt care for these looks, her looks to me, at me. She looked at me. Oh well. She came and knelt at the side of my chair. She kept me going. The woman and the children, husband as one of them, the other child. In the old days the women didnt eat the meal, they gave it to their husband; if not could they have completed their shift? Maybe not. Or was I waxing sentifuckingmental; oh dear, mental as fuck, oh dear again.

I allowed her to hold my hands. Her hands were smaller than mine. But she had these long tapering fingers which surely were longer. It was the mass. My hands were of the male mass, born to shovel shite. You wore that skirt to yer interview? I said.

Of course.

I smiled. I smiled again.

She stared at me. She leaned to kiss me, was kissing me on my mouth. I needed up, up and off, and tried to get up, get out of my chair but she grasped and held onto my hands and I could not, could not rise. Good god, powerless. I need to go to the bathroom, I said.

Wilma stared at me until I met her stare. Dont be so silly, she said.

I didnt know what she meant. I was not able to withdraw my gaze. I was a fish. And she studied me. Dont be so fucking stupid, she said, so stupid.

I nodded. But I did need a piss. When I came out the bathroom I waited in the lobby for peace. The cistern was a noisy piece of crap. It had to go through an entire clanking and juddering process in order to empty and refill. If I didnt wait for the racket to end before opening the door it would have wakened the kids. I was wanting to see them.

Kids. We believe in them. Me too. I believed in them. This was me in the world. This was my humanity, not the existence of weans but the belief in them. The measure of my 'success' if survival may be described as such, e.g. 'He negotiated life to a natural conclusion, thus may we judge him a success.' Without such belief this individual who is myself would not have survived.

I opened the door to the front room. Moonlight and their breathing; my nightly fix. Their beds side by side: I walked to them but that scratching, the scratching. What was that scratching. Fuck sake. What the hell was it? Rats. Dear god. More than mice. We had had mice. I knew mice; little fuckers, but not this, this fucking scratching. It was bloody loud. I stared at the wall above the cots. Wilma had arrived next to me. Is that it again? she said.

Yeah.

It's through the wall, the neighbours up the next close.

Ye reckon?

Yes.

They're making the noise? I said.

Yeah.

Thank god. Better than rats. Annoying, okay. Neighbours were annoying. Rats werent, they were like scary as fuck man. Although this time of night . . . What the hell time was it at all! How on earth could they be making a racket at this time of bloody night when weans are trying to sleep, that is like fucking outrageous! To hell with it, I said, I'm going round to see them. Nay wonder the weans are so bloody nervous with that racket going on, it would drive anybody daft never mind a toddler. Really, it's shocking.

It's been like that for a while.

Has it?

I told ye about it. I told ye.

Sorry.

The kids are used to it now. They're used to it.

I'm no. I'm going round to see them.

I wish ye wouldnt.

Even if it is just mice they should be doing something about it. They might be dropping down the walls.

I dont think it's mice.

Well what then?

I dont know.

Wilma watched me pulling on my boots, lifting my jacket. It was late November, and cold, cold. My feet had been freezing for days. I wish ye wouldnt go, she said, it's too late to go chapping people's doors, especially if ye dont know them.

I thought you did?

Yes but not to talk to, they're elderly. I just know them from being out the backcourt. They're okay. Wilma smiled. Really, they're okay.

They shouldnay be making a racket but.

It's not a racket.

It is, I mean there's kids trying to sleep.

Yes and they are sleeping.

We cannay just say nothing. We've got to tell them. I tied my bootlaces and lifted my jacket.

Dont upset them, said Wilma.

I'm not going to. Keep the door locked till I come back.

Wilma sighed.

Downstairs and across the street I stood on the pavement to see up to our building and our front room, where my son and daughter were asleep. There was a dim light in the window in the front room through the wall from them. This was where the noise was coming from. That was the room. I climbed the stairs to the third storey. Donnelly was on the nameplate. I chapped the door. Inside there was some sort of movement. I chapped again, though not so loudly. A man called: Who is it?

I'm yer neighbour through the wall.

Now the locks and chains were unbarred, and a key turned. An elderly man wearing jeans, vest and baseball cap. The stub of a cigarette stuck out from one corner of his mouth. His vest and jeans were spattered with lumps of plaster. By his side an elderly woman dressed in a sort of housecoat or else a dressing gown. I live through the wall from you, I said. Look it's just that my kids sleep next to your front room and they keep getting wakened at night with the noise. Nightmares too they're getting and it's because of this. My girlfriend thinks it's rats or something though to be honest . . .

The old guy interrupted me. Come on in, he said.

He held the door for me and I went in. The woman locked the door behind me. The man led me into the kitchen and she followed on. He saw me looking at the cigarette stub and took it out the corner of his mouth, leaned to tap ash into the sink, then looked to make sure it was not burning and dumped it in the rubbish bin. The smell of old tobacco was strong.

The tea's infusing, said his wife.

He nodded and took another cigarette from a pack on the mantelpiece. He didnt light it but stood near the window. What's the matter? he said.

It's just the noise through the wall, I said, I mean like it's just eh . . .

Ye talking about the front room?

Aye well that's where the weans sleep. It's their bedroom.

He glanced at his wife. I'll take him ben the room hen.

I'll bring yer tea. D'ye take sugar son?

Eh, I dont really want a cup.

Ye sure?

Aye, I'm fine, thanks.

In the front room a wardrobe, a dressing table and a tallboy were stacked along one side of the room. No other furniture, and nay wonder because the floor, the slope, what a slope! Christ! The floor was bare. Maybe ye couldnt have laid down a carpet, it would have slithered into the wall.

Near the window lay a bucket containing a kind of cement mix, and there were trowels and a wine bottle with water in it. My daughter's bed would have been through the wall from there. Mr Donnelly saw me looking and walked across. I followed him and it was like walking up a hill. He pointed at the corner of the wall. There was a crack from the ceiling to the floor and it was open in places. Christ almighty, I said.

He crouched a little and stuck his hand in, and through beyond his wrist. He said, If ye were standing in the street ye'd see me waving. He withdrew his hand and wiped it.

That's a nightmare! I said.

He gazed at me. After a moment he took off his baseball cap and scratched his head.

Have ye been filling it in?

Aye, he said, that's the noise ye're hearing.

Huh, yeah.

He lit the cigarette, sucked in a lungful of smoke. He gestured at the crack down the wall. It isnay structural I dont think. Mr Donnelly watched me, waiting for a response. When I didnt say anything he added, Otherwise it might have fell down, the building.

Jeesoh!

I've been keeping it blocked. Trouble is son it's never-ending; a Forth Road Bridge situation, ye spend yer life doing it; by the time ye get to the end it's time to start back at the top. He frowned, noticing something about the crack; crumbly-looking concrete or plaster. He lifted a trowel and knocked the stuff out. It's mine, he said, probably there since last year. Needs replacing. Same with this here, he said, tapping another spot with his trowel, and he glanced at me. Maybe if I changed the mix a bit, got a drop more sand or something. I might be using too much cement. I'm no great at the concreting, being honest about it.

What about lime? I said.

Lime? He puffed on his cigarette. Lime . . . He nodded, looked at me again. D'you know the building game son?

Eh naw, no really. I mean I did my brickie's labourer for a few months.

Did ye?

Aye.

Right. Ye think lime . . . ? He scratched his chin, gazing at the crack then frowning at it.

Well I dont know, I said, I was just eh I was just saying. What about the housing association like I mean have ye been on to them about it?

Hoh!

Naw?

Naw son ye dont tell them nothing. A big big mistake that.

The very excuse they're looking for. They'll fucking demolish the place.

Jeesoh!

That's the very excuse. He sniffed, shook his head. Naw son I think it's the mix, if I got the mix right. There's a resin I've heard, it'll stick to anything. He knocked at the top of the crack with his trowel. See by the time I get to there I've got to start back down the bottom. I know it's the wrong way round. But I used to start first at the top but it just didnay finish as well. How I dont know.

I thought ye started at the top and went fast down the way like if ye were concreting.

Aye, only it starts crumbling out the way, like I say, it doesnay take the grip or something.

The water dries in . . .

That's how I was thinking about the resin.

Right, yeah. At least it's no rats.

Rats?

My girlfriend worries about them.

Fucking rats, he said, rats are easy. Just batter them ower the skull. It's the front door with them anyway son, know what I mean, they ring the fucking doorbell, rats, open the door and in they stroll. Usually they're wearing polis uniforms. He glanced at the door. I thought she was bringing tea . . .

He saw me peering at the floor and furniture stacked at the end wall. I said, That's some slope ye've got.

Nought to ten and three-eights. Cannay put a stick of furniture anywhere bar the wall. Ye want to see it in the house up above. Murder polis.

Do they no complain?

Does who no complain?

Up the stairs.

There isnay any cunt up the stairs. There's a nest of doos. I used to have a set of keys but the bastards changed the lock. It's got worse too. Ye stand across the street ye see them all sitting about, all the birds, they're all fucking in there; it's like that fucking movie son know that one. Some racket they make too. Do ye no hear it?

Aye, yeah.

Fucking billowing and cooing. It started the same time as the slope, the crack in the wall. It's a bugger too with the decorating. Ye cannay paper the walls. That's how I shove on a lick of paint. Them down below tried to paper it. It all fucking fell aff. Ye would need to be a mathematics teacher to get the lines. Mr Donnelly laid the trowel on the floor. Come on ben the kitchen, he said, and paused. Dont mention rats.

When we entered the kitchen Mrs Donnelly was sitting on a dining chair with a newspaper on her lap which she was not reading. What like's the crack now? she said.

Much the same.

She nodded. There's tea in the pot. Ye for a cup son? I made extra.

Eh naw, I better go back.

Mr Donnelly walked to the sink and switched on the tap to rinse his hands. Did ye make a sandwich? he said.

Mrs Donnelly didnt reply. She said to me: What age is yer kids?

The boy's three the girl's two.

Is that his mammy with the fair hair?

Yeah, Wilma.

She looks awful like the lassie our grandson married, she has the fair hair too. Mrs Donnelly called to Mr Donnelly: Billy's wife.

Mr Donnelly frowned at her. I'll need to change the mix.

Aw.

The boy here thinks it might be lime, if we add some lime.

It might be worth trying, I said. I stepped to the doorway into the lobby. Anyway I'm sorry to bother yez at this time of night.

Och we're aye up late, said Mrs Donnelly.

She'll be wondering what's happened to me.

Mr Donnelly had poured himself a cup of tea and was stirring in sugar. Mind what I was saying if any of yer mates were in the building game, they might know the score ben the room.

I'll ask around.

That'd be good.

Nay bother.

Mrs Donnelly smiled and got up to see me to the outside door. Back up my own stair Wilma had the television on in the kitchen. What happened? she said.

Nothing.

Ye were gone a while.

I filled a kettle and shoved it on for a cup of tea. Wilma was watching me. I forgot ye were out! she said.

That's no very nice.

So what happened?

Nothing. I grinned. The outside wall's falling down.

Ha ha. Was that the noise?

Yeah, the fire brigade.

Wilma smiled.

I shrugged. He's doing a bit of plastering; the auld guy, he's good. His wife was there.

What's their name again?

Donnelly.

Is it okay?

Yeah, I said.

BRINGING
HER TO THE
LIBRARY

Then her feet. How come you're not wearing socks? I said. She stared down at her feet, mulling over the question. There were alternative answers. Is it because you have been wearing sandals? I said.

Yes! She laughed. That's it. She stared down again, wiggling her toes, then frowned. Only if it rains how you get the water in and your feet get slippy.

Definitely, I said. Sandals are out the question in this weather. She looked at me.

What did you do at church? Did you take them off?

She grinned suddenly. Yes! Did you know I did?

Of course.

She chortled, but cautiously, covering her mouth to muffle the sound, seeing a punishment possible.

Dont worry. Seriously, I said, there's no need.

But it wasnt her so much as me; I was worrying about her. I was exhausted. It was so draining. Everything. My energy. Intellectual energy. Did I have any? If so it was gone. Always having to think about it. Oh christ, I told her again and again to join the library. Never again would she have to involve me. All that information one can access. It was wonderful and can be even more wonderful just going online if one cannot access a book on the shelves one might find it there, depending on one's tastes, given that one is a reader, and one does not have to be a genuine reader; those of us who only browse will find libraries a haven.

She listened but didnay know what I meant. Maybe she couldnt read. I thought she could but maybe she couldnt. Maybe she lost it. So once inside the library lobby she wouldnt know what to do, where to go, whom to see. Watch me, I said, I'll be there with you. Just watch me. See what I do and later you can try it on your own. Computers or books. Whatever. Computers are good. Sometimes ye switch one on and it is like a curtain getting drawn back. Then outside ye see everything. With a computer it is inside but it takes ye outside.

She gaped at me, getting the image and amazed by it. She smiled, or seemed to – her face entered 'smile' mode. In this context I dont know if she knew how to smile. Not at first. But dont worry, I said, whatever ye do. You'll see these other folk and see how they do it. You'll work it out and you'll get behind the smile instead of outside looking in at it. And ye'll see this as progress. I know ye will, ye definitely will. The library is not only good as an end in itself, it offers a way ahead. The likes of you and me. Winter is deadly as ye know. Me as well as you.

Yes, she said.

When it is freezing cold, snowing, raining, dreich and miserable, you go into the library and get a heat, keep warm. Meet people. That is that. Most important of all is you get entertained. I always think that and so will you. When it happens you know for certain you are alive and living in a world of other people. That is the great thing.

She was watching me.

I knew yer feet would be cold, not wearing socks. I knew you would take off yer sandals.

Did you?

Of course. As long as you didnay feel it was blasphemous, I knew you would.

Oh. She smiled, covering her mouth.

So then ye dried them?

They dried in.

Dried themselves ye mean?

Yes. Did you know?

Of course.

She smiled. I craned forwards to see her feet again but now she was self-conscious and raised one foot to cover the other. She was staring down at my feet. Comparing them. I watched her, ready to smile. Mine were bigger than hers by some way. Big clumsy things, I said, that's my feet. Yours arent, yours are neat.

Yes.

Her hands were small too. I hadnay realised how small they were. Really, they were delicate-looking, soft. A man would have had a hang-up about this. Small feet, small hands, small penis. Not me. It didnay matter to me, small nose, small ears. To others it did. The way of the world. People I knew made a joke about it. In here they made jokes about anything. I thought it unforgiveable. A person's dignity is to be preserved at all costs, I said.

She didnt look at me. It was difficult for her. I was being totally honest with her but how did she know I was? Except through trust. I was advocating the library because I believed it the one place she could relax in the proper proper sense of what that is. People dont know what relaxing can mean to a person. They just dont know. I would want people to know. Come on, I said. I patted her on the shoulder. She closed her eyes and laid her head against my chest. I was not comfortable with this but pretended all was fine and okay. She remained with her head to my chest for several moments. Too long really, I didnt like her doing it for this length of time. But it was not self-consciously done and that made it easier. Things will improve, I said, one day you hope to marry and you will marry.

She nodded but it was not a responsive nod, more absent-minded. I doubt if she knew what I meant. She knew marriage but not in regard to herself. This form of relationship was new for us both and I was trying to put her at her ease but none was there for me, to help me, and in this sense maybe it was not working. But I was not going to blame myself. What else could I do? Nothing that I could think. She was used to defeat. Of course she was. Me too. Or what amounted to defeat. Maybe there was no defeat. Not for me not for her, in the sense I would have thought, and this did not sadden me although for some maybe it might have. But it didnt me. If I was so it was natural and I couldnay stop the feeling. Give me your arm, I said.

She reacted cautiously.

Let us walk, I said.

I dont want to.

It will be good. We need to walk, walking is moving. Come on, I said.

Do I have to?

This question brought a lump into my throat and I was not able to speak for a wee while. It made it worse that she could not understand my silence. Eventually I said, People need to move.

Not everybody.

Oh but this time of day, it is a time for moving, a time when we all, we all . . . we all move. I smiled. I reached my right hand to her and she grasped it. She sighed in the act. What courage. It was true. You underestimate yourself so much, I said, so so much. I touched her wrist: Another thing too; you think I know your life but I dont.

Yes you do.

Honestly, I dont.

Her smile was one of relief.

Are you weary? I asked.

Yes.

Hang on. I began pulling her onto her feet. She allowed this. Once upright she only stared at her feet. I waited for her to walk, or try to walk. She glanced at me, expecting a form of command. Where are your sandals? I asked.

She nodded.

No, I said, where are your sandals?

Perhaps by the door.

Good.

May I go?

Yes, that is what's happening, we're going to the library.

May I?

Yes.

She smiled. You always think of me.

No I dont.

You do. You are a kind person.

I was not kind and did not feel in the slightest that I was kind. There is expediency but that is not something, certainly not. I tugged at her wrists. She had become stubborn and would not move from the spot. I tugged again. No, she was not moving. She studied our hands. Yours are big, she said, expecting an explanation.

People are different. Some are stubborn; others have big hands, some walk in sandals, others in their bare feet. I apply honesty in my dealings. Others dont. I desire it on the personal level and in every level too, of human engagement, levels of it, it is level.

Oh, she said, gazing at me with great sympathy, while awaiting my reassurance. I found this not challenging but presumptuous. Blamelessly so. I could not have blamed her. I could not have blamed her. She closed her eyes, allowing me to tug her forwards. I did. She did not totter. I could leave her stand alone. I allowed it and stood threequarters onto her that she might also walk but that I could support her if necessary. She smiled but not sheepishly. Are we going to the library? she said.

Of course.

What is your part in it?

What do you mean?

Am I to trust you?

Of course, I said.

She chuckled and touched my hand, and trod forwards daintily, in a typical style, grasping the side of her dress.

DID THE PIXIE SPEAK?

The house was over the southside and it was to be quite a walk when I got off the bus. I missed the stop and that made it longer, then it was right down the end of the street. It turned out to be a wee backwater, a cul de sac; in other words, a dead end. But I could see how folk would like living here because of the privacy, the peace and quiet. People liked that and paid money for it. Back in those days the flats here were worth a fortune. Ivan Johnson was the name of the guy whose flat it was. As usual the top storey. The same everytime I went on a delivery. There were a few other names at the secure-entry.

It took ages for the security buzzer to be answered. Nobody spoke, it was just a different echo sound. I said, I'm here to see Gerry.

Nothing happened. I waited a while then buzzed again. This time I heard a funny noise, like somebody going do do do do do do, as though mimicking an engaged tone on the telephone. I listened for a few moments: do do do do do do; then it stopped. Did I hear breathing? I'm here from the printers, I said, is Gerry there?

Now somebody whistled but the door unlocked and I opened it and went in and on up. The stationery I carried was packed solid in three plastic bags and was heavy. Awkward too: I had to watch the bags didnay bust; I stopped a couple of times to change hands.

But this building really was something. I had never been in a tenement like it before. People left potted plants out on the landings. Apparently nobody stole them. Fantastic. My Granny and Grandpa stayed in an auld yin but it was very different to this and didnay have the fancy trappings. Here were tiles all through the close and stained glass on the landing windows and ye got the feeling the people here were all quite old and rich. It looked like the design had been done by hand but how could it have been?

There was only one door on the top landing but next to another buzzer it had five names, including Ivan Johnson. The door was ajar. I thought about going in. But no, that was a bad idea; I just had a feeling, and I hit the buzzer. Even doing it, I dont know, it didnay feel right, something about it, even if it was a kind of trap, but what could that have been, how come? I had to buzz a couple of times. Then the footsteps down a creaky staircase and the door opened and it was a guy. I made the mistake of asking him if Ivan Johnson was in. He gave me a total rigmarole. Who are ye, what is it ye want, is the business urgent, did ye say ye were coming – all that kind of stuff. It was sarcastic what he was doing and when I showed him the stationery bags and told him it was a message for Gerry he just about shouted at me. Oh Gerry! oh! oh! Gerry! Then he looked me up and down: And you are?

I'm from Thomsons.

Thomsons?

The printer.

The printer the printer the printer. Obviously you take precedence.

What?

What! he said, right into my face.

I had never met this guy before. What was it all about? Total crap. He was supposed to be an artist. To me that was the last way he acted. Artists dont get involved in petty crap, not like this. It annoyed me too because not only was I in a hurry, I didnt even need to be there. I had volunteered to make the delivery. Somebody had to and I offered because it was Gerry. He needed stuff urgent for tonight. Flyers and leaflets for the march that was on tomorrow. It was an important one. A demo and a public meeting were to follow. I was going on it myself straight from work. Saturdays I finished at the back of twelve noon.

But from the way this guy was talking I knew Gerry was there. I held up the stationery bags. Look, I said, I'm just delivering this, that's all. Gerry phoned me at the printer to say he would be here. It was him gave me the address.

Oh it was you, he gave you the address?

What?

What! he said.

He stepped back and gave an exaggerated look at the three bags. He was waiting for me to show him what was inside. But it had nothing to do with him. We only finished the printing two hours ago and here it was, for Gerry and nobody else. Marie in the office had told me that but even if she hadnay it was what I would have done myself. Is Gerry there? I said.

Oh are you in a hurry?

The guy not only gazed at me here he started kind of rolling his head from side to side with this big kind of gaping maniac smile. I didnay know what to do. I thought he was crazy or else just being absolutely sarcastic. He was probably the same age as Gerry or even older. I dont know. I was nineteen so he could have been twice my age. I wasnt used to somebody acting like this. It was like he hated me.

He was a total arsehole, plain and simple. And taking a chance the way he was carrying on. Some guys would have got angry and would have been entitled to get angry.

He left the door ajar and I heard his footsteps on up the creaky stairs. I stood waiting. It went on a while. I felt like an idiot. He wasnay coming back. What was I supposed to do? I wasnay on overtime here. The owners didnay pay extra for stuff. It was just a favour I was doing on my way home from work, not only for Gerry but for them, the husband and wife that owned the business. They were committed to worthwhile causes. All different people and groups used them; community projects and campaigners, wee political groups, even political parties. Some thought the owners were too committed. It meant there was always 'rush jobs' and we were having to leave one order and jump to another. Then everything got rushed and last-minute. It was an irritation for the folk that worked there. It meant too that ye couldnay be too particular. Ye wanted to do a good job but ye didnt get the chance. Everything was here and now and rush rush rush, so inks were out and so on, and ye were supposed to not worry about it too much. Except if it didnay operate in a business-efficient way then there wouldnay be any business. That was my Dad's opinion. He was a storekeeper. The same happened with 'paying the bills'. The people who used the printer didnt always have money upfront. The owners were always harassed but coped with it. They seemed to cope with it anyway.

But this was another thing wrong with Ivan Johnson's attitude, acting as though it was some big global business enterprise. People like him annoyed me. They had no politics but pretended the opposite.

Maybe as much as five minutes passed. I knew he wasnt coming back. I lifted the bags and walked in.

Some place right enough. Huge big ceilings and a massive big hall. To the side was a door with a sign, The Ivan Johnson

Suite. It was nicely done but, no doubt about it, he had a good touch, for what it was worth. More calligraphy than italic. Actually it was good, so at least he showed that.

This door was open. Inside a wooden staircase led up to the attic. The bannister itself was a bit shoogly but nothing that couldnay have been put right. I didnay know ye got attics inside tenement buildings. Fantastic. Very elaborate the way the walls and the bannister were painted the same red and yellow colours.

At the top the landing twisted round a corner. Up here the ceilings were much lower. In a wee room I saw furniture stacked. Ivan Johnson was either coming or going. Stuff was packed every-where; binliners and cardboard boxes. The wood on the walls but it was real old-style panelling. Ye wouldnay have got wood like that nowadays. It was a very deep colour, almost a red – beautiful, ye wanted to smell it, run yer finger ower it. I would have taken a piece of that wood home with me just to have in the house. There was also a lot of pictures stacked back to front, oil on canvases and all sorts, and it would have been great seeing through them all. Art class was the one thing in school I ever liked.

I found Gerry in a large room with a sloped roof, he was standing inside one of the window alcoves. This room was chokablok too, junk and piles of newspapers, more pictures. There was a weird clock on the wall. It looked like a handmade effort out of tin. There was something about it I didnay like, except ye wanted to look at it and see how things fitted. It didnay look that old. I doubted it was anything special.

Gerry hardly looked at me, he just nodded his head when he saw the bags. Is that the rain on? he said.

Surely he could have seen for himself if he was looking out the window? His head was away somewhere. I wanted to leave the stuff and go but I didnt. He stood there, whatever he was thinking, I dont know.

Sometimes ye looked at him and it was the guy ye knew from the media. Ye had to remind yerself ye knew him personally and ye said his name if ye were talking to him, just like he said yours. He wasnay what ye would say good-looking, but maybe he was. He was different. He had a different type of head. He was quiet-mannered but could give certain looks. Ye didnay want to be on the receiving end of them. I suppose they were threatening. But what did they threaten? I couldnt imagine him punching anybody. I thought he was good. Other folk thought he was arrogant and only out for what he could get. They said he was ambitious for a career. That sounded crap because what age was he? He must have been thirty or like thirty-two or whatever. When do ye get careers? To me it was more how some criticise the ones that go out on the street and try to do something. Okay if things are bad in the world but ye have to try and change things, not just talk about it. Gerry was one that did go out. Ye would expect people to respect that. If they did they had a funny way of showing it.

I dont think he had forgotten I was there. But it was getting that stupid way; maybe I was to speak or else just maybe go away, I wasnay sure, or else maybe if he had forgotten. I felt stupid and started getting myself up to say if he could check the stationery so I could leave, but then came a loud crash from another room. I jumped but I dont think Gerry budged an inch. Then footsteps and in came Ivan Johnson with a packet of binliners. He was wearing a different T-shirt, a red and yellow one with his name printed; his own actual name: I AM IVAN JOHNSON.

He ripped off a couple of binliners and started filling them with stuff that was lying about. He was so nervy. Acting like he wasnay but ye could tell a mile away just by how he was packing it in; trying to do it properly but not able to make a job of it, but not letting it upset him. At the same time he was acting for effect. He definitely was. He was like a kid showing off. Never once did he look in my direction. Then he came right close to me and I had to step out the way. It was like he hadnt seen me. I was invisible. So stupid. He had this new binliner and couldnt find the right end to open. I thought he was goni rip it the way he was gripping it and pulling it, trying to get the thing open. Ye wanted to take it off him before he got too worked up. When he got it open he grabbed a stack of clothes from the top of the bed and dumped it all in. The clothes had been neatly folded to begin with but he didnt care about that.

I had a cigarette out and was about to light up but he noticed. He looked astonished. Oh you just start smoking? he said. When you're in somebody's house? You dont ask, you just light up? Is that the way it works?

What?

What! he said.

I looked at Gerry but he didnay seem even to have heard.

Sorry, I said and put the cigarette back in the packet.

But now he kept on and on with really daft patter. Stupid nonsense no worth repeating, except it could have got embarrassing. I was his target and I dont know why. Even like it was personal, he was trying to give me a showing up in front of Gerry. How come? I had never seen the guy afore in all my life. He was acting like a huffy wee boy. This was a guy in his thirties. All the time he was doing it he was banging about with the binliners and I just really wanted to get away. I thought Gerry would say something but he only listened. He looked totally fed up. Then he said, Hey Calum, Ivan wants ye to give him a cigarette.

Oh Calum! The guy actually shouted.

Yeah, that's his name.

Now Ivan Johnson stepped right in front of me and I thought he might punch me. I was ready for it. I wasnay scared of him except I was worried he might grab something or if he had a knife maybe. He looked right into my face: Who the hell do you think you are?

What, I said, I dont know what ye're talking about. I'm only here a message.

Oh! A message!

A message for Gerry, aye.

Oh a message for Gerry. Indeed, yes.

I looked for Gerry to say something then but he didnay, he just stood there.

Ye just march into somebody's house! You think you have the right just to do that! You think I'm going to stand here and let you do that! What do you think, that you're going to walk over the top of me! Is that what you think?

What?

What! Yes, indeed. The guy laughed.

Gerry, I said, what is this?

Gerry shook his head.

Ivan Johnson laughed. Gerry Gerry Gerry! He laughed again and did a wee dance shouting, Gerry Gerry Gerry, Gerry Gerry Gerry.

Gerry said, For christ sake Ivan. Just leave him.

I'm not touching him.

Gerry sighed. Calum, give him a cigarette.

I took out the packet and offered him one. But he didnay take it, only stared at it. He scratched his head and stared at me, like he had hit a blank spot in his memory; how come I was standing there, he couldnay remember. Gerry's mobile rang and he went to the window to answer it, staring out. The artist guy smiled at me, not a good smile. I am Ivan Johnson, he said, dont you ever forget that. He tapped himself on the chest pointing to his name on his T-shirt.

I dont know anything about this, I said, I'm sorry. I dont know . . .

I know who you are.

What?

Yes, what.

What d'ye mean?

Now he took the cigarette and waited with it in his mouth like I was to light it for him. I passed him the lighter to do it himself. He did but kept the lighter. He stuck it in his pocket and turned his back on me. It was even funny. I held out my hand for it but he ignored me. Give us the lighter? I said.

He didnt reply.

That's my lighter.

He started opening another binliner. It was one of these things where all ye can do is look. It would have been funny except it wasnt. It was actually terrible. Really, it was. How come? I dont know, except it was. I couldnay have explained how terrible it was, or even why it was. Maybe a bad dream. Ye wondered if it was really happening.

Gerry was standing over by the window alcove, phone in hand. He called, That's Mac arriving in the street with the van.

Oh goody, said Ivan Johnson.

Gerry ignored him and started on another phone call, staring out the window.

I was glad he was sarcastic about Mac. It meant it wasnay just me that was getting it. Mac was Gerry's pal. If Ivan Johnson was doing it to him he would do it to anybody, so it was like nothing to do with the person he was attacking, it was just him and his twisted stupidity. He started giving me weird looks. Even how he done it was weird, like it was behind my back and I couldnay see him, except it was right in front of my face so of course I could see him. And he did daft things with the cigarette he was smoking. If ye were watching it would have been comical but no when it was happening to ye. I wanted to leave but I needed Gerry to say about the delivery and if it was all okay and everything about it, and he wasnt doing that. He was supposed to sign for it too but that wouldnt matter because it was me to him direct.

Who the hell was Ivan Johnson? How come Gerry was here helping him? I couldnt remember seeing him before. I would have if he had been involved with Gerry politically. He was carrying stuff to the door now and looking at me as if I was supposed to help. I might have if he hadnay been so hostile. Then he was babbling. What was he babbling about? He directed it to Gerry but it was meant for me, to do with the name Calum. Scotland the brave and blood and soil patriots; bonnie Prince Charlie. His ancestors werent Scottish. His name was Ivan and I was prejudiced or something. Racists in his own house. It was mixed-up stuff; not worth repeating. He was trying to bring me down, using big names from history and showing off like he was well educated and I wasnt.

I couldnay have cared less what he thought. It was the first time I had seen him and with a bit of luck the last. He didnay know me at all. How come Gerry ever helped him out? I dont know. I just wanted him to check the stationery and I was off.

The buzzer sounded. Gerry held the phone away from his ear and said to Ivan Johnson, That's Mac at the foot of the stairs.

D'ye expect me to fly down the stairs and let him in!

It's you that's flitting.

So?

Gerry shook his head and went back to the phone conversation. But ye could see the guy was angry, staring daggers at Gerry. Gerry didnay notice, leaning with his back against the window alcove. The buzzer sounded again. I said to Gerry, Will I go down?

Yeah Calum thanks.

Oh yes, just take your orders. Ivan Johnson shook his head. You're such a nice little boy!

What? Cheeky bastard that he was, I would have told him to fuck off, getting at me, how come he was getting at me!

Mac was right down at the foot of the close. Ivan Johnson could have opened the security door from the buzzer but hadnt bothered. He was surprised to see me. Hoh Calum! How ye doing? He had two plastic bags in each hand. A big carry-out; cans of beer, a couple of bottles of wine and another bottle, maybe whisky. Plus nuts and crisps and stuff. He nodded at it. This is for when we finish the flitting. Ye giving us a hand?

Eh naw, I wasnay eh . . .

Friday! Ye're playing football.

Supposed to be.

Mac gave me a bag of beer to carry up the stairs. I wanted to ask him about Ivan Johnson. Instead I told him about the stationery. So far I hadnt had a chance to tell Gerry about it. So far he hadnt even asked. He hadnt even looked inside the bags.

Maybe ye can pick up the rest of it yourself tomorrow morning, I said.

Yeah, said Mac.

I would do it myself except I'll be on the machines.

Okay.

Or if ye talk the owners into having it delivered.

No bother, said Mac.

The owners were funny about deliveries. For wee deliveries I was expected to take a bus. Usually if the job was political they gave it priority and might let me take their own car if it was urgent. But they didnt like people driving it. A twenty-five-year-old Volvo Estate. A great old car. I would have asked my

Dad for a loan of his except I didnt think it was right to ask it for somebody else's business.

Before we reached the wooden staircase to the attic Mac said, So ye've met Ivan?

Ehhh . . . I was going to say something else but why bother.

Is he been giving ye a hard time? said Mac.

I shrugged.

Dont worry about it. Ye might say he's got problems. He's an old comrade. Hey, when's kick-off?

Half seven, I'm supposed to be there for seven.

Dont hang about here then! Mac began whistling and moved on up the stairs. I followed. There was no need to stay. If Gerry wanted me for anything he would say, maybe, maybe he would. With Mac there maybe he wouldnt; probably he wouldnt. Unless if I helped with the flitting but if so it had to be soon. I could give a help, if I wanted to. Gerry wouldnay have asked, not directly.

He was helping Ivan Johnson stack the stuff by the outside door. The flitting hadnay been scheduled for this evening but now it had to be because there was some sort of problem. This didnt surprise me if it was Ivan Johnson. According to Mac the more serious problem was the van itself. The clutch seemed about to pack in. With a bit of luck we'll not have to shove it, he said.

Four of us, said Gerry, we'll manage!

Mac glanced at me. Three. Calum's got his five-a-sides, eh Calum?

Yeah well, supposed to be.

Aw. Gerry nodded.

I'll be fine to help but if ye need a hand.

That's okay, said Gerry.

It's okay I mean if ye do.

Ivan Johnson laughed, for whatever reason; more like a snigger. Gerry looked across at him and shook his head. Mac said, The van'll be fine Calum you go and get a game of football.

Listen to goody-two-shoes, said Ivan Johnson.

That was exactly what he said. It was the most stupid crap shite of a thing to say. About Mac too, imagine saying it about him. Just weird. Ye might have laughed. I didnt. Gerry smiled. Mac did too and gave him a wee salute. Just as well Mac reacted the way he did. He was a heavy guy and went ahead with anybody. Ye heard stories about Mac. Even the polis. He had been lifted a few times for street affray and breach. One time he got done for assaulting a polis van. They drove it into a crowd to break a line. Mac was one of the ones that stood their ground. It passed him to within an inch. Then they opened a door and knocked him to the ground and grabbed him. They gave him a kicking then done him for assault – assaulting the van. Gerry and them went to the polis office to get him out but it was a Friday afternoon and they kept him in the cell till Monday morning. They said he kicked the door. The polis were laughing about it in court.

Mac was good. Ivan Johnson was just so wrong and the disrespect. He was an idiot. I couldnt believe he would have said something like that. He was looking at me now. It was me, and a smile, the way he smiled, and the most stupid thing ever he called me – not worth repeating except what happened next I went red in the face, just really like blushing because with Gerry and Mac there it was the worst of all. I couldnt think of anybody worse to be there and hearing it, and when he saw how it affected me he pointed at me and said it again with a name at the end, a woman's name, he called me a woman's name: the woman's name then the highland waif! Oh look at her, the highland waif, she's blushing oh she's blushing oh dear she is blushing, she is so red.

It was just stupid and horrible. I couldnay handle the damn thing at all what he was saying, I couldnay and it was like I would start greeting, him pointing at me and smiling the way he was smiling. Oh the highland waif, she's just so upset.

How could I not handle it? I couldnt. I wished I could fly out the window or just disappear. What it was reminding me of was the patter ye get with guys that are gay or like if they are drag artists, just the way he done it, digging in at me and hurting me, he was just hurting me, that is what he was doing, how could he hurt me like that, I wanted to punch him, just batter him, pick something up and just batter him with it, Gerry there and not stopping it, just letting him do it to me. It beat me. I couldnay do anything. I was used to fighting and here I couldnt, like I was stuck there on the spot and it was just the worst ever and I felt again I was going to start greeting and maybe I dont know, if I was, maybe I was and Gerry being there and hearing it and just seeing me like that – and Mac, the two of them, what they were thinking, it was so so bad and the worst ever there could be.

I felt like I dont know just if I lost my temper, what would happen, but I didnt lose my temper or get raging angry, I was just in a state, just shaking, I think I was – and how too what I knew, they werent telling him to shut his mouth. They should have, they should have told him. They just were looking at me, not smiling, whatever, just looking.

It was just so bad, ye couldnay describe how bad it was. But why did they not tell him? They could have made him shut up. Even battered him, I would have battered him. Because they were old comrades, if that is what it was, so they wouldnay hit an old comrade. But what about me? How come they didnay see me? What was I? Okay if I was just young and hadnay been around much except a few months but I was always there and went to meetings. Usually always I did. What about him? artist guy, an artist guy. I had never seen him at one single thing. Never. Not on any march or demo or any solitary damn thing ever. Things that needed to be done, I done them. It was me. I always helped. If there was any stall or any damn thing, helping set it up or bringing in all the books and cards and stuff from the van and even two times I looked after the stall and took in the money. Usually but I was giving out the fliers and leaflets. Whatever, just what was needed, I done it. I just helped. Not just me, there were other ones. Women as well as men. We just did things to help, like tonight I delivered them the stuff. The printer's was my full-time job, I was typesetting and line-editing and doing all kinds of other work. That was what I got paid for. Not for doing after-work deliveries.

Naybody asked me to do it. I just did it. I didnay look for any thanks either. Things were needed. That was all. I just helped. I knew they needed stuff for tonight. The most of it would be for tomorrow. Gerry was glad when I said I would bring it because the van was needed – needed for here. I didnt know why it was needed, I didnt know it was for him, Ivan Johnson. When I phoned Gerry he told me to come round with it and that was how it happened. They could collect the bulk of it first thing in the morning.

I was a help. I dont know how this was happening. Where was the guy, I dont know, he had stopped talking. He was maybe out the room, I dont know, I wasnay looking. I wasnay looking at anything. Just the floor maybe, I dont know. I dont know.

I dont know even if my eyes were open, all what was happening, how come even it bothered me it was all just stupid shite nonsense. That was in my brain. How come this even bothered me? It shouldnay have bothered me at all, just so shite, so shite, and went on all the time with guys and everybody,

everybody. The five-a-sides, it was always like that, then ye were having a shower and everybody, and that kind of daft patter, skelping yer bum and pointing at ye, yer dick or whatever, all shouting things, it was aye there and ye were ready for it because ye were used to it and ye were never blushing, not at all, no since school ye would never have blushed, that was like – what was worse than that? No much. That was like the worst could happen and the guys would have got ye, they would have, they would have got ye. Imagine them hearing about this? If ever they ever heard about it.

My mouth was all dry now. It was like I didnay have the power to do anything much, except stand there and maybe shut my eyes but that was the last thing, I wouldnay shut my eyes, I wouldnay have done that, as if that was me completely finished because I wasnay, I wasnay, fucking arsehole bastard, saying that about me, getting at me like that, and I looked up and Gerry was looking, just looking, that was something, just like looking at me. I couldnay cope with it. I couldnay cope with it. Whatever he thought, that was the worst thing, him and Mac, what they thought. It was all inside going to roll down, if I blinked, all the tears.

Then what happened next was Ivan Johnson. He had a beer out and he pulled off the stopper. He said something. Then he said something else. I dont know, I didnt hear, if I was listening.

He drank the beer and put the can on the floor then was filling a binliner with stuff. He tied it up and walked out with it. Now Gerry said to Mac about the van and how was it running, stuff like that.

It was as if I was in a movie and now almost I thought I was deaf, I could see stuff and no hear anything like maybe I wasnay even there. What a strange thing the way it all happened. A dreamscape. All out of nothing. Ten minutes ago it was all fine and everything was okay and now it was this. I didnay even have to be there. It wasnay overtime. It was nothing. I didnay even have to go the message, it was just a favour, that was all it was, I was doing it for them.

That daft clock up on the wall, it was going on ten past seven. The guys would be in the café having a juice or something, just relaxing before the game.

So it was a taxi. That meant watching the money for tomorrow. A taxi was stupid but what else. If I didnay leave soon I would be too late even then. Ye had to be on the pitch at 7.30 p.m. and if ye were late it didnay matter, ye still had to be off at 8.45. The next teams were waiting.

Gerry was on the phone again, leaning against the window alcove, staring out. Mac was carrying some pictures out the room. I was able to get a grip of myself. Mac came back in and passed me a beer. Ye'll sweat it off later, he said. Unless ye want a cup of tea!

Ivan Johnson was in the room again. Mac said, Cups Ivan? In the kitchen?

Generally speaking, yes, this is where we find the fucking cups, in the fucking kitchen. Ivan Johnson looked at me. Is that not the case Hector, that one finds the fucking cups in the fucking kitchen?

Gerry looked over.

Ivan Johnson said to me, Dont look at him for support, he's got a habit of leaving his friends in distress. God knows what he makes of you!

I dont know what ye mean, what d'ye mean? I dont know how ye're doing this?

Oh you dont?

No.

Hey man, why dont ye give it a rest? Mac said, Ye're going over the score as per usual.

If it's as per usual why tell me about it? Why make a comment about it at all? If there's nothing to say dont say it, ye know the old saying. Hector here knows what I'm talking about, dont you Hector?

His name's Calum, said Gerry.

Yes and a fine upstanding name it is. It's a fine upstanding name. Ivan Johnson stared at me. So ye're back in the land of the living eh! Well done. He sighed and lifted his beer from the floor. I had been trying to figure it out, he said, it took me ten seconds. Now Ivan Johnson glanced over to Mac, and raised the beer to him. Old goody-two-shoes!

Mac saluted in reply, while on his way out the room.

Ivan Johnson saw Gerry was watching him. How's Emily these days anyway? he said.

Emily's fine. Gerry smiled. Hey Calum, this is one of the wildest men ye'll ever hope to meet.

Ivan Johnson shut his eyes.

Ye are though. Gerry winked at me. He is Calum, one of the wildest greatest guys you'd ever hope to met. Eh Mac . . . ?

Mac had come in with three cups and a jug of water balanced on a tray.

Just saying about Ivan, one of the wildest greatest guys ye could meet.

Mac nodded. I'll go along with that.

Shut up! shouted Ivan Johnson. Just fucking shut up!

Mac made a face at me, set down the tray and lifted packets of crisps out a bag. He opened a bottle of wine and poured into three cups. He looked suddenly at me. Hey did ye want a glass of wine?

Naw.

Wise man. That's how I didnay bring ye a cup!

He didnay bring ye a cup because he forgot about ye, said Ivan Johnson.

Mac smiled.

That's me now anyway, I said. I looked over to Gerry. So is that okay with the stuff I brought?

Ivan Johnson turned to Gerry. How come ye still hang around with fools?

I looked at Mac again but he didnay bother. Gerry was checking the print work I brought in the three bags. Ivan Johnson had left the room. I cant find the promo cards, said Gerry. He checked back through the packages: I dont see the promo cards? We need them the night for the gig we're hitting.

I didnay say anything because I didnt know anything.

There's no advice note so I cant double-check it against the stuff ye brought. Did ye not check it out before ye left the shop?

Who me? I said.

Yeah.

Well naw. It isnay really I mean it isnay my job. I just eh, it's no my job.

Did you not pack it? said Mac.

No. It's Marie does the packing I just eh . . . I mean . . .

Maybe ye left it on the bus? said Mac.

What?

Gerry sighed. He looked down at the packages and I thought he was going to check back through them again. Now Mac spoke. He said, Did ye take the stuff out on the bus?

Take it out?

Out the bags I mean.

Out the bags?

Mac shrugged. Well if ye took the stuff out ye could have left one, one of the packages. Ye could have left it on the seat. Mac glanced at Gerry who had his phone in his hand and was about to make a call. Gerry ignored Mac and spoke straight to me: Could ye not have looked inside to see what ye were bringing? Eh? Surely ye could have had a look?

Well no because I didnt know what I was bringing, I just knew it was a rush job and ye needed it, I mean I dont do the packing or anything; it's like the printing I do and typesetting kind of stuff.

Gerry nodded, glancing down at his phone. He reached for a cup of wine and sipped some.

Mac said to him, Can we phone Marie?

She'll be away home, I said.

Ivan was standing watching from the doorway. What's up girls? he said, is the revolution going to be late? Who's driving me by the way?

Me, said Mac.

Well for fuck sake stop drinking.

A glass of wine.

A cup of wine. And a can of beer.

Mac grinned.

It's not effin funny if the cops stop ye.

One cup of wine and one can of beer?

Yes, it is over the fucking limit.

Ssh, called Gerry who was back in the window alcove and flicking through contact numbers.

The trouble is I've put something down and I've lost it. Ivan muttered, Now it's gone forever, the same as the rest of this world.

Gerry wasnt listening. Ivan Johnson gazed at me but spoke to Mac. What's up with poor wee Hector? he said. The burden of life hangs on his shoulders. Some talk of Alexander but the Hector fellow was aye the man for me, at least he used to be.

Leave him, said Mac.

I take it he forgot something?

It's nobody's fault, said Mac.

Everything's somebody's fault. I'm always overwhelmed by these demonstrations of efficiency.

Ssh, said Gerry.

Dont ssh me.

Ivan shut the fuck up I'm trying to phone. Take the stuff down to the van and start loading.

Oh mister orders.

Gerry raised his hand to silence him and began talking into the phone.

Mac grinned. Now Ivan Johnson looked at me and held his hand out. Are you keeping the cigarettes to yourself?

I took them out and gave him one but didnt take one for myself.

Mac said quietly to me, Is it worth phoning Stephen?

He'll be away home too. Him and Marie live together.

Ivan Johnson chuckled.

Well they're married, I said.

Ivan Johnson shook his head. Mac smiled. I knew my face was red again. I dont know why. I dont know what they found funny. I dont know what I said except just the basic. I didnt want to be here now, not any longer. Gerry was talking into the phone but looking away and keeping to himself what he was saying. I really did just want to get away and hoped he would finish the phone call and say what it was, whatever, I didnt know what would happen, it just was nothing to do with me. I just took what Marie gave me, I said to Mac.

Maybe ye should have checked but.

But I didnt know what to check because I didnt know what was supposed to be there.

Maybe we can get it first thing in the morning? said Mac.

Yeah, I said, but if it was supposed to be for tonight?

Mac shrugged.

I saw Gerry was listening now too and I called to him: Could we phone Stephen and maybe I could get a key and go to the shop and maybe get the promo cards, I mean if the package is there, if it's lying waiting, Stephen would tell ye.

Gerry said, D'ye think ye left it?

What – naw I mean no left it I mean I didnay pack it, it was just eh, I just brought it. I just offered to bring it because ye needed it.

Gerry gazed at me.

I knew ye needed it. But if it wasnt there, I wouldnt have noticed because I didnt know what it was I mean the actual contents. I knew it was a rush job.

Poor little Hector, said Ivan Johnson.

Give it a rest, said Gerry.

Well because as yoosyoooal you are blaming the message-boy. Imagine blaming the message-boy. Tut fucking tut. But hey, if the message-boy has a message to go, and he does not go that message, he does not fulfil the obligation. In some countries they shoot the messenger. Eh Hector, did ye know that? They do it to appease the leadership and to let them off the hook. If the leadership stays on the hook too long they start to wriggle. Wriggling leaders are the last thing we need in a revolution, d'ye not agree? Hector and Lysander, some of Hercules. Some talk of Alexander eh, some talk of his boyfriends.

Gerry just smiled, shaking his head.

Why dont we all get drunk? said Ivan Johnson.

Aye, said Mac, forget yer flitting.

I'll just leave this place forever.

Did Picasso not do that? I said.

I beg your pardon? said Ivan Johnson. Did the pixie speak?

Gerry smiled.

So ye know these things? It's true. He outgrew the house and outgrew the rooms and outgrew the cupboards then he outgrew the whole fucking kit and caboodle, the house. He just fucked off and left everything. Every damn thing. How wonderful. All your work. Every damn thing. Every damn damn fucking damn fucking damn. He stopped suddenly and shut his eyes.

Hey you, said Gerry.

Ivan Johnson shook his head. He still had the cigarette in his hand. He took out my lighter and lit the cigarette, returned the lighter to his pocket but almost as though he had forgotten who it belonged to, not deliberate like to steal it. He took a deep gulp of smoke and breathed in deep too, with his eyes shut.

My advice is go and get drunk, said Mac. Then ye go and start in a new place. Getting drunk is the answer to everything. D'ye know that Calum? if they ask my advice that's the answer, that's what I tell them, go and get fucking drunk and give us peace. That's what I say to them. Or in your case go and play football. Mac grinned.

Ivan Johnson glared at him. We're talking survival, do you actually know what survival is? Do you actually know what survival is?

Mac didnt answer. But Gerry had heard although he just stared out the window.

Was that a reaction? said Ivan Johnson.

It's in yer head, said Gerry. Ye want me to laugh out loud?

Well it would be something.

Gerry glanced at his watch.

I said, I'm sorry about the stuff Gerry. It's just I didnay know what I was bringing so . . . I mean I'm working tomorrow morning and I can make sure like eh I mean I can get Stephen to let me away early or else maybe, I dont know, whatever, maybe he could give me his car.

Isnt he sweet? said Ivan Johnson.

Give it a rest, said Mac.

No but he is.

You just fuck off, I said.

Ivan Johnson laughed. The worm turns.

It's no me that's the worm, I said, I never done anything to you.

You certainly did not.

Give me my lighter, I said, it's my lighter and ye've taken it.

Instead of giving me it he took another deep draw on the cigarette.

Give him his lighter, said Mac.

Miss goody, said Ivan Johnson. He took the lighter out his pocket and looked at it, then put it back in his pocket. He gazed at me. I turned to leave. It was time for me to go now and I just wanted to go, just leave. Even the things I had said to Gerry, he wasnt listening, just staring out the window, not bothering about what I had said about tomorrow morning. It just seemed not to matter to him, it didnt make any difference. He was going to do it himself, whatever it was. Even like Mac, he wasnt listening to Mac either. That to me was something. Mac was good, and a good guy. Gerry didnt seem to listen to him either. I just wished he would say something because if he did I could have helped. It was twenty past seven. The football didnt matter now anyway. I hated this and wanted away. Mac opened a packet of crisps and offered me some. No thanks, I said.

He admires the cut of yer jib, said Ivan Johnson.

Mac grinned.

If he doesnt I certainly do, said Ivan Johnson. Ye dont mind me admiring the cut of yer jib?

I dont care what ye say. I really dont care. That's me away now Gerry, I said.

But you have a beautiful jib, said Ivan Johnson.

Shut the fuck up! said Gerry.

You shut the fuck up! said Ivan Johnson: You know nothing.

I know I know nothing.

Absolutely nothing. Not about sexuality. Not about nothing. You just know nothing about nothing about nothing.

That's a lot of nothings.

Ivan stared at him. Gerry glanced at his wristwatch.

I said, It doesnt bother me what he says. I dont care.

Ivan Johnson laughed to Mac. He doesnt care Mac do ye hear that?

Gerry folded his arms.

Ivan Johnson said to him: Ye really are a bastard, d'ye know that?

There's a lot of us about.

Mac said, Alright Calum?

Yeah.

Contretemps! Mac grinned.

Is he for real! Contretemps! Ivan Johnson shook his head and took a last draw of the cigarette.

Give it a rest, said Gerry.

I went to leave but Ivan Johnson stood blocking the door. If only ye knew him better, he said, if only ye knew him better.

Aw come on, said Mac, leave him alone.

What is it? I said.

What is it? Ivan Johnson looked at me a moment then grinned. To the side of him I saw Gerry shrug.

Aw for christ sake, said Mac, that's enough.

What is it? I said and my face was red now, and so red, so red.

Gerry swigged at his cup of wine. Ivan Johnson said to him: You fucker. He doesnt know what I'm talking about. Then Ivan Johnson looked at me again, and he frowned. He does, he said, he does.

But what? I didnt know. I didnt know at all what it was. Ivan Johnson stepped closer in to me and grinned right into my face. I wanted to crash him with the head, right on the bridge of his nose. I really felt like that, just to bloody kill him. I thought I was going to faint and maybe looked like I was. Now he put his hand on my shoulder. I jumped back from it ready to punch him. You touch me, I said and passed round him to the door.

Calum! Gerry called after me.

I stopped then didnt and walked on and just like walked on down the stairs to get out of there. I carried on down the stairs. I really didnt want anything to do with him, any of them, I just didnt know and hated it all. It was just Gerry, it was only Gerry, if him, it was only him, if he thought, if it was something, what did he think, it was only him anyway who cares, who cares.

VOLCANIC
MATTERS

My facial muscles had erupted. I traced the thing with my right index finger, touching gently, softly, tracing the outline and inner swelling, finding the ouch point. Volcanic was a more than adequate appellation: astute even, for how else to describe the tragedy. My face was a gigantic pimple decreasing to a globular shape complete with eruption, the volcanic protuberance, great fucking irritant, producing an unpleasant sensation when touched, as now, even in such soft, soft . . .

I was groaning, afraid to seek out the mirror. That was funny. At any rate amusing. Obviously it was ironic and could only ever be ironic. I looked this way and I looked that way. Suddenly I moved, scampering, I scampered about the room, oh what will I do what will I do.

What will I do now.

One thinks of these things, and other things too. And I stopped the scampering in the act of uttering the words. So often it comes like a question, *what will I do now*. Well is it a question, not just *like* a question, it is one; that is the form it comes in. And the question takes one by surprise to the extent that it is not even a question.

Yes it is a question but having such force it travels beyond that, it is a segment of one's being that is fundamentally central to one's essence and in grammatical terms is designated 'verb'.

That is the truth. Verbs are at the root of my very essence; my heart and my soul. I am a doing person altogether.

Forget preparation. What is 'preparation'? One is better off diving head first into one's life. One meets a potential partner, so meet her, just meet her.

One thing was clear, I knew where the mirror was, if I wanted to find it. Did I want to find it? No! Not just doubtful: NO. I had no intention of finding it, now when my face was the very last thing ever I wanted, never ever never.

It is true. There was the mirror. I cocked my head to the right side. This was a habit. It was not a bad habit although one might have wished it on another. An elderly relative once advised me that such was my Father's habit. Oh god my father jesus god love us, in short, I preferred my Mummy. Now here I was cocking my head like the auld bastard, auld dadikins, dastardly dadikins. O he was alright, simply that the annoying habits, annoying habits, that was Dad, him and his

o well, so I was like him. Well well. I was gazing into the mirror, this way and that, quirks of the eyebrow, the hairline. Oh Daddy Daddy!

But matters of a volcanic nature.

Life takes one by surprise. The poor auld fizzog. *What will I do now?*

In the form of a question a statement is mere rhetoric.

Hang on a minute: this question does not imply action, it *contains* it. It is not a question at all but a statement, supposedly of intent; a stated intention. God love us all.

This action existed that I was to perform.

The theory of relativity in a sentence. How does that happen? Often I appear a genius. The old Scotch thinkers created mechanical devices to test metaphysical systems, going all-in on Newtonian physics.

I sighed and sighed again, cheerily. The recognition of this induced a smile. That smile! In the name, I was my Father, who art in an urn, unnir the grun.

Verily there is an astonishing difference, an effortless gulf, between what will I do, and what will I do now. And a distressed person who makes such a distinction is on the road to recovery. That was my own feeling, staring into that mirror. Forget the bloody volcanic tip. This is a temporary physical blemish.

If I had been a male of average, a male of, an average kind of, if I, I would not have seen it like this at all, hardly – an average male, not an average male, I/he would have plowed on and done it in that average male manner where every decision being one's own decision done by and for oneself in the absence of 'the other'. But not this male, never this male here here here, thinking of how one is in the world and blemishes, always blemishes, blemishing the body. I saw into my eyes. I had invented the word 'blemishing'. Before me there never was such a word, for such an activity, blemishing the body. O if only I could live in a different manner.

staring into that mirror, staring onto that surface, the surface of a mirror

Does the surface of a mirror exist? What colour is the surface of a mirror? In the absence of colour does anything exist? When we stare into a mirror do we disappear?

The pimple had grown. My god. It was all the time. Gender characteristics, and so unfair. Anti-existential. Why should this distinguishing feature of humanity effect such consequences on living one's life, surely life is conditional on existence, the existential condition. That might be a defining truth about females but here was I, a male not so average yet at the same time yes, merely, merely myself, when all is said and done, myself, merely a male. O what am I to do, what am I to do now?

Thunderstruck.

No.

Yes.

THE
PRINCIPAL'S
DECISION

The Principal here was known to have hesitated before lifting the dishcloth which he used to wipe clean the blood. I did not witness the hesitation. It was reported. When he had wiped clean the blood he glanced to where I was standing by the door. I was his associate and waited there. The body lay crumpled in its own heap. This was approved. The Principal reached towards it but only for purposes of evaluation. He was not being observed, not as such. But I saw that his eyes closed. This part of the practice is found wearisome by some. In those days I supposed that its continued existence was for decorative purposes but I took part in it. My interest was genuine. It had occurred to me that if decoration had no part in the practice then aspects of it were mere obsession. Allowing for this, if it were a form of obsession might the Principal have employed it for decorative purposes? If so I thought it admirable. I have to say that I did. At the age I then was it brought a smile to my face. It later occurred to me that he wished to be rid of it altogether, signified by the hesitation before lifting the dishcloth.

Music in the background. A nocturne by Henry Rocastle sent the Principal into a dreamy condition. Art was his passion, or so he maintained.

Would he wait until it finished? No, not him. He used his foot to manoeuvre the ruffled edge of the corpse's clothes. The untidiness made him grue. Yet his facility to operate in the most trying circumstances, withal, was here to the fore when he could never have stopped himself reaching downwards, and seemed to notice his own fingers curl in preparation. Whether he approved or not I could not say.

He had a degree of self-consciousness that I knew to respect. I watched how he sighed yet easily lifted the corpse's arm, let it fall. The arbitrary action might have made it the more natural, removing a general untidiness, so to speak. But this untidiness could not be removed from himself, not altogether. Arthritis would have him cornered in not many years hence. This was reported to me. By then I had advanced in a manner that demanded he be placed on retreat.

The Principal's very professionalism allowed the distance between truth and appearance. It is not enough to state that I respected this quality. I was experienced in the field but not expert. Whether this was enough to secure the primary position time alone would tell. I saw that the elbow of the corpse had bended. Should this have been corrected? Queries of this form can be posed objectively. Workable inferences may be ascertained by examination of the interior. A course of potential activity, from either or both, is safely predicted. Patience did not enter into these proceedings. He expected objectivity if not indifference. Either was a reward, having its own significance.

The arrangement of articles displayed on the shelving inclined towards order, irrelevant to the overall picture which was already contained in the above. Severing a limb was pointless. Such a possibility had presented itself. The result would exist as inconsistent. The Principal would not accept such. The result would further illustrate a pattern. The pattern would appear perfect, after its own fashion. Perfection of this type is not what is required. Thus the Principal looked to myself. I knew this as a ruse. I glanced at the large wall-clock. His decision belonged to an earlier generation. In these harsher times alternative courses of action were hypothetical. This was the nature of the Principality. On another occasion, and in less immediate circumstances, I might have smiled. The next time he glimpsed the clock it would have stopped altogether. Not through any action of his. Such would never happen. He would look to me. Any decision of mine required due process. I might have smiled. My pulse had quickened and I wet my lips. The proper matter I should have happen is what would happen and what must happen, and in the correct time, but to no avail.

The Principal studied me. I knew reality and hoped that a truth lay between us. Nevertheless I departed the room. I strode into the adjacent room. I then witnessed the Principal stand alone. There would be no private smile. It was as it was and his practice dictated a practice. It was nothing to him. Personal detail is of no account in situations of this nature. Our work concerns extensions, parts and bodies. The Principal peers at the corpse, now comfortable in its presence. He could have filled a kettle, made and poured a cup of tea. Such moves enabled promotion and were victories. Their nature would enable my own promotion. It was no thanks to know that his had depended on my absence, but perhaps not.

WORDS AND
THINGS TO SIP

I had to move on. The main question concerned Anne: where was she? I gave up the highstool at the bar and carried my drinks and bag to a table, accompanied by my brains. That was alright; I needed them to think and I was wanting to think.

The nature of the thought, the content. Forget one's father. Had I been thinking of my father? Not in so many images, simply a sensation, a sensation of daddy – poor old fucker, dead for the last twenty years. We think of the dead, even fathers, they are always with us. Even when we are thinking about all these hundred and one different and varied matters, business matters: will one ever make a sale again in one's entire miserable existence? Shall I ever walk into some fellow's office and chat him into an irreversible decision in regard to a sum of money large enough to guarantee one's job for another fucking month? No wonder one sighs. My old man never had such crap to put up with. He was a factory worker. One contends with all sorts, all sorts.

Life is so damn hectic, especially the inner life. The dead and the undead. And thoughts of Anne and myself, our relationship.

I groaned again. These days I groan out loud. People hear it and look at me.

I didnt need pubs like this in which to become annoyed. Although they did annoy me. I get annoyed at myself, by myself and for myself. Leastways irritated, I become irritated, breathe in breathe out.

Having said that, I was turning over a new leaf. The short-tempered irascible chap had gone forever. Recently I had been prescribed aspirin; anti-coagulants. One's blood. Henceforth I was to be a changed man, a veritable saint of a fellow. Never more would I lose my temper over something as trivial as bad service in a hostelry of questionable merit, a bad boozer in other words, who cares? Not me. Never more. Those parties who ignore a body they perceive as a stranger. Erroneously as it so happens. Little did they know I was a fucking regular so why not treat one as a fucking regular? Who cares, of course, me or not me, it dont matter.

Unpunctuality whether in barstaff or one's nearest and/or dearest.

A bad choice of language. But never more, never more.

What never more? What the hell was my brains on about now? These whatyacallthems did not deserve the name. Brains are brains. Whatever I had, tucked inside my skull, those were unclassifiable, certainly not fit to be described as 'brains'.

Oh god, God even.

Yet Anne was rarely punctual. Why worry about one's nearest and/or dearest.

Odd. I recognised where I was sitting. This was where I typically sat in this typical bar, of all most typical bars. It was side on to the door, avoiding unnecessary draughts.

I had books and reports, the smartphone alive to the touch, even sensing the touch. And an old newspaper too, a – what the hell was it, a something Planet – what a name for a newspaper! Was that not Superman, here at the Daily Planet with Clark Kent and that old chap, the irascible editor, what the fuck was his name? Who knows, who cares, Perry Mason or some damn thing, so what, I could have read the sports pages.

Maybe I would. Whether I did depended. I was drained –

drained! Yes, washed out, exhausted, weary, deadbeat, shattered; stick adverbs in front or behind, all you like any you like; mentally, psychologically, physically, sexually, emotionally, socially; then quantify: totally, wholly, almost, just-about, a small amount, very much. Had I strength to spare I might read a report, book or newspaper. Alternatively I could sit and sip alcohol, insert the earplugs and listen to something, something! Or view television, or watch the world go by, neither intrigued nor bored by thoughts of a downbeat nature. Mum too – if it was not the old man it was her – why was I thinking so much about my parents? Maybe I was about to drop dead and that was a sort of roll-call of one's existence. Hell's bells.

Anne would be here soon anyway. It did not matter if she were late. I had not seen her for six weeks, had not slept with her for my gad three months, three months. One could ruminate upon that. I enjoyed lying with her side on, her eyelids flickering. She also with me. This was our favoured position. We relaxed. I did anyway, being without responsibility for eight or nine hours, barring texts, emails and even phonecalls for heaven sake, but I could not switch off the phone, though her breasts, her breasts.

I disliked myself intensely. Nevertheless, one continues to exist. A small something in my pocket. A piece of jewellery nonsense for the one I loved. Gold, gold I tell you gold! I screamed it hoarsely, in the character of a crazed Humphrey Bogart, unshaven, unkempt – what was the movie? the mountains and gold.

Anne liked gold. Women do like gold. Golden jewellery. Joo ell ry. I kept the piece in my trouser pocket that none might steal the damn thing. England was not Scotland. Given that forgetfulness was a greater risk than theft. If I took it out my pocket I would forget to return it.

But I did enjoy gazing upon gold. Gold was a pleasure of mine too given that in my position I could not aspire to the unkempt unshaven look, being as how the state of one's dress, the label on one's suit, the subtlety of one's timepiece

Oh my dear lord. Panic panic panic.

Defective memory banks. The mind dispenses with petty data. The clock on the wall. I checked my wristwatch against it, and the phone, checking both, pedantic bastard. And not panicking. Never panicking. Never, never never never. I was not a panicky fellow − never used to be − besides which the anti-coagulants, lest the dropping-dead factor . . . Jesus christ. I groaned again. I was glaring, why was I glaring? I studied the floor. One's shoes. One's socks. Tomorrow was Monday and I would buy new ones, new socks.

Oh god god god.

Three gods = one God, the way, the truth et cetera et cetera, breathing rapidly several intakes of what passes for air, for oxygen because one's head, one's brains, what passes for the thingwis, the whatdyacallthems.

Where however was she? One would have expected punctuality. And the barstaff:

barstaff are typically interesting. We try not to study them too blatantly lest personal misunderstandings arise. But we do study people. We are people and people study people. Humankind is a reflective species. Two had been serving in this pub for as long as I had been using it which for heaven sake was a long time; seven or eight years. Certainly a long time for barstaff to remain in the job. They assumed they had never seen me before. They were wrong.

But who wants to be a regular? It means one is alcoholic, near as damn it, an alcoholic geek, one who gets sozzled in the same bar year after year.

Neither barworker allowed me a second glance. I was a nobody. They might have qualified this to 'nobody in particular' which would have been better in the sense that a particular nobody is better than a general nobody. Still it would have been wrong.

Regularity need not operate within a brief span of time; twice every two years is also a pattern and such an event can be enclosed by mental brackets. I might only have come to this pub six times a year but I only came to the damn town on said half dozen occasions. So is that not regular? Make the question-mark an exclamation. Six out of six is not 99% but a fucking hundred if one may so speak. Of course I was a regular. Some people are so constipated their bowels only move once a month. But at least it is not irregular.

That crack once landed me an order. They were feeling sorry for me. Once a month every month is measurable, is regularity. A hundred per cent. A man had his dick cut open without an anaesthetic. Having to have one's dick cut open! Oh god. One could only shudder. Without an anaesthetic! That was just like – wow! Why even had it come into my mind! But it is such a fact; its incredible nature has it jump into one's mind apropos of nothing whatsoever. It was in the papers, stuck away on page 7, 8 or 9. It should have been front page news. I must have been reading a quality. Unless it was a lie. Even a sexual disease, a serious one: none requires that sort of operation, a severing of the skin. Getting one's penis sliced open without anaesthetic. Dear lord.

Move on move on.

Sliced was my word, not the newspaper's. It just said cut, cut is cut, sliced is sliced and severing is, of course, severing, he intoned gravely.

One considers punctuality. Why?

The main question: why did Anne even consider a fool like me? It was beautiful she did but why? I was no looker, I was no nothing.

Truly, I was not. Yet she had considered me.

Come the cold light of morning this question continued to arise, to haunt my very being as the author of Gothic yarns would have it.

I had one daughter. We never communicated. She used to tell me the books she was reading but due to my critical commentaries she stopped doing this, and stopped telling me about movies she enjoyed, plays she appreciated, painters that

forget it. The main question, or should I say answer, to our lack of communication

forget it.

The only reliable method of knowledge is literature. I was a reader of books. Truth comes in books: we cannot trust internetual information, nor other human beings, obviously, given the chap sitting at the next table to me was reading a quality newspaper so-called, given that in hostelries of this nature such newspapers, not to beat about the bush

But what could Anne ever see in me? In the final analysis I was a prick. Upon my tombstone let it be writ: Here Lieth a Prick.

Prick rather than dick; dick is a pleasant term.

In contemporary jargon I would admit to having 'fucked up' my life. One should admit such matters and not conceal them if such issues are thought to be the ones, the main perhaps questions, while Anne herself, she was never a blinding flash, what do they call it, love at first sight, oh this is the girl for me, it was not like that. I was in sore need of female companionship. Males tire me eventually. On guard and have at thou. An acquaintance of mine was fairly camp, well, really a friend rather than acquaintance and not 'fairly camp' but wholly so if not blatantly. Male company exhausted him. He told me that. I was pleased he trusted me enough to so confide. I didnt wonder: how come this guy is telling me such stuff? Rather I confessed to a parallel feeling. He nodded, not at all surprised. I appreciated that somebody else felt the same even although I caught him observing me during a lull in the conversation. I respected our friendship but distrusted it. Certainly there were times male company repelled me. Males are uncharitable. Younger males too, perhaps especially. One would expect tolerance. Walking into some factory or warehouse and them all looking and sniggering, what is he selling, fucking fool.

On occasion I need to sit, only to sit, to sit still, to sit at rest, to just be be be be, just be, and unaware of my breath. Without a woman this was impossible. Another friend was an ex-alcoholic and divorced. He told me the major boon concerning alcoholic friends is how they relax together; they share basic acquaintance, occasionally drink tea together, occasionally not. But they lapse into silence. They do. I found that remarkable. I should have expected a headlong charge into confession, each outshouting the other, listen to me listen to me, the poem of course, who was that now? Coleridge.

Silence. The leaves doth grow, doth shed, falling.

I first met Anne on the other side of town. She was in company. I was introduced to her and we got on. We met the following evening. The sexual attraction was mutual. My heart skipped a beat. What is beat? The assignations began and we lay together. She chose the rendezvous. This bar.

Life has the habit of booting one in the testes. Anything might happen. I checked my watch and, instinctively, my belongings. A man had risen from his seat, cigarette already in his mouth, making for the smoke exit. He was a shifty-looking bugger. An older man but older men can be shifty given they are less suspicious, immediately that is. Once one ponders a little one has second thoughts, these bastards are just cautious, seeking the slightest opportunity.

The truth is that I did not care. If someone wished to steal my goods and chattels they were most welcome because I did not give a fucking shit one way or the other and that is to be blunt about it.

I had become an afternoon drinker, an imbiber of false hopes, false dreams. Even one's fantasies are false. What is a false fantasy? I once had a boozy conversation with my daughter. Unfortunately I advised her of my secret desire which, at that time, was death. Nothing false about that.

Oh fuck.

I reached for my briefcase to check the report. I had 'a report'. A REPORT!

Jesus god.

I also had an anthology of short stories by writers from Central America. I left it concealed. Instead I would read the walls and read the tables, read the chairs and read the floor. Truths are where you find them.

I opened the report once again, he sighed wearily.

The sort of fucking garbage one is fed at head office. Not that I cared, I did not fucking give a fucking rat's fucking arse, bastards. Even if they did fire me. I did not fucking care. Not one solitary particle for all their lies and dissembling: should one be cast onto the heap of forgotten souls? Never!

They no longer pretended respect. But I had none for them so there we are. Whatever I had was gone. Such incompetence. They were unable to back a chap! They wanted to sack me but could not. Ever heard anything like that! At my age all one seeks is competence, efficiency. People who do their work in a consistent manner. They do not fall down. They do not leave one high and dry. They do not forget the most important component of any business. Salute in passing oh colleague. Do not fear. One's hopes and dreams will not fall on stony ground.

It does not matter how gifted the scientists are, how advanced the products, if those cannot be sold they will sit there in the warehouse. These are not planks of wood and tons of gravel. Wood and gravel will be of use in a thousand years' time. For new technologies all it takes is six months, if these cannot be sold in six months let them be consigned to the heap of forgotten ideas.

On a daily basis fevered spasms struck my brain. A customer said to me: William, your brains are palpitating, look! See the sides of your head: your temples are banging together. Look, look at your whatdyacallthems!

How does one spell 'forever'?

The new technologies are of a certain order. Technologies do not change things in the world they change the world.

I had a proposal for Anne; not wedlock, of slightly greater importance than that. But she, however, was a woman.

What do I mean by that?

Nought may be taken for granted.

I had one ex-wife and one who – well, the reality, I had been a widower when I married her. My ex-wife was my second wife, my first wife died a heck of a long time ago. So so long ago. Mother of my daughter. Yes I thought of her. Parents, mothers, fathers.

It would be wrong to say that I did not think of her. Yes, I did, after so many years. I no longer felt like her lover because I had been her lover. I carried a photograph of her and had scanned a couple too. My daughter kept most of the photographs. She was quite remarkable really. She had a smile – what would one call it? – beautiful, the most beautiful smile. Girls are so damn open, they are so damn generous! In fact

move on.

Women regard wedlock in a favourable light.

Vodka and water. A typical drink. Not my favourite. A colleague described it as a 'working drink'.

Things that are truths are no longer truths. This type of mental whatdyacallit peregrination. By the time one remembers the context one has forgotten the word. It was age. Ten years ago I would have followed the thought, wrestled from it the sense. My line of work destroys the intellect. I was a university graduate. Now look at me. I glanced round quickly, having spoken aloud. I did. I thought I did anyway, maybe I did not, maybe it was

oh well, and if I had, what odds, what odds.

The reader of the quality newspaper appeared to be concentrating unduly. He must have heard me speak.

The reference was freedom. I saw it as a possibility, as substance. When I was a student, many years ago, I lived my life taking freedom for granted, intellectual freedom. Enmeshed in that assumption is the concept 'progress'. Students assume progress as a natural state. A false assumption. Nor, if it does exist, need it be chronological or should I say linear, geometrical rather than algebraic, in keeping with the digital thingwi, revolution.

Vodka and water.

Once a widower always a widower. If one's wife was one's first, one's first love. Not just a relationship, a marriage, complete with child, finished. One wee girl. It was nice having a wee girl.

It was a pleasant drink aside from anything. In the past I used cola which had become too sweet so then lemon, bitter lemon, stressing the bitter. A vodka and lemon please, bitter. Vodka and orange, bitter orange. Gin and bitter orange. Gin and lemon of course. But not gin and water. Why! And of course Spanish brandy and water, I had a fondness for Spanish brandy, if only to annoy the purists.

Drinks that do not stain the breath; which does not refer to the Spanish although it too renders one too eh well now how to say it, pissed.

Life is strange. Context is all. Without context where would we be? Where would the world be? This question is the most real. One might consider much. But, howsomever. Then when the context is human, a personned-entity, another person, i.e. not oneself. When another intellectual being, repository of humanned data, has become the context. Love is indicated.

How does one define love? Anne is not at all in the image of my first wife and yet and yet, needless to state, I, well, perhaps, ah, perhaps, indeed, may I love her, do I love her? do I do I – a song by Blossom Dearie, oh Anne do I love you, do I do I.

essence of woman

Language turns a man inside out. The world through Anne-tinted spectacles; today William is wearing his Anne-tints.

Having said all of that, ignoring reports and briefcases, if not for university I would not have read and appreciated Monsieur Sartre. I did appreciate Sartre. People condemn universities. Not me.

I was so looking forward to seeing her. I had failed to appreciate how much. If she was not going to turn up, and let us face it

Why was she not here? She was not here. She was not coming. Ha ha.

I was not a man for the one-liner. I enjoyed proper jokes. More jape than joke, and japer than joker. I performed japes. Allez oop. Just sign there madam.

Yet when it came to it, thinking about how much time I gave to her, to thoughts of her. Not all that much. I thought about everything else. But she was never faraway, lurked within, inside of the brain old gel, she was at the root, her presence determining negative space. Mine was the most healthy negative space one could discover: so much so it was the opposite of negativity where negativity is an unpositive element. Anne was the direct opposite and inside my head she was like that. My head had been full of vile bitterness, a composition of bitterness and anger. And rage, irritation and frustration and bloody hurt sensitivity, hurt sensitivity, too much even to think about; such that it drove a man to distraction. Soon she would enter the bar. She would place her hand upon my brow. In a former life she was a healer. Upon the brows of the ill and dying, and they did heal. She has retained this ability through various transmigratory peregrinations. Peregrinations, a damn fine word. I would to construct a monument to my love, this woman of the balm. Vodka and water. I gestured with the glass as in a quiet salute to the dearly departed, the yet-to-arrive.

A barworker was gazing across. I nodded to him but my nod was not acknowledged.

I was an interloper.

People's lives are sacred.

Through the side window the street lights blinked. It was early December yet still warm. I liked the north of England and Lancashire in particular. Jokes abounded but I found it okay. It was not dull and it was not dreary. Ever stepped down from Wigan Central and not enjoyed a large brandy in the bar of the Station Hotel? or am I thinking of Rochdale? The old Station Bar had gone of course, like community fellowship, the days of which too had gone, yea. One crosses the road to the licensed grocer as once we termed the mini-market, a half bottle and a couple of cans for the rest of the trip home, perchance one avoids the more obvious error, madly dashing back up the stairs into the station and stumbling onto the slow train to Fleetwood, or Blackpool, or where was I when the conductor came calling? Never mind sir.

It was two and a half hours since the text. Anne was most overdue, let us say – albeit her life, her life was complicated.

Other than Anne and my first wife I have had five women as serious presences in my own life, excluding my paternal grandmother with whom I had an early bond. My ex-second wife, my present partner, my elderly mother, my daughter and Joan Richmond with whom I had a lengthy affair some years ago. It struck me that these six women, in fact seven – eight including my grandmother – shared characteristics yet nevertheless were so different

In fact it was eight women. Dear god!

This was predictable.

Eight women.

My daughter did not count, being of myself. I was attracted to aspects of myself. Yet at the same time we two were so different! How could we be so different and at the same time be aspects of the one?

Shared characteristics and traits. Such a cliché to say that I loved most all but I did, nevertheless, I did. I do not hesitate to use the word, 'love', for what is love? The indefinable, he said with a cheery grin. But Joan Richmond? I could not have loved Joan. Joan was just

I set down the new vodka and water, what was left of it, very little.

My ex-second wife was generous.

My god almighty sometimes it took her ages, bloody ages, we are talking ages. If somebody said to me are you coming and I said yes I would be there in two minutes, but that did not work with one's spouse. Nor did it work with Anne. If she said two minutes it was two damn days by the time she took care of everything so I had to advance her notice beyond reasonable limits. But of course. What was wrong with that? People cannot be expected to drop everything. Especially women; which is no sexist joke. I do not like sexist jokes. Women require greater segments of space and time.

Hell's bells.

The shifty-looking smoker had returned to his seat and the door opening again. Whoopee. I was onto my feet and to her, grinning like a madman, taking her by the elbow. Anne Anne Anne.

Sorry I'm late, she said.

Oh god, dont worry dont worry. I was laughing now and trying to put the reins on it. I showed her to where I was sitting, assuming she would sit on the chair next to me but she pulled back another, to sit facing me. I waited for her to talk. It was important to do so. She looked so great. She did! She glanced about the room. Same old place, I said.

She grinned.

Oh jees. You are looking wonderful my dear, my god you are, you are, you truly are.

Anne whispered but too low and I couldnt hear. I asked her to please whisper it louder, more loudly.

I couldnt get away, she said quietly, self-consciously. She gazed to the bar and added, You look tired.

I am. I'm going nuts into the bargain: g & t?

Thanks.

Imagine forgetting the damn drink!

I ordered another vodka and water for myself, a packet of crisps and a packet of nuts. I was looking forward to the night, looking forward to a meal. Where would we go? I hoped she would opt for Indian food. She preferred Chinese or Italian. I preferred Mexican or Indian. Grub needed bite. One for the notebook that. I smiled and shook my head. Grub needs bite, I said to the barworker who didnt reply but smiled vaguely which is always fine by me; if I get somebody to smile then half the battle be o'er, I shall get them to buy, for 'tis my job, the modus operandi.

Anne was signalling to me; munch munch. She was wanting a packet of crisps!

Allez oop. I abracadabrad at the bar where lay the bag of crisps side by side with the nuts. The barworker smiled honestly while handing me my change. Thank you most kindly, I said.

Anne ate her crisps in a mechanical way. But it was interesting. I was chomping a nut. Nuts for me and crisps for her. Aha! Hey! I said, a wee test.

She chuckled, and it stopped me in my tracks. I had been about to say something but her chuckle, her chuckle. You're laughing at me, I said.

Wee test . . . ! She shook her head, smiling.

My Scotteesh voice señorita eet knock you for seex? Seriously, I said and I snatched the packet of crisps out her hand. Without looking at the packet, what flavour's the crisps?

What do you mean?

Nothing, I'm just asking.

Could you repeat it?

What flavour's the crisps?

Aah . . . Anne frowned for a moment then studied me. I know it's a trick.

It's not, I said.

Mm. She frowned again. Is flavours a noun or a verb?

Pardon . . .

Is flavours a noun or a verb? she asked.

I looked at her. She was smiling at me. Anne smiled at me. Her hand was to her mouth, and she reached for my hand and held it, she studied it, turning it palm up, examining it for personality indicators or signs of the future. When do you go away? she said.

Tomorrow evening.

Are you working tomorrow?

I've got to be.

She nodded, she now was holding my hand with both of hers; both of her hands, she kind of cradled mine. My hand. What was I? just a damn man.

That's why you're here, she said.

I couldnt reply. I was the best part of I think what is thunderstruck because this is what I was and felt like crying and felt as if I could cry right there. The whole of life was too good to be true and I was the luckiest man in the whole world and that is the God's truth, the one God the only God, so help me my Lord, the one bright star in the dismal night sky. She was the only only thing. She pushed aside the crisps and studied her drink. She raised her head to look at me but only for a moment.

What's wrong? I said.

She smiled but kept her head lowered. You are always so sharp, she said.

I saw the worry in her. My hand went to hers, rested on it. It was above her nose where the worry was, in line with her eyebrows. I wanted to stroke there, easing it, the burden there. I glanced at the empty seat beside me. Come round here, I said, please. Come round here: sit beside me. She shook her head and continued studying my hand, which I made to withdraw, it was strange to me at this moment. I shifted on the seat, edgily, although there was nothing wrong. If anyone had asked me, nothing.

HUMAN RESOURCES TRACT 2: OUR HOPE IN PLAYING THE RULES

The Crime has Occurred.

A crime is a criminal act. We should not have committed the act. If we had not committed the act the crime would not have occurred. We did it. Thus we committed the crime. We cannot 'take it back' as some will suggest. Colleagues think it possible, it is not possible. Actions cannot be undone. We can regret the performance of such an action if it is we who performed such. The deed, however, is done and none travels back in time. We might wish to withdraw the action but that is impossible. Actions may not be withdrawn.

Of our guilt none may know. Not in this world. This is a remarkable feature. We should pause and take proper cognisance of it. Some will ponder the causal relationship. Might we have effected the end result? At all costs it will be known that no consequence shall be suffered. The action we have performed will be known by others. It may or may not be considered a 'crime'. Whether or not the action accords to the term 'crime' is a judgement in itself and outwith our scope. Should this prove the case it will be recognised as our decision, acknowledged as our decision, respected as our decision.

Others will not judge for us. This will not happen unless so allowed. Whether or not people agree with us is of a certain significance but without bearing, unless so allowed.

We may believe ourselves guilty of having committed an action that we should not have committed. We know that in the judgement of other people our action was no crime. But this is not enough for us. We know that we committed a wrongful action and further may believe ourselves guilty of a crime (see para 1). Our quest begins from there and will reveal inconsistencies. Nothing is more certain. In petty detail truths are revealed. Our more risible judgements will have derived from sentimental generalisations.

If we remain in guilt we cannot be with God and may not enter His province. The process of absolution begins with our acknowledgement of guilt. We confess our guilt. It is only through this confession of guilt that our guilt becomes known. In order that we may be absolved our guilt must be known. We confess our guilt to God. This is achieved through direct communication by prayer and other spiritual methods. The magnitude of God's greatness is forever beyond our ken and cannot be a concern.

In many religions there are human mediators who assist us in our quest for absolution. If we are uncertain how to go about matters then the mediators will advise and guide us. A list of those is readily available. They are thought more knowledgeable than ourselves. They are to have received training in the ways and means that direct communication with God may be obtained. The ultimate end is the ultimate mystery. Mediators are taught this most difficult of roles; that which appears to approximate to an acquisition of the will to win the attention of God.

Confessing the crime in theological terms is an important solution and we should not hesitate to embrace such. Our preference is towards these religions into which most of us are born, that place humankind close to the heart of the universe. The heart of the universe is God and His is a beating heart. The centre of the universe is the province of God. God is primary and ultimate dispenser of justice. This alone is our foundation.

Yes we committed the crime. Our examiners may be notified.

THE TWITCH

She was staring the question: What was I doing? what did I think I was doing? I just looked at the floor, shifting my weight from one foot to the other. My hands were out of my trouser pockets and I put them back in again. I was frowning, I knew I was frowning; she had criticised me for it often enough. Now the telephone was in my hand. How come? And I was going to dial somebody. How come to that too? If she was opposed to it. She was, really and truly she didnt want me to dial the number. Put it away, put it away. That was in my head. Fuck that. I did not put it away. I was not remotely interested and was happy and content just standing there. Till kingdom come. I believe I thought that. I shall stand here forever. I did think it! There is a statue. What statue? Where? A mega larger-than-life figure, the size of a huge tenement building, faces the setting sun.

Thy kingdom.

The twitch in my left eye, above my left eye, the lid of this, nerves jumping. It had started again. What was that twitching? I didnt like that twitching. Maybe she would see it. I hoped she would. I went online about it. Nothing. This was my question:

When I scratch my right side temple the curved bit at the ear makes an echo.

Is it her fault? And if it worsens, forcing me to continue what I am doing, what then?

And *robtoforeau* replied. He is strong. One hour later he replied as he does, he does it for most every post, each and every, he is like tentacles tentacles:

What are you doing wrong?

I doing wrong.

I winced but that was a smile wince, that was like ironic ironic ironic. He said the things and they were the right things. I needed the phone in my hand now now, but she wasnt allowing it, she was not allowing it and I cannot beat it cannot beat it how can I be expected to, I cannot cannot beat it. I was not about to speak. Even if I didnt not want to, if I would. I went to the window instead, strolling across. Her thinking I was acting cool but I was not acting cool, acting nothing, not cool not anything, not acting anything, only me myself being myself, being me; only me, it was me being me.

I was not sure what else; or to say if I did speak. She would speak first. She would have to, always she did. What I was doing is what she would want to know, what I thought I was doing. That was her question and I thought it shocking. It was. To me it was. I had my back to her feeling it so strongly, the hostility of her stare. She hated me. So much. If your woman hates

imagine

like for *robtoforeau*,

I see now that my woman hates, that she hates, that it may be me, it might be, if it is me, if she could hate me, despising, if she could be despising and I, if I

oh God.

How did I know that she was doing that?

I just did.

What was she trying to achieve?

I do not know and never ever could know, always and always, what she was thinking. She could not see my face and would assume the worst. I smiled. But if smiles have sound this would have been misinterpreted. She was waiting. I shrugged at her whatever it was, a question, yes a question, always a question questions questions.

Please, she said.

Surely I was not laughing at her! That is what she was thinking. She thought I was and I was. I was. As though I couldnt laugh at her. Ludicrous idea, if it was possible. But I could. If she thought I could be so so

I dont care. Fuck that. She thought something, I dont know, what she thought she always did, she always did. It must be so if she thought it. This was her arrogance. A woman's arrogance.

What was the question? *robtoforeau* replied. Oh was that the question! I was smiling, I could not stop myself. She wanted to fight me. So I was to her immediately. Immediately. My arms were round her, restraining her.

Oh, she said, oh . . . and was not able to break free I was clasping her, the sides of her arms, upper arms. Until she calmed, calm, calm, she would not calm. Her breath rasped. She shook her head, not looking at me. Oh never never never never. If not her eyes. I hated her eyes. They could not be trusted. Her eyes made it happen. They were closed when she spoke, what she said, Oh, oh.

I would have told her honestly. Simply to say and have said it. My right eye was twitching. I could not stop it. She did not push me away. I held her and thought to whisper to her how people may whisper and speak together and nothing need ever be intentional, the act of communication, intending that we might communicate but nothing beyond. Switch off the machine. Nothing else is necessary. She knew that as I did, we both of us. She knew it. And you must, I said. I said it to her, the phone in my hand, you must.

UNTETHERED

Then I saw the field.

How many days had I been here? Now I saw it, and knew that I could walk to it. There was no reason why I couldnt except I couldnt. I might walk to there. But I could not.

Had I no power? Had they stolen everything? It wasnt a dream. I was taken and I could not move. I could not move. Is that a joke? It seems like a horrible irony.

I didnt enter that so-called field and I wouldnt enter. Was it mathematical? One day two day, then three, four and coming now to the tenth day, my senses said no, I was not going to be controlled by these damn forces. You know, fuck! It was not to happen. I was not going to allow it to happen.

What to dominate? Or even me; me to dominate. Okay I know myself and know my capabilities. I can rise to the occasion. Of course I can. If they thought I couldnt, if they thought that man they were wrong, they certainly were wrong. I would have challenged them there and then. I always challenged them anyway, I didnt worry about that.

Why could I not enter that field? That to me was like a religious question, certainly logical, as though a logical field, therein the key man that is what I was thinking

You know I didnt have any trust in them. Why ask? No faith, nothing. Of course not. It was only a political position; there is no thing other than that, no morality, no goddam fuck all man so I did challenge them, and challenged them on that. Always. My very existence. There and then at that damn time man right in front of that so-called field, their so-called field, you know, what did they think! Make it a question and I shall answer: Of course, of course I saw it.

Were I allowed. I am not allowed. Even this, to have challenged them on this very point. Prove it! I shouted at them. Prove it to me. As of right you have got no authority. Any power you have you have stolen, you have stolen from people; peoples, plural. All the people of the world. I shouted that to them.

But something was spinning. Near to me. What is spinning? My fucking head! I could not discern. Was it near to me? Spinning near to me, if it is near to me.

I had to search. Then give in to it. If I had to sleep then remain where I was. It was no chair. It was no chair. Damn chair man it was not a chair. I know what a fucking chair looks like.

My finger too, fitting snugly; into my nostril, my ear, between the fifth and third toes of my right foot. That was my finger, talking about my finger, how come? The point of consciousness. I was not being tortured.

Where now here now. Such reflection. My feet were bare. I might have laughed at that. Even being there, and that field, what was that field, did I see a field? is this significant? or was it so? I thought Yeah, none of this is by chance.

A time passed. I rose from my chair. It was a chair!

My thoughts no longer raced ahead. What is reflection?

I would not have believed it possible. The place itself, the surroundings, these had changed me. And these long weeds, long long weeds, each time I saw them I wanted to lay me down to sleep, not even to sleep but lying there, with the long stalks, angling above to enclose me. This was a proper field. It had grass rather than symbols, a natural form, if logical.

I knew what to believe. They told me. It was a command. Believe what you know. Such was their advice. These bastards had no shame. They said to me: You have nothing.

I didnt seek information. They gave me it, what they wanted me to know. I preferred to discuss death and that other concept, that concept uhh humiliation; humiliation, of a people, peoples the world over.

I should not have acquiesced. If I did acquiesce. My reaction was if believing what you know was the more important, which surely it was.

What followed. I cannot remember.

But my reaction then was less than immediate. I acquiesced. I agreed to my own, my own

I do not accept 'degradation'. If the field was there to be entered. What is a field? A simple area, bounded area. I too was bounded, I too am an area. My body is a fucking map of fucking humanity. Who is to deny that? The degradation that I suffer is the degradation of humanity.

If the affirmative can one deny it? Would one deny it? I put thoughts up to thwart more difficult thoughts you know and mediocrity, mediocrity is not the result.

Although one may predict the unlikely, as to the nature of it, grasping that, it is not feasible. Or is this also a banality, rooted in tautology. We go back and go back, and again.

The mind of a human being, this human being.

The field.

How many days? I think of days man I dont know and I am here and facing the field and I can enter, I could enter and I fucking do not man it is like the one and only the sole thing man, that area of conflict, ultimate one.

The brain is also composed, its constituents, each a field, stalks, weeds

One is commanded not to think but not to think becomes to not think which is activity of a cerebral kind. Thought in itself. My state is secular. And if I am part of a community, of a class or a caste, ethnic or communal division: state of mind. It is a fucking state of mind man I can forget what I am, a fucking human being man part of fucking humanity, of peoples, an individual.

I smile. I smile at these things. These things; such things. 'Such things' is discriminatory. I might have chortled, chortled equalling to laugh aloud in an ironic manner, a manner approaching sarcasism, sarcasism – if not internalized to the extent it had to be. In order to exist it begins from internalization. The challenge is within me. My inner form is logical, not mathematical.

But what meaning does this have? Something lodged, existing within. A thing of myself, purely of myself.

The inquisitors. Those who foment

What is inhumanity? I do not fucking know what it is man I do not know what the fuck it is.

The gaolers cannot control this, you men of the state. Chortling is to be of humanity. Pushing authority, pushing

To be alive is the assumption of control, for this is reflection.

So the place had changed me. This was the fact, how do they say it, these foreigners, they have a way, that the 'ah' sound is 'ay', 'é'. I am not a foreigner. They said I was.

These conundrums. Oh that you are, you are not; contradictions. They give me the language.

These logics, disappearing fields, the shapes, dissolving, disappearing dissolving, battered from my head, so gone, psychological truncheons and hammer blows. French terms for these assaults. I gave them the answer. These are the pillars. They sought the answer and eventually received it, received it from me. I absolve myself. Said with humour. Is there a question? I am no foreigner. Allow me to move. I moved.

THE TRUTH THAT TIMMY KNEW

The storybook about trees was good and the man was looking at it a lot. The one where the children found the biggest tree in the whole world. This tree led into a magical world. The children had to climb or fly to the highest, until they arrived at the very top. It had to be the very top where branches were thin as twigs, the most fragile twigs. The children had to balance there.

Somehow they managed it. But they had no option. If they didnt what would happen?

On windy days clouds were chased across the sky. We saw how clouds went. He watched them too. How they merged, changed and shifted. He could not see one for long. We watch as long as we can. Then they are gone. People lived up there; not beyond and not above but within their own strange lands where every manner of thing dwelled, and dwelled by right. His wife did not know this but would learn. No cloud returned. What about him? Could he jump up? Then his wife could see, she would have to see and have to suffer them.

What if the children did not want to go? Surely they would fall! But they would have to go. They could not float. Not if there were no clouds. So then what would happen? Something bad. He did not know. He had started in on the act and did not want to stop, reading quickly, as quickly as he dared. He found it exciting; sure, but there was something else about it. Just something. He didnt know what, or why; nor why they should have been doing what they were doing, out there and on their own and just relying on whatsisname, Timmy.

The man did not know what his wife thought and was not interested. It was up to her. She went her own way anyway. Good riddance. Her and her family. All the rest of them, they could do what they liked. It was the children, and just uh what, just the children.

He turned the page. It was exciting, almost excruciating. They were beyond the first layers of cloud and unable to see in front of their noses. How had they managed so far! No one knew. Only that this was the place, and the only place.

God it was frightening. He almost had to cover the page. There were pictures; did he dare look at them? Yes, and so he did, oh God, all peeking out: that was the kids, just youngsters. He felt like making a coffee and just, just thinking about it, like savouring it, what was happening. Really. He was nearly rubbing his hands.

A special cloud might come. What if it did? The children waited for it anyway. That was the one they waited for, that special one. There was no other like it. It was a unique cloud.

A unique cloud.

But he knew clouds and knew the truth of it. Clouds were unlike human beings. People said they were alike. Clouds are never-ending in their change and transition, or transformation, and this is the way of people, their lives are endless motion and he saw it in his children. He wanted to end it then. Their mother had not appeared. Their mother did not appear. This was characteristic. She did what she wanted. Who cared about her, she hardly cared about anyone anyway and so what. Not about trees either, and storybooks, even the ones belonging to the kids, she cared about nothing except herself.

There was only one tree. The children waited there and would jump. There were eight in all. Eight of them. Children. How might they jump? Dare to breathe, they held hands as in a chain. Timmy was eldest. The man did not like the name Timmy. Jimmy would have been preferable. But he was Timmy, and was always Timmy. He held the hands of the next two in line and they each held a younger one who each held a younger one and the last one, the little two-year-old whose name was Maggie, she climbed onto Timmy's shoulders. Wee Maggie, she was great, a wee fighter, and to the bitter end!

The children settled, awaiting the cloud.

They wanted to know about this cloud. Were people living on board? Were they hostile? What was the game? Friend or foe! Was it even a game? The man would not have thought so, not if he had been present and with a say in the matter. Timmy held charge and said nothing. Better to bide one's time. Or was it? The man was uncertain. He would have chosen a different course of action. But boys such as Timmy are not found in storybooks. He was too ordinary. About him was a quietness that reassured the youngsters.

Some would have risked all for that, for that ordinariness.

The children watched and waited. No cloud touched close enough. They knew not to make a jump. How did they know! By studying Timmy. The decision was his. The children looked to him. He knew it and accepted it. They would not jump without his lead. Nevertheless they were restless: even nervous. Timmy whispered to them, Hush, you must hush.

They settled. Not one inch should they move; one solitary inch. One paltry inch.

No sound, no movement. Sound is movement. Cease whispering, this whispering, sssssssss, oh a breath, a breath and the slightest such may alter a cloud's formation. If that were to happen the outcome was horrific, too too horrible; unthinkable, almost.

The man turned a page and shivered. The children would not stop whispering. Surely Timmy knew the dangers! The slightest breath! My God! He was responsible for all these children. Surely he knew what this level of movement might signify! Timmy had answers to most everything but not this. A brave boy but a boy after all. How could he cope with this number of dependants? Ssh, whispering again, he was whispering again.

It was heartbreaking. And happening in front of or under – so to speak – his breath. Saliva at his mouth. It was true. This story held the man in thrall. He did not 'enjoy' being in thrall.

The cloud itself. The special cloud. But would Timmy even recognise it? What were its distinguishing features? None.

Are clouds of infinite extension, indefinite extension?

How could he recognise a cloud, such that this cloud was the cloud? Not via observation. Only from a form of inner operation, an internal process. Timmy would recognise the cloud by means of intuition. But how would he get from 'a' to 'the'? In forming the question one recognises its immateriality. Timmy would know. Simply, clearly. He would. Younger children relied on that. They were correct. Timmy closed his eyes, but only for a moment till once more he was alert as ever a boy could be.

One saw the picture. This child!

At last Timmy had impressed this upon them. The children would not move, they could not. If they were to move! Oh no.

But this story was life itself! The injustice palpable. The very foundation of which is that: injustice.

What would she have said, his wife? Nothing. Another form of denial, that would have been her. And had she been the boy's mother would the denial have stood? She might not have been his mother but she was a mother and mothers have that in common.

An overwhelming injustice. The man hardly dared look. Six children clinging to this one child through hand grips. The seventh was wee Maggie who sat on Timmy's shoulders. How could he manage? No one could have. How could they allow him to try? They allowed it.

Contempt surged through him. The actions of people.

Even these children. Just waiting there. What the hell were they waiting for? The man did not like how they waited. He found it intimidating. Children can be like that. Holy terrors; they can be.

He didnt know what his wife believed. Perhaps she didnt believe anything. Perhaps she was incapable of belief. Men believe. Women dont. Women dont believe. Women. If she could be called a wife, he would not have called her a wife. What did she believe? Even children. He doubted she ever had. Whoever did she care for? She would never have suffered a child. She had children and did not suffer them. It was him, always him, he suffered the children and watched them. Not her. Never her.

Oh my God yes and he also waited. What did she know, she did not know, not that he waited. He could have laughed at that. The children would have heard him. He had the children. He also could have laughed. He also, and seeing them and how they were, waiting and just waiting and their reliance.

Timmy was a good boy. The children relied on him. They relied on his intuition. Yet to rely on the intuition of this one boy required strength. These were resolute children, having a strength of their own. Without this strength they could not have relied on Timmy. This was plain and the man could see that and grasp its significance.

But why had there only to be one cloud? He could not understand that. Children suffered because of it.

No one should carry such a burden, yet these children had the obligation. They took care of one another. No adult could help.

No adult was there. Adults were in their own world and could not help the children, try as they might. And there were those who would have offered support, would have wished to, they would have wished to offer it. He knew that and wished perhaps that somehow he could, somehow enter into their world but that was absurd it was absurd. Oh God and one worries one worries.

Simply that their way was barred. They hoped to find a way but couldnt, they could not find a way. There was no way. The world of children is its own structure and might not be disturbed on pain of annihilation.

But it was a nightmare. These were children's stories and they represented the worst conceivable horror which was their world in-itself. No adult entered there. Any who tried must fail unless on the children's own terms. And what were these terms?

He read further and discovered a solution. The solution was revelatory, yet all too apparent. The one source of entry was imagination. Not that of the adult. It was through the children themselves. Of course. He should have realised this. He himself was a parent. Of course there was no other route. We enter through them. Not as figments. We adults had substance, we were a type of being, recognised as such. The man could see the clouds. Some were inhabited by adults alone. Colonisers. There were no children on those clouds. Colourless places; hardly places at all in their vapidity, and were to be guarded against. The children could see them from their vantage point. When one passed they stared with a vague interest, perhaps sullenly.

Timmy clutched the hands of either child. They glanced at his face and were reassured by his steady gaze. They leaned forward and smiled across to each other. In this way the younger children clutching to their hands also were reassured and so too the remaining pair who were not yet of school age and trusted only siblings, while wee Maggie grinned, clutching Timmy's ears. Adults were not trustworthy beings. They knew it. An adult may have been surprised by the knowledge, not so children. Once upon a time he too had known it. He must have forgotten along the way.

So many questions. Even turning the page. He did not want the children to jump. Where might they land? He could go with them only so far. Beyond there he could not venture.

The children tensed. Certain cloud formations had appeared on the immediate horizon and among them surely the one, surely the one was among them! They stared out from the heights, gripping onto each other. Occasionally one glanced to Timmy who was one of them; he was; he too had tensed, he too stared to the horizon; making his own preparation, thoughts racing through his mind, if the land was there what land might it be? Could one return from such a land? What if the children went to see, spent too long and were doomed as a result? It was too late by then. None might climb down. The cloud would slip away. Clouds did not return. Beyond a moment they did not exist. One had to be aboard to be there.

This was the sigh. It escaped. The boarding point would exist for one fraction of a moment. The world of adults. Ahead lay danger. They were being guided toward that. How could this be!

Timmy too, even him, he could not understand what was happening. Timmy was unable to understand. By now he had acquired the necessary knowledge yet even so, even so. The boy was lost! What was to happen? He was shaking his head. The younger children watched him with an obvious bewilderment. Who would be left with them?

Questions upon questions. The children waiting. The man had to look away. It was not to be borne.

OUT THERE

I had to do something new. My way of operating was not so old yet I seemed to have forgotten how to do anything else. I didnay like that. My eyes kept closing too. I was not requiring to sleep, not thinking about sleep at all. Although it was in sleep the thoughts came. I didnay want these thoughts but I got them. And I could not care less if I was caught in the act. I had given up worrying about this months ago, several months ago, last year at least.

Mental preoccupations, I couldnay afford them either. Waves of sleep but I would not allow them to engulf me. Waves of sleep.

I looked for my diary.

It was round somewhere, roundabout – where?

Reflections.

My diary, reflections. Also the usual aches; how come these aches all round my right ear itching and fiddling footering scratching and oh jesus the back side of the head; right side, and just aching, oh fuck. Finding myself in the same old situation was less than helpful. I needed something new and to hell with it.

But in a new form? No, I didnay think so. I didnt think at all, I didnt, just that, no, not such that I couldnay handle it, and readily, reserving my energy for the struggle itself, not the conditions toward it, setting them for what lay ahead, that was the danger, constant temptation similar to giving up, the concession to it oh god I could no longer just be here, and just being here.

Although I would be walking into the new place soon. I would be arriving there. So I would keep on. I would. This is not proper decision-making, only a function, continuing as a person.

I knew more was demanded. So what? I knew myself inside out. To be upright, the one deep breath, opening the eyelids to greeting the day. Extant, that was what I looked for, having become, become it: extanticity.

But the temptation oh god and to make it as a question: Why do my eyes close? No, I do not believe it; I do not accept it. All the time they were closing. So what? That is nothing, that is bloody nothing.

I wasnay supposed to sleep. I knew that I could, if I lay down and the scene had been set but how, how, colder, to sleep.

I didnt want even to be doing that, and if it was cold – colder, okay, then my eyes

GOD LOOKS DOWN

I was living these many stories above ground level which is sea level. I knew that I was, that it would remain so. Here then the river, and this river flows to the sea. And the sea.

This is the torture.

I would have looked out upon this river. I would not enjoy seeing it. In earlier days I did and its existence offered hope, offered escape; that possibility. It was then my belief that were I to jump from the ledge I would miss my landing. It could not be guaranteed that I would land in the water. I would land in the earth. Solid earth. This river is a thin line burning through the earth, the landscape which is the earth.

Contradictions are a distraction. I was not allowed to talk. To think there is only so much. It may be the best one can do. I accept this. I did not always. On another occasion another may prove better, prove 'the' better. Ways we progress, continue, unto. Another truth: truth is given as a relative entity. Take from the fascists. For each one of us the truth. Some saw the river and considered the jump. The sea. The ledge. To miss the water. In earlier days I was with them. They hide it. We too. We hide from it. In hiding from truth, we hide from ourselves, concealing truth from oneself, hiding from ourself. I could not stomach the cowardice which was my own.

Our assumption that truth is best is a proposition; perhaps a proposal: if so to whom? Am I talking to you or to someone else? I have not the belly, am nauseated; intellectualisations. I get many such. What to do with them. If propositions, proposals, to whom do I propose, do I make the proposition? If it is you, if I am talking to you, then surely it must be you. If these 'intellectualisations' arise within me they are not only of me.

And if I frame these sentences in a question to you and another person is posited. Who might it be? I do not have 'a person'. It must be you, you must 'have' the person, where 'have' means 'to know'. Others have. They have 'friends and loved ones.' But I do not. I do not have those.

Those persons. Who are those persons? If there are such persons. They must resemble someone. Whom do they resemble?

I was in the other room and people were far below and suddenly these were persons. This was my summation.

My chair at the window, this window, where rays and beams cannot enter. Across the valley below the motor cars, trucks, buses, vans and vans and motor cars, buses, trucks and vans non-stop and forever and ever forever. And I would land on one were the wind to carry me. But here the wind is cornered. This is the rear. The river flows to the side of the building and cannot be seen here. If I dived outward, the cornered wind, how could it carry me, it couldnt carry me unless maybe if I were to catch, to be caught within it, the rush of it holding me within, becoming part of the force thrust round and round the walls.

The other side for some the finest most graceful high dive, bypassing way above the surroundings, the walled surrounding

'If' qualifier.

The radio played and I was listening to it, a political talk. The guests talking of matters current, current affair matters; tripping the language. The anxiety. I was hearing neighbours, these are neighbours. I wished for other than other, whomsoever they might be, if I were to have others, these others, if God allowed it. God might allow it, His decision, effected by His wish. Between my area and immediate others was the wall. I saw only from the window, shoulders and heads, angled lines, slanting light. These lines were arms, legs and even bodies though bodies might have been points, so that these figures – human beings – were composed of mathematical marks and one might have set them in motion, into motion. God looks down. Or not?

God cannot 'look' and only can know. God only can know. All that He may know is known only by Him. The Godly context. Progression, in itself.

Look from the window: figures are moving. They appear stationary but are moving, these are moving. I was looking too, I was seeing the figures. Older metaphors making use of the insect do work here where we see a stain, blob or blemish and upon closer examination we see that this is no blob, no stain, this mass of points where each is in motion, and each its ownself true to itself, tiny wee structures living matter. This is truth and truth of its ownself, each one a person, each a truth. I saw that, I saw it from my window. This is a proposition, so formulated as to one other person, it required this other, this one person who may look. A proposition formulated by my ownself and proposed to another. Perhaps it is you. Only perhaps. Only allow it, allow the perhaps, of the person who is other than yourself so that you, you and I and I and I, here we are doors clanging, if they come for myself they come also for you but we are the one.

BACK IN THAT TOWN

for
Mia Carter

I had things on my mind this day and took no chances on the road so wound up a couple of hours over, and too late. They would have the truck loaded tomorrow morning, as early as I cared to make it, but no sooner than that. I didnt mind the overnight as long as they contacted the contractor. I wasnt long enough in the business for that sort of communication. It smacked of decision-making. That was to risk human error. Business operatives deleted all such potential. I was prone to it. The bastards would have deleted me. They had done in previous how shall we say it, sorties.

That is like working nowadays, going into battle. A brief glance at my track record, my Life record, my Life. Oh man, I got weary. Which state was I in anyhow.

Okay.

I had a wash on the premises. They wouldnt let me use the shower. They said they didnt have one. I did not believe them. I was a smelly bastard. Three days' sweat, and nobody sweats like an overweight trucker. So they say. I changed my clothes. Was I overweight? Yeah. The weather was good. I set off walking. A long walk but a big town. I used to know it pretty damn well. Locals termed it a city. Nowadays it was in the doldrums, according to the information I got over breakfast this morning, a distance down the road.

I enjoyed walking. I did so little of it. I was like a cowboy or a biker. Get a man walking. The body isnt geared towards it. Let me crawl, let me crawl! When did human beings get up off their all fours? A million years? In these parts it was six thousand, no more no less. If the Lord didnt rest up on the seventh day we would have another thousand. That is no joke, just what we call a faith-fact. This long walk reminded me forcibly. Churches. Places of worship. The tallest sturdiest buildings. Built to endure. In towns like these there seems a church to every six people.

Two miles later I was still walking. Buses passed. I knew nothing about buses any more. In this town, yes, I used to, but that was years ago. In a past life I worked in this town. Back then it suited me. I thought then if Life proved too difficult elsewhere maybe I could return.

And so on.

Okay. Sentimentality. But the sense of a past belonging was true enough. Whatever, here I was. The truck took over one's Life. Good for people like myself; difficult relationships and all that, like the rest of the planet. Weary sigh.

What is a failure? One who doesnt succeed in what one intends. One who doesnt survive by doing what one wants to be doing. Okay. I enjoyed a certain way of living. I just didnt earn money doing it, that was the issue. But that is not to say it couldnt happen one day. One day! This driving crap was temporary. Temporary! he screamed.

Yeah, of course.

But it was possible a couple of guys from my own day were still around, and if they were? If they were what? Most of them were crawling brown-nose fuckers who always took no for an answer, of the three-bags-full persuasion, yessir nosir.

The landscape was not so familiar where now I was walking. Higher buildings, glass and metal flashing in the sun. How many years was it for christ sake it seemed like a century!

Things had changed so drastically. The buildings is what I noticed. New money. New money in old hands. New people too.

But there was money in the past. Dont fool yourself.

A couple of street names were familiar but not the streets themselves. The new buildings made them unrecognisable. Man it was busy busy busy. Office-worker clothes dominated. Folk all out their little offices having a five-minute smoke break in front of their buildings; white shirts and blouses, smart skirts and trousers, arms folded and shivering – no! trembling, on the breath of freedom. The cusp man!

Let me back to the truck!

Jees I was one arrogant bastard! I had become so. Patronising. My world was on the verge of collapse. Maybe it had already and I was in denial. The night before I left my wife had cornered me with the old ultimatum.

Maybe I would write a song. Notepad in pocket, sturdy pencil. Gone to pot. What a title! Losing my wife and losing my children and if I didnt act fast I would lose my fucking teeth. I set aside a week to pay the bastard. Dentists. Truly, I was ripe for conversion.

Okay.

This trudging would have been good for the walking muscles, the legs and so on. I stayed along the central artery, crossing many streets and one river, into crowds of people. Nobody would know me. It was too unlikely. So many years gone by. I used to be young; bushy-tailed. Now here I was. Broken dreams? Forty-four years of age. That is not old. But it is certainly not young, it is not young. My old man was a grandfather at the same age. I needed to phone him and my mother, she would know how he was. Keep an eye on the kids, check it out with the wife. Ah fuck, problems.

Okay. No, nobody would know me in this damn town. Not any longer. A pity, some fond memories.

But where were they going these crowds of people? They were going somewhere. Saturday afternoon in the spring, some event or other; and looking smart too, dressed for an occasion. Plenty people, families, children. Children are currency, emergency fodder. I waited on the corner to get my bearings. Parkview Road. Yeah, I remember that one. Parkview? what was that? that was something for sure.

All this walking, I could have done with a rest. I leaned my shoulder against a streetlamp. In other circumstances I would have washed my feet. Somebody could have offered to wash them for me. Hereabouts they took the Good Word in the old fashion. Oh but the feet ached. At least massaged the toes, sat for a minute and taken off the boots. Jesus.

But the atmosphere was fine, it was fine. A couple of bars were doing business, guys on the outside at the smoking places, sipping coffee, coffee and brandy, a glass of iced water: old-time civilization. This is how people should be at weekends; out there sharing their lives. I didnt see many tourists. Indigenous all sorts. At the next corner a guy appeared right at my side walking. That situation where one of you moves on quickly or slows down? If you dont you are walking together. I slowed a little but he maintained the same pace as me. I glanced at him. He held my gaze a moment: a desperation, whispered fast and urgent: I got a sister will suck you off for twenty.

What, what was that?

Agitated and nervy, not able to talk and a worry if he was holding; knife or a gun, something. Not slurred speech or like that, but the desperation. I dont like seeing the desperation, a particular kind. When you do you walk away, just walk away. No, I said in a quiet reasonable manner, not wanting to upset him, me not being local either. Fuck. I didnt want to upset anybody. How would a resident have handled this? How did he know I wasnt one?

He didnt. Maybe nowadays this was normal. You approach strangers downtown Saturday afternoon and try to sell them your young sister. He was still walking beside me, taking my 'no' as a negotiation, whispering urgently: Twenty, only twenty; my little sister man.

I shook my head now not wanting to talk any more but keeping walking all the time walking.

Twenty is fair, he said and now the irritation was there in him and that spelled danger. I walked on faster. He kept upsides me. I slowed he slowed, slowed right down, yeah, him too. And he was restraining himself, grabbing for my wrist, he managed not to lay a finger on it. I said: Hey man . . .

His head jerked sideways, he squinted at me, he was focusing.

I stepped away from him. Calm down, I said. I stopped walking for a moment. I was annoyed; not so much angry, which was probably better for me. He saw that too, staring at me as if working out who I was. When I resumed walking he matched strides with me again and said: My young sister man, you got to pay for her. He shook his head at me in a weird kind of affronted style, as if I had rejected his baby sister in a marriage proposal.

Look, I said, I'm not interested. I told you already.

That agitation was back in him again and he reached suddenly for my wrist.

This was danger. I pulled away from him. He knew he shouldnt have done it. I kept walking, keeping on. This place too, hidden dangers, maybe not so hidden. A place for transients, like passing through. People like me. The bus station wasnt too far from here, if they still had one, and the old market where I was thinking maybe for something to eat. No time to look for it now. I was ignoring him but on he came. She is my young sister, what do you think man you take her for nothing! You dont take her for nothing. He stepped alongside now and into my face, beyond negotiation now, as if a relationship existed between us. I would start hearing sad tales about his starving children. You have to pay, he said.

No I dont, I dont have to pay nothing.

I have a brother, he said and was looking about now when he spoke.

What do you think I'm a tourist man, fuck off, I said.

He stared, not knowing what I was talking about, hardly listening. It didnt matter what I was saying he was planning a move. Across the street a crowd had gathered for a guy standing up on a chair, he was hectoring them with religious messages and I saw that the street had changed, had become an open market whose stalls featured arts and crafts kind of cultural stuff, bric-a-brac

– and this guy was still here. How come? This was turning bad. Potentially. Just something. I knew it, like sensed it. How come he was persisting like this? It was past time to cut the losses. Minutes ago he should have done that. So why didnt he? I could not figure it out. How come he couldnt call it quits? This was making me irritated too like not so much fearful, wondering what it was, if the guy himself was in danger and this was why he stayed there. That was it. It was him. It was the guy himself in danger. He was under orders. People watching him, waiting, they were waiting, they were watching him, jesus christ this was why he came back man *he was scared*. He was not past the stage of reason but he was scared, and I looked around and saw nothing – except this town. Cops and preachers.

Yeah, I remembered this damn place. But if he was in danger then it was him. It was only me if I allowed it. I needed out of there fast. It was busy across the street and anybody could have been there. The guy saw me looking, knew what I was thinking. I had been identified by other bastards, he had been sent across. It made sense. He would have taken no for an answer if working alone. It wasnt up to him. This was another kind of business. No decision-making here. What is your problem? Me. I was the problem? He wont give you the money? So take the money. You want a resolution? Here is the resolution. The knife in the belly.

These fuckers across the street would be here in a stride. I would be found in south river. There were two rivers in this town; north and south. This time of year both dried in long stretches, unless maybe flash flooding, except that was towards the end of summer as I recall. They met four blocks north from here and this juncture separated also the east of the town from the west. Over west was money; east was not. Follow the north river west and you met the big river; return south in the easterly direction and what would you find? My truck is what you would find. Yeah, and my sense of direction had returned; it was never the worst.

The one thing this guy did know about me was I was neither a stranger nor a local. He came at me again as if convinced I was negotiating and again that hand going to my wrist. I raised my own hand. Maybe it calmed him a little, but only a little. The desperation remained. He sniffed, hanging back, wondering the options. I heard music from someplace; religious-sounding. Didnt he guess I could have smote him down! I should have told him I was there on religious grounds, religious business in his damn town and he should not interfere with this: such business is sacrosanct, is God's business.

But carefully. In towns like this sarcasm works in reverse if it works at all. The guy was no coward. This type of desperation makes the question redundant.

Now it got me, the truck, it was the truck, they wanted the truck. What was in the truck? There wasnt anything in the damn truck. I unloaded it this morning and now at this very moment it was being loaded for the run east – I think east, maybe north-east. What was the load? How the fuck did I know? Hereabouts it might have been chickens. Or whisky, or guns.

A woman in a doorway. I saw her peer in my direction. Unless she was hustling too jesus christ the little sister!

What a town, it pains me to say; maybe it was like this before and I hadnt noticed, too busy with chillun and wives all over the place.

Ahead and to the side was a charity store. One of these big stand-alone buildings with a major carpark attached. The guy walked to my outside which made it easier. What could he have done anyhow? Nothing. I did it suddenly, abruptly, no warning, nothing, a sideways turn and off, striding fast fast across the forecourt until reaching the double doorway entrance this grumpy old man like some antiquarian codger raised an arm to stop me in my tracks: What you blind boy?

Okay, okay.

Yeah okay, he said, hit the bucket! He pointed to this bucket which had a sign that read: Entry by Donation. You dont see the bucket? he said.

No, otherwise I would have donated.

Sure you would.

Of course I would.

Oh yeah, he said shaking his head and looking elsewhere. But I was glad to see the damn bucket anyhow, it was another obstacle for the guy with the little sister. By the doorway another sign read:

Got a Gig?
We'll Give You One!
Volunteers Run This Show.
Come Join Us!

I dropped a bill into the bucket, gave the codger a nod and entered. Mobbed inside. Immediately here was a long table. I stopped for a look and shifted to be facing the street window for a double-check on the hustler guy. Nobody nothing. This time he had to have given up. If there was people over the street he would check it out. Cut the losses cut the losses. Unless if it was personal, if it was personal it was the truck.

I checked the long table. Twenty-four bodies could have sat down round it, maybe thirty. This was from an old-time bunk-house kitchen.

All sorts of people and all sorts of ages. A preponderance of young folk; infants, babies and buggies. Oh yeah, and the look! These young couples had 'the look'. I identified this years ago when I was half of one such. 'Fervent' is how I described it. Yeah and it still obtained. No matter the political reality they will live their lives and raise a family and will fight to the death to preserve this. They will make that Life a full Life or they will die, they will breathe their last, in the attempt. This is them setting out for the long haul, picking up their furniture and white goods where they can. Okay they come here but next year who knows, who knows.

I saw the sign at the far side of the room: Husbands Corner, where the men were dumped among the old PCs and DVDs, old books and old vinyl, and I saw old cassettes there too and hell, who knows what, 8-track stereo systems. But the books! I could not believe my luck. These books were proper, I am talking proper books. I could have bought all day. Instead I bought three, to fit into my jacket pockets. I needed my arms free.

Okay. Three women chatting behind the counter. They gave me the amused look. Essentially patronising but I dont mind. I like it. It annoyed my girlfriend. Other guys do not get that reaction, she said.

Yeah they did, she just didnt notice. She said I gave a signal. What like a scent? Yeah a scent. She said I gave a scent. Well yeah, like male? Okay. Was that a fault? I didnt see that a fault. That was gender difference man and I could not care less about that. I enjoyed it. I was as predictable as the next guy and these books were the goods to prove it.

The woman examined each of the three in turn, glancing at me and drawing a line of consistency between me and them. Weird guys read books. That hurt my ego. I figured myself a cool sort of guy. Who cares. The truth is she amused me, this woman with the good smile who did not know what to make of me. How come? Because I did not look like a reader? I could not believe how cheap they were. That was that nowadays, nobody wanted books. Not nobody; some did. The three of them were about fish. No wonder she thought I was weird. Unless an actual fisherman. Probably that is what she thought. I smiled at her. Yeah, I said, I read them, I read these damn things.

I know you do.

Yeah? I also do fishing.

I guess, she said. You want a bag?

If ye've got one, yeah, that would be good.

She got one from beneath the counter; an old one. We have to charge, she said, it's policy.

I paid the money, dropped in the change to another donations' bucket and saluted the woman. They had a little café in one of the side rooms. Only a couple of people were there. It had that hostel feel to it. I chose a table to the far side wall, carried over my coffee. This was me getting things out my head. Life was tough enough.

I had the books on the table. The books the books. One by Herman Melville, <u>Great Short Works</u>. I might have bought <u>Moby-Dick</u> but it wasnt there. People talk about it. I tried it years ago thinking it was a kind of Huck Finn. I gave up. Call me Ishmael, it was like the bible or something. I should have stuck with it. Stories about fish is what I like. One I got seemed like a <u>Moby-Dick</u> for children, about a huge porpoise. My daughters would like it. They enjoyed adventures, like every other kid, and swimming too. So a story adventure with a swimming theme. Well now. But I would enjoy it myself. It reminded me of a movie. Maybe it was a movie and this was the book version, about a porpoise and how one spring she was swimming down from the Antarctic in pursuit of the cod who were all swimming down in pursuit of the small bait, a little thing like whitebait but called something else. My daughters would tell the story in class. Their teacher seemed like an enthusiast, she got them to read and discuss stuff from home. The porpoise was a girl and not a boy. My daughters would love that. I was wanting to read it now myself. It didnt require too much concentration. If I could regain concentration, and not go worrying about stupid things; stupidities you meet on the street. Any street any place somebody wants to do you in.

I picked up the third book. This was by that hard-drinking fat guy with the zeezee beard and how he came to set some world record with that one fish-rod cut from birch or something. His old ancestor showed him how from way 'up on high', and this rod won all the major championships. He smoked that old pipe too; one belonged to the same ancestor, and drank his whiskey neat, yessir. Him and his ancestor's pipe man that was sick. Let the old guy rest in peace. This one was about big game fish off the west coast. I hadnt read anything by him. Everybody all talked about him. They played his stories on late-night radio stations. That native guy who goes with him who spends his Life seeking the 'spirit fish', this ghostly apparition, symbol of mankind thrashing around in a foolish attempt to defeat the natural order. Shit, it doesnt interest me. I listened to these stations driving. Maybe they kept me sane. The gaps in my brain. Music didnt fill them. I needed the words from other people. These stations done it. Except penance was necessary. Supernatural crap man you got to put up with it. What do we give? In exchange for our soul. I did my penance.

Take the water out your whiskey. Drink it neat like old fat boy with the zeezee beard, him and his fucking fish-pole. One radio guy went on and on and on about him, all through the damn programme: Hey now you got to read him, read him about the fish-pole and that native guy seeking the spirit fish, he goes looking for the spirit and what does he find? el diablo. Philosophy for crackpots all jumbled in with religious notions. You would be as well hitting those places right here and now, we all know them; joining the freaks who want to get the 6,000 years fixed into the school curriculum; an alternative theory of In the Beginning. Forget the Holocaust man I want to deny the entire outside World. I want to disappear. Where to? Everywhere the same, give or take a fucking nuance. Spiritual native guys were only there to make the front man look good. Fuck them. If I was going mad, at least I knew it and that was something.

Okay. I was enjoying thumbing the books, taking a sentence here a sentence there, savouring what I could; late 18th early 19th Century novels, seeing whole paragraphs. I liked doing that. I wanted to shout them out. What I hoped for, what it might give rise to. Like a whole new politics and way of living, linked into some ethical code where people are people and fuck the capitalists man, these billionaire bastards man, let us wipe them out and lead our Life. I could shout it out, I could get the soap box, I could shout it out: Why sell your sister asshole, buy yourself back instead!

They did that already, and had a name for it: redemption. Redemption!

A woman was watching me. I had laughed aloud. Giggled more like. At one point I had to. About what, hell, what was I giggling about? My own grandfather who knew fuck all about fishing, what was I thinking about. My own grandfather who loved John Wayne.

In the midst of everything. Where did it come from? This is my brain. Ever looked at a brain? Up close? Had he slipped something in so now you found yourself away someplace else? Talking about the writer: what was he, God? John Wayne, boy how fucked up was he! Except he wasnt. Only naïve, like the rest of us. What goes on in the world. How can you be so famous and buy into such shit? be so ignorant of the ways of the country? How can people be like that? My grandfather man how could he buy into that? A few days ago I was stopped in this place eating breakfast, sitting with these guys and they were doing just that, John Wayne, and I had to keep my trap shut listening. The politics of our country.

Acts of contrition.

Maybe it was personal; me sitting there this spring day, not knowing a soul in this town that I used to know reasonably okay. That was long ago. This was now, and that stupid hustling bastard thinking he had found one, found me.

If the truck was loaded I could drive it out right now, right now, is what I felt like doing, drive to hell out of this place. This is how things were. Sometimes we pretend otherwise. My memories of this town were based on a lie and it was my own. I had ignored the reality. Candy floss. Where was my head? White-rite strongholds. How come? This phrase from some-place, lodged in my head. Where had it come from? White-rite strongholds.

An eerie scent charged my nostrils. An elderly woman gazing at me. I didnt feel uncomfortable about that but I felt uncom-fortable about something. She would see I was not from hereabouts. How come? She was doing a real stare like she was smelling me too: Oh you from up north? Yeah, you got your own smells from there son – fresh! That right?

Fantasy conversations. Back to the porpoise story. How come the north is up and the south is down? My daughters would have answered that one. Down south, up north. Over east and easy, across the west. So where is hell? down below and heaven up above. Okay.

She was watching me. This old lady had been around this town so long she not only knew everybody by sight she knew their smells and their pastimes too. She saw me and knew me for a stranger immediately, this guy with the books, what books, sitting here with his coffee like this, who is he? What books is that he's got, he aint from here. She would sniff out a stranger at two hundred metres. She was the one. Anybody not from there she sensed it and knew it. That was one fearsome thought. She had the apricot pie. A big slice of it, full of juice and syrup, a dollop of cream. She attacked it. Elderly people eat things different; they begin passive but are not passive. That is the last thing. They are aggressive, like a machine is aggressive, they are involved in a struggle, they are fighting for their lives, chip chip chip chip, chip chip chip. No let-up there. This old lady was no joke. And the way she looked at me! Those eyes! Jesus man who was she! Here I was. Recovery. Now this. Her.

Everything connects. Were they connected? Anything is possible. Ma whatshername with the kids; gangsters and butchers, machine-gunning the cops. You hear the stories over this side of the country. Things that should be stories arent stories. So what does that mean? Real Life? No but reality, that is the horror. You see the guys inside the gas station, ordinary guys, heading into the diner, crossing the parking area toward their truck and you know they have their stories. Nobody knows them. How come? These stories are important. Their stories. How come nobody knows them and are listening to them? Even if they are bad stories. What is bad stories? Stories about bad things. That is what stories are. These people too man where do they stay? Who knows where they stay. I got a little sister man, you want her? They stay miles out of town and their families been here since the 'purchase days', maybe where they got decent beer or maybe like from the Indian states, their ancestors came down to fight with the white-rites.

These people in the charity store, I was angry about it. Young families. Going the same way, end the same way. What was their stories. We dont know their stories. How come we dont know their stories? They have them to give and sometimes they give them but nobody listens. How come nobody listens? Even if they cared but they dont, one way or the other man they dont give a damn who listens, it never crosses their mind, that is their history, that is the history of their people and they dont give a damn who listens, it isnt for telling, they keep their stories, they keep themself to themself. This is how they live and been so living for hundreds of years. That is their culture, that is their tradition, that is how long they go back. Thousands of years is how long they have been around; dynastical systems, what are we talking about – 7,000 years? is that what that means, 7,000 years before Jesus Christ was born? Tell that to this old lady with the apricot pie, who saw me glance at her and smiled. I smiled back. Why? God knows. But now she took the lead and I knew she was going to talk. She began by smiling at me. How come? I was too polite. I was a stranger. Strangers are polite. Or should be. In these parts especially; even ones with blue eyes, getting mistook for locals. Did I want people smiling at me? No I did not. Old lady or not. Life is too fucking tricky. I didnt want that at all. Not here and not now man I was not right for it; stuff like the hustler guy, it wasnt good for the confidence. He chose me. How come he chose me? What did I look like man a tourist? Hell. I opened another book just to see what it was, and to end these thoughts, the elderly woman and the charity store regulars, these young families; broken dreams, broke the law. If there was any truth to the tale, his little sister, the horror of that, he was mid-twenties so she could have been anything and where was she, locked in a room. Except it was a line. That was a line, it was not the truth.

I was too polite; the old failing. I should have told him to fuck off. I did. Yeah but too late too late. What if he had gone for it with me? I knew he was holding. Then the working compadres on the other side of the street. I would have wound up in the river.

Okay. A book or a beer? I needed something. A book, concentrate on the book, but I was thinking because one thing how people do not take the lead like this elderly woman was doing. They wait for you. People react. What are you doing. They wait for you. Once you do your thing then they respond to you. I saw this as a key into the character of this place. Are you a friend or foe? I did this on the road into a town near this one time where a bad murder had been, and I didnt want to stop there, just keep driving but this once I needed to stop and just rest, I needed to rest and through this wooded land, passing by a pond, thick forests, how do you see through the trees, you cant, all small places there, decrepit shacks and broken-up automobiles, and you didnt need to see people to know who was living here; this was them and if you aint one of them or related to one of them you should drive on pretty damn smartish and dont risk any blow-outs on your own vehicle, make sure about them tires, you dont want to stop here man you really dont want to stop here.

Taking a truck along here in itself was the gamble. Why ever did you come this way anyway, well you got to go some way or other, what road you going to take? the fucking highway of Life? like Billy Joe says, well dont you be mistaken mister you want to go some different route and see different ways of making it through because this can be of real service in the future, and this is where I was coming from. It is how I drove the truck, and I shall call it my truck. Because that is what it was. That guy who was murdered, black guy, in his own place too, in his own time: that preyed on my mind; east someplace, Texas maybe into Louisiana. Some tragedies you always go back to. That murder was one most shocking horrible thing, it was, if you can say any one is worse than another, taking the Life of a human being. It makes you sicken, dragging a man so long and so bad that his poor body falls apart; how do we cope? his family, how do they manage it? People would see me and know that too. People would see me coming and know who I was, who I was not and so what if I had those blue eyes? Some blue eyes are different. You got blue eyes in this place does not mean you sanction horror. What do you mean sanction horror. No one sanctions horror. Not that old lady smiling at me. I looked up from the book and enough. I smiled back at her: Hi.

She stopped smiling. You a teacher?

No.

You seem like one.

Well, I'm not.

She nodded. You sure seem like a teacher.

Yeah, okay, but I'm not.

We got teachers here.

Yeah?

She waited on me. I was to add something in of my own. I was not going to. There's room for more, she said, there's always room for more, if you love the Lord.

She was waiting on me again. No, I was not going to add one thing more to that. She was not bullying me, the white-rite shite man. I held up my hand. Pardon me ma'am, I dont want to be involved in this conversation.

She squinted at me.

Not at this time of the day, I said, smiling.

Her head shifted position as though for a better view of me, that she might see every move I made, hear every last utterance, uncover everything, get it all. She frowned. You love the Lord mister?

Me . . . well, really, it is no concern of mine, as I am to you, of no concern. It wont do any good for us to talk. You believe one thing, I believe another. You want to test your belief against mine but I am not going to allow that to happen.

She smiled. I dont test my belief.

I drive a truck.

You think about these things.

I do, yeah. But why not think about these things if all you have is your own head and your own stories, that is driving long distances, your brain is working and begins from there and makes what it can, if you allow it to, if you dont seal it off from interference.

I smiled at her. She was listening; wanting to be talking but needing me to talk so she could deliver what it was. People talking to me is interference. What I'm saying is be a listener, a true listener and if I was a teacher that would be my one exhortation. It is what I want in my own life, and other people too, pardon me, yourself included, should maybe seek the same, be a listener, be a witness in your own town right here, this very place, your own place, be a witness. This town is a difficult place. But I dont want to be a witness to that. I aim for something in my Life, but my Life is a solitary thing. That is how I see it, only with development. I see it as a development. Okay, a solitary development, always personal. Look around and see them here, young couples. Even their kids, they are with them too and they carry the goods out to the car and dont look this way or that, just getting on with their Life, they get on just living, and if you want to talk to them they will listen and maybe you get a smile from them but not much of a smile.

I seen you were a teacher from over there, she said, pointing at the door through to the long table by the front window, the old guy with the bucket, the double doorway escape. I seen you from there.

Well okay. But I think what you saw was these books. I lifted the one with the porpoise. This one for my daughters about the Pole and the cod fish hunting after the little whitebait fish what-you-call-them, I've forgot their name that they come chasing down here, all the way down – caplin – that long chain of existence, through all the species, down through the Southern Ocean, the great whites, supreme predators, giant squids, these ones where the belly entrance is through their brain.

The old lady smiled.

It is true, I said, they got a brain like a doughnut.

She got up from the chair.

That was my story with most everybody. If I managed back to the depot I could get the truck and just leave, leave.

Where was my head? I dont know except it was okay; nothing a cold beer couldnt cure. This town was not dry. Or was it? Maybe that was the problem. I saw guys drinking outside bars but these bars might have been alcohol-free cafés. That would make me smile. Yes.

My Life was like anyone else's: full of exits. I would find one. I had a nose for such detail.

I took the books from the bag and distributed them into my coat pockets and headed through to the double doorway, checking it out while I went, not too fast, not too slow. No old lady. No woman on the door – who flirted with me. I think she did. They all had gone; all gone. Oh man except him, the old guy who sought entrance fees into the bucket, he was watching me, he knew I was there. Coming through, I said.

He glanced at me and didnt smile, he was unable to charge me for leaving the damn place. Here, I said and passed him the empty bag.

I needed that beer but closer to the depot and newer haunts. If a bar existed, a proper bar, dark, dank and dismal, with music playing, and I could say, Hallelujah.

A NIGHT AT
THE THEATRE

I was watching and trying to engage, but I could not. It was near the end of the performance when Christine asked the question. I could not manage an answer and could not explain the reason. She held my hand. I loved when she held my hand. My bones were weary. How she did this imparted life. Yet I could not raise my head. She was waiting for me to do so and had been so waiting. When I did not she did. She did, she managed it. I could not. I tried and I could not, god almighty, why could I not manage it? This was all I had to do and could not do it. I tried again, knowing she would have been staring at me, willing me on. No, I said, and smiled – I hope! I hope I did. Christine would cope now that I could not. Still I tried. I think I did. Go on man go on! The roaring in my brain my brain my brain. That same roaring. I could stroke the side of her face. I reached to her; the line of her chin. I managed to reach and press my lips to the side of her mouth.

The rest of it was nothing to me. Such a poor performance, it was impossible and caused only anguish. I hate theatre, I said. I smiled, still with my head lowered, avoiding her eyes. But I should have screamed it here and now, right here and now, in this damn auditorium, repugnant place.

To engage, how to engage, I could not engage. I tried and I could not. I saw her eyes, man man man, her eyes, her eyes, the smile there, my God and that life. Yet if I had raised my head I could not have avoided the stage, and the actors there and if one, even one were to peer in my direction, poor bastard.

Was it only me? Surely not! Impossible! I concentrated on my shoes, poor things, the wrinkled leather, scuffed. The shoes next to mine were silver with lilac trim, and heels of perhaps two inches. Those shoes had their own existence. I whispered through gritted teeth. What did I whisper? What in God's name did I whisper? These were Christine's shoes; had marched onto her feet. I was in the shoe shop when the phenomenon occurred. That expensive shop we visit annually for the January sales. I had experienced a most peculiar sensation. This was in Glasgow remember. The strangest most peculiar sensation the strangest, and I told her, Quick! I cried, Quick! Yer shoes. Get them off!

I was laughing and she chuckled. She always trusted me.

No sooner done than the new pair enveloped her twice over. These shoes appeared the epitome of feminine frippery yet they were tough tough tough. Oh man! These shoes! Tough wee bastards man I knew them inside out with their lilac trim and silver fulsomeness, fuck! these two-inch heels. I breathed deeply. I knew I was smiling. Her beautiful feet. The warmth too. Christine gave to me a warmth. What was happening beyond! I gave nothing for that, nothing. Never.

I am not a masochist. Yet there I was. I grasp the concept where ye put all of yer trust in one other human being. It can only be one, only ever one. I can see that. I can. If something goes wrong does not enter the equation. I see it. Not the other nonsense it is nonsense and not real at all but a masturbatory pastime of sorts, hoods on yer head and getting dragged along the pavement, bow wow, lick me lick me, where's the apple?

I raised my head. The poor actors. A fine troupe too. I would have argued the point. But oh God almighty my inner world was more startlingly dramatic than that performance. This level of quality was quite outrageous. Glasgow had a reputation, once upon a time. I stared at my shoes again. Concentrated the stare. Two human beings on stage.

Yes, I saw that. What else?

Not a thing. Sorry, I could not make head nor tail of it and shall not apologise. Never mind their relationship, whatever that might have been, a situation maybe. Folk say that. There was a situation between them. It is what the cops say giving their evidence. Let's have your report, says the Chief. Well Chief there was a situation.

A situation? Good or bad?

I do not know sir I aint filed my report. Well see that you do officer.

Christine glanced at me. I smiled as though interested generally, but why had she withdrawn her hand. I had been holding her hand and that hand now was gone from my grasp. I was to think something but what? What was I supposed to think. That was my question. I made art but did I know it? No. Fuck. What a realisation!

Perhaps it was art. Perhaps it was me. Perhaps I was outwith my perceptions. My perceptions, it would appear, amount to shit.

But what was the point? There did seem to be 'a point'. If so was that it? If yes, fine, I accept that. I know little about theatre, art and performance other than what I have learned in its practice. Generally a context exists. In this case it did not. This is the crucial element, the absence of context. One is left floundering: Oh where am I!! if there is no context.

Slice of art, slice of life. People are supposed to think that way in its presence. I doubt anybody does. It seems daft. If human beings are involved how can there not be a context, even if it is one's parents? One's parents allow a context, and a primary context at that.

For all one might resent the very idea as a massive attack on privacy! I resented it strongly. I saw it as opportunism. You may discuss this with the older generation. Not to me. Do not drag me into it. Under no et ceteras.

I had lowered my head. Amusing to witness. Hiding my head. How long had I been hiding my head?

Oh Christine Christine this is the moment. We must leave leave leave. I am raising my head, raising it, from the floor. My head has been on the floor, it lolled by your shoes.

How can our parents be dragged into it, never mind the older generation, whoever they might be. Strange ancestors. They knew who they were but not in history. They are who they were and helped make us the persons we have become. Listen to the breeze, the swish of the leaves: Oh so this is why I am me; my great grandmother was a seamstress in a wee village northwest of Donegal town and my great grandfather was from the depth of south Ayrshire who joined the Foreign Legion thus establishing his own place, making of himself a statement. That is the way I saw it.

Of course that is the whole point of the aesthetic so-called situation if one might call it that, that a context does not exist. I know that; I know it now and knew it then and that was how come I concentrated my stare so long, thinking 'What if the one acting the aggressor's role takes a dislike to one in a personal capacity?' This would result in getting hurt; perhaps tortured, depending which side of the border.

Then if one is the perpetrator, the person doing it, if one is the aggressor, and it is all in that typically semi-pleasant manner, what one might call 'unctuous'. It dawns on one finally that this is for real and it is frightening.

The idea alone, being a sadist, oh no, no sir, that is the most dreadful horrible sort of nightmare, twisting somebody's arm so that it is painful beyond belief, wrapping both hands roundabout the higher wrist area of the other person's forearm setting one hand against the other, twisting the skin in opposite directions and agony of the purest form. Does the skin snap open? Then too the eyes. In another drama the narrative conjectured a hair-raising experience involving the military medical corps and soldiers brought into the ward with foreign objects inserted into their penis for which they themselves were responsible.

I was listening to an old soldier in a bar down by the Wyndford, Maryhill pretending I was intrigued. I was not intrigued, I was sickened. His stories were sickening. This part of Glasgow was known as 'Armytown'. He watched me while recounting the anecdotes. They left me aghast aghast aghast sinking fast fast fast, oh God I was sinking, gasping for air so not to be fainting right there and then, even conceiving of such such horrors, really, it is just too much. I cannot listen to stories from war zones, overseas containment struggles and these films smuggled out onto YouTube about some bastard's big brother, a soldier fighting alongside the Yanks in some place, the middle east or something, Asia, who knows, dealing with something or other. One saw it from a few years ago but the likes of me I cannot remember too much about it. I was not able to watch it for long. I could not. Horror upon horror. This is sadism, this is masochism, this is the real thing. There is no negotiation here, not towards a deeper sexual gratification. This is horror.

And Christine too, I saw her watching news reports on trust-worthy television channels. I needed to scream and scream scream. But she was fine. She sought tickets for the evening performance thereafter. In the foyer I saw art books on the bottom shelf of the little shopping area. Photographs of Vietnam, of Iraq, Kosovo, Somalia, photographs photographs. Brave camera men entering these most dangerous zones to bring us the images. Languishing on the bottom shelf, unread books, bringing us the images. The images. What are images?

What exists is not skin-deep. Images as images. Images. The colour of one's skin is no image.

Nearer my God than thee.

The phrase had entered my head. I turned to Christine who was engrossed in the performance. I could not have asked her and did not ask her. I did not wish to ask her, not even to be seen by her, that she might have seen me. Why had she brought me here?

Who is this sad fellow?

Me!

Why did I bring him along! Wringing her hands! Why!

Except she was engrossed in the performance. I was alone.

Nevertheless.

But I could not stand it. I thought I could. Until I tried. I could not. Some seek an excuse. And if I say I can understand that, fair enough, but not that I might act in the same way in the same circumstances. Back to contexts, if it is that context it might happen to us all.

The worst torture

defined as torture

One peers into the mirror, in that studied fashion we have when shaving our upper lip. See the concentration. A woman can never. Not even Christine, in all her extraordinary humanity. It is achieved in the act. And once one sees oneself in the act it is gone. Anything other than that is a contradiction in terms. A male can only achieve it in the act of not seeing himself, if his concentration is authentic. Staring at yourself cannot work. The body becomes a problem. We cannot move beyond. I watch my shoes. My shoes do not have a life of their own but that is not to say that they do not exist. Yes they exist of course they exist of course they exist. Christine, I whispered.

What is it?

Nothing.

It will soon be over, she said, referring to the performance. I wished to stuff my fingers into my ears. I could not listen. I wished to gouge out my eyes, I could not see. In the manner of the scientist, how it would be

how it would be

Christine recognised this reality, when one rocks in one's chair, one rocks in one's chair, one rocks in one's chair. So then frightening. Frightening. Because one is resisting the urge. Not for oneself but another. Because one can not do it alone. One requires another. So that is S&M, and how I too resisting the so-called performance when it came to that most crucial most fundamental point she turned and she touched my cheek and stared into my eyes, that I might whisper, Oh Christine we have to leave we have to leave I cannot abide it, I cannot abide it, oh please, please.

And all I then could do was stare to the floor and shake my head. It was not the time, it simply was not the time and I knew I would gain the understanding through this, the way it had to be, this form of enlightenment, watching the performing pair in that knowledge, alongside Christine and in such a manner, and too it being what it is. I was a member of an audience. This needs to be remembered. I could not watch. I could not watch

Whether to make the apology for that, setting it out clearly, what more could I do.

ITEMS
PRECARIOUS

I knew the judgement had been arrived at and this judgement was theirs. People have that right. This is the way life is. What is wrong with that? Nothing. Prerogatives exist and people take them. If certain prerogatives belong to those who consider themselves guardians of children then sobeit, we must ahem let it be without reaching for weapons of self-destruction. Every game cannot be won. The mother of my childs appreciates this fucking stuff. Or she would, certainly she would, if I so informed her. Bloody hell.

Probably I would inform her but if not so what, whose business is it. In the long run definitely. In the long run, however, everybody is there and one is not, you, you are not. By you I refer to oneself, me, to hell with it. We all know this. My youngest child knew this, third of my three, at three years of age; yes, she did. I saw it in her. The girl would learn about suits of armour, forms of irony, levels of ambiguity, in other words self-deceit: for so she will come to perceive of it and recognise that in me. In me she knows the concept may exist but if not there was a practical reality. Dad.

Yes I saw it in her. She escaped her mummy into my arms. Then she escaped me. She did. She began by escaping my embrace. Same as mummy oh mummy. Horrible to see and countenance: can one bring oneself to that point? One cannot. I cannot. But I, he said, am going mad.

Three, three, of three.

My youngest was not so much escaping other people as seeking solitude. She appreciates and respects solitude. At three and a third years of age – as happens again at the age of fifteen – most people enter a further and rather interesting stage in life, the realisation of the existence of other intellects. I refer to its effect on one's emotional development. How to be with others. To recognise the pain of another, the hurt. Prior to then children do not comprehend. That incomprehension; we note it in them. There are those who never achieve this stage.

Then of course how to be in the world. The child resists this too. It is forced upon her, as deceit is forced upon the rest of us.

When everybody is there and you are not. I think of that with pleasure. One attempts honesty. At least that. Even as a young man I went into rooms on my own and stayed there for interminably long periods. Mine own company was required. Not so much company; company was not what I wanted, not even my own. I was locked for a period, up and into, and thought to become a better human being. It did nay happen. Mental chaos sums up that experience. There is nothing about it I want to remember. Any memories I have are negative, which under-states the reality. It is nearly wiped from my brain, this secret part of my earlier time on the planet. I maintained the secret. The mother of my children knew nothing of it. I am eleven years older than my wife and shall carry the secret to my death-bed.

One day I might inform the weans. The youngest especially. I have come to favour her. She remains in a state of innocence that might last the rest of her days or so I believe, or appear to believe. What a fool I am. I wonder if I relax with her. It would be to her sister and brother I make my first confession.

There is more than one way to live one's life and I chose wrongly. There is a heroic element to this, but where and what might that be! I cannay find it. Except in the long run, it remains a to b, always, a then b, a then b. I wonder if there exists a language where the first letter of life is 'a' and 'b' the first letter of death? The composition of the concept 'and' is what exists between. There is a language pertaining to the algebraic that somehow achieves

quaternion

Lest one falls to the ground in the throes of death. Where I stay we say 'drapped deid', as in 'the poor cunt drapped deid'. I prefer 'drapt' deid.

I could not get away from death for long. Even if I wanted.

The short rejoinder is that I did not. Nor did I want to die in a condition of intellectual dishonesty. Even at my advanced age. I would like to have said, Above All! Yes, complete with the capital letters and the mighty exclamation mark. Above all else I wished for

What? Not truth. I could not describe it as truth, the object of the wish. A life that was true.

When I became a parent I realised that the days of my own life were numbered. That was common sense. Not for them it wasnt. My life was a joke to them. My wife and childs did not so much conspire against me as enter a type of solidarity that excluded me. They told me to fucking 'stop fucking moaning'. They said it to cheer me up. Or so they liked to think. My wife advised me of it. According to her they were well-intentioned, assuming I wished to live forever and familiar jibes would help smooth the path – the path to immortality presumably.

Even if it didnt, that the act of trying might.

Not for me. For other folk it might have worked. For myself but, forms of 'cheering me up' acted as a depressant and served merely to aggravate stressful situations. I could have done without it. We live our lives. Along the way we discovered that it wasnay a question of ownership. If I had said, Shut the fuck up it is my life: if I had said that, it would have made it appear as though 'life was mine'.

Except of course life is mine. A statement deserving at least two exclamation marks. But I was always a sensitive soul, and liked to underplay the hand.

But oh oh oh. 'Life belongs to me.' What an absurd load of pish. Cowardice masquerading as sensitivity. That one's weans believe such refuse shows merely the extent to which the propaganda chiefs have won. And we, as the adult generation, have lost.

Why could I not get talking to my offspring? Why are such barriers erected? Who in God's name is responsible? It isnay me anyway. They put up these barriers. People do. How come they never listen? They never listened to me. I exclude my youngest. At three years of age she listened, it was the other two didnay. They never listened. Never. Why was that? Their stupid little jokes, ripostes. How come? One asks: How come?

Because they had been programmed.

We enter life full of goodwill. We do. There are no grounds for cynicism here. In good faith we begin. I give that to my child(s).

The propaganda chiefs have destroyed the ability to learn. I know what I would have done: lined them up and shot them down.

When my colleagues spoke to me they uttered excrement ingested from television. Some fascist celebrity off a reality programme spouting the worst sorts of rightwing nonsense in that general spirit of smug ignorance that infuses the British Broadcasting Corporation. They listened to them and their lickspittles, washed-up entrepreneurs, DJs and rockstars, retired football players. They took their information from such sources. They knew nothing of politics and didnay want to know. At least not from me, nor from anyone like me. They listened to nonsense, regurgitated nonsense, then regurgitated the regurgitations, like licking up somebody's bile, spitting it into a cup and trying to use it to construct a picture. Even if it works it is the wrong colour, too similar in density, the catarrhal and spittle strings and it breaks one's heart, it breaks one's heart. They were deceived by these rightwing arguments and paid no heed when I called them fascist. They assumed my use of the word 'fascist' was the same as theirs, which amounts to 'killjoy'. Hitler was a killjoy. Nowadays the person who breaks up the party is called 'fascist'.

When my youngest gets older she will move towards their line of thinking. I should be mad to expect more given that she is her mother's girl. She is a fighter yet daughter to myself. As she moves towards their line of thought she will at last recognise my lies for what they are.

I wouldnay have wanted her any other way, nor her siblings. Of course not. I have lectured people for years. I should have kept my trap shut. They didnay listen, didnay hear, and eventually I came to realise – after I discovered I did not care – that life is short and maybe even too short which is altogether a concept or detail I have had to learn on pain of becoming a grandfather, scheduled eight years hence, on my reckoning. At twelve years of age my first child bears the most extraordinary resemblance to my father who begat myself at the age of twenty years, and whose elder grandson, my eldest child would no doubt conceive his own first child at that same age, eight years hence

and came to realise, to conclude the proposition, that I preferred the way they thought to the way I thought, and the reality amounted to nothing anyway, I cared nothing for reality, being unable to live with their mother except in a state of bemusement structured on the realisation that she married a fool, an absolute and irredeemable fool, that gem of a woman.

She was the one they would emulate. Surely to God! Definitely not me, I didnay want it to be me. I was never a good example; not for children. And my ideas werenay worth a brass farthing which has as much of a relation to my life as a plugged nickel. One sighs, but must continue. There are ways of being, honest ways of being, ways of being honest, ways of living our life, lives, the space in between mine and yours, this is truth, a balancing act, like all clichés. And one wonders why one sighs, sighed, while the one in between, my second child

THAT WAS A SHIVER

for
Tom Leonard

It happened on the Sunday him and Tracy were down the Barrows. Originally they were going a walk but there were things she needed and they hadnay been for ages. They split up when they got there. She couldnay shop with him around, so she said. It suited him anyway; it was a rare day, the sun beating down. Robert set off looking at this and that, no bothering. Maybe he would buy something maybe he wouldnay. It was relaxing. Really he was just passing the time till they met for lunch. If he did buy something it would have to be quite good else why bother? Even if he liked something he didnay always buy it; no if it didnay fit in his pockets. That annoyed her. No so much annoyed as irritated. But ye like it so why are ye not buying it?

Cannay be bothered.

Dont give us that, it's because it doesnay fit in yer pocket.

Exactly.

God!

That was what pockets were for but to carry stuff. Women carried stuff, men didnay. No if they didnay have to. Ye needed the fists free. What if something happened? Ye had to be ready. His granddaughter said to carry a rucksack so then he would be okay. A good idea. She was a bright lassie. Maybe he would, a rucksack, ye just shoved it on yer back. Today it was a polybag in the jacket pocket. Tracy made him bring it in case he saw something. She felt better shopping if she thought he was shopping too. So he kidded on he was. Although he did buy stuff occasionally. Auld vinyl maybe, a CD. He still bought music; especially vinyl. He was into country, a wee bit of blues, a bit of jazz. Mainly it was country but. One site he visited described what he liked as 'specialist'; 'Specialist Country'. It made Robert smile. At the same time it was right enough. A lot of it ye only found on vinyl; it wasnay available elsewhere, unless some wee snippet on YouTube. Apart from that what was there? No much.

He liked wandering about. Tracy didnay want him trailing eftir her. She was good at shopping, smelled a bargain at a hundred paces: take aim, fire. She aye bought stuff. At the same time she needed it. If she didnay need it she didnay buy it. It wouldnay have bothered him if she did. Whatever; he would carry it. If she let him. Some stuff she didnay. Oh you'll just bash it. That was cakes and vases, antique vases. She liked these telly programmes where folk tried to make a few quid 'buying wisely'. What does that mean, 'buying wisely'? Did she make any dough? No that he noticed. Never mind if it kept her happy. Except ye couldnay get near the computer for her checking out silver fish forks from the 18th Century.

Flowers too, she wouldnay let him carry flowers. He could hold them if he was standing still but no to walk. Flowers, seeds and plants; she liked all that. Their ayn garden was tiny. It wasnay theirs officially. They just had a ground-floor flat. There were six families up the close; three one side, three the other; and two gardens out the front. Tracy stuck a fence round theirs. It wasnay to lock out the two upstairs families, she did it to stop the boys playing fitba outside the window. If folk want to come in they can come in, she said, but not for football. She was thinking about the summer and aw that, a glass of wine with the neighbours in the evening sun.

It didnay bother Robert that much, being honest, he wasnay brought up with gardens. Tracy made it a joke. Oh dont talk about gardens, he hates them. Naw he didnay. He just didnay care about them. Oh you've got a phobia. Phobia fuck all. She called it soil, he called it dirt.

He would be under it soon enough. Unless he got cremated. He quite fancied that, the ashes scattered. Except he couldnay think of a place he wanted to go. Resting for all eternity, it was a pleasant thought. The ferry to Arran; they could toss the ashes ower the side. Right in the middle of the water, open the tin and shake it loose, let the wind carry them. Speed bonny boat. He aye liked Arran.

Mind you ye could just fucking save time, wrap them in a freezer bag and toss them off the Jamaica Street Bridge; watch them chug their way down the Clyde. There go the ashes. Ye would be on a cloud, a wee whisky in one hand. Then the stars at night, the Atlantic. With his luck they would get caught on the current and wind up in Orange Lodge Province, King James and all his rebels; shudder shudder, even thinking about it made ye claustrophobic.

The slow boat to New York but imagine, floating across the Atlantic. He didnay want Canada. Too cauld. Nova Scotia! Oh christ naw. Out the fucking frying pan.

A garden phobia. Maybe she was right. It was aye tenement flats with him. He was born in one and would die in one. Unless he drapt down in the street. Or coming up the steps at the front close. Or down the steps. Weans left toys and ye had to watch ye didnay trip ower the cunts.

Mind yer language!

It was the toys he was talking about.

She liked auld cutlery as well. Good stuff but, high quality. If it didnay have the makers' marks she wasnay interested. An auld

Polish woman ran the stall she liked. Tracy chatted to her. The auld days in Poland; the Communists and the Second World War, the Holocaust. But that was her with another bunch of forks. The kitchen drawers were jammed full. It became an issue after a meal because doing the dishes, the fucking cutlery drawer wouldnay close. He counted the teaspoons once. Thirty-two! What was that a joke? Thirty-two fucking teaspoons! So then she had plastic containers for the excess. So what were they keeping it all for? The boy didnay care. Him and his wife had their ayn stuff.

Och it didnay matter anyway. Who gives a fuck. Live and let live. Tracy done what she wanted. He was happy with that. She was another human being. The Barrows was a for instance. Gie her her head and off she went, ye never saw her again.

He didnay mind browsing. Good seeing the tools. Amazing the number ye got secondhand. Did people even have tools nowadays? How come there were so many? Ye looked at them and thought about the guys that used them. When did they die? at a fair age or was it young? Was it an accident? Robert had worked in all different jobs right throughout his life and there were aye accidents. In the fucking army as well; some admitted some denied, all covered up; they were all accidents too, even the intentional ones. Then if ye boxed a cunt. Robert boxed. It wasnay a game. Guys got killed boxing. People forgot that. Yer fists were weapons; they were classed as that if ye fought, like if ye were a boxer. Tools were weapons too depending how ye used them. Cunts took hammers to the dancing in case of problems. A fucking stanley knife could slice off a cheek. A wood chisel; the damage ye could do with that, a wood chisel! fuck sake.

Ye saw tools down the Barrows ye couldnay work out what they were for. Then ye thought about it: all these different jobs down through the years. Tools for every last one of them. Some ye had never seen before, for jobs that didnay even exist. No in Scotland anyway. Maybe in places like Africa or Asia, South America. Ye saw them on the antique telly programmes. Antique experts like tools. Nay tools nay antiques. Nay tools they would be out a job. These upper-class cunts, where would they be? On the fucking broo same as the rest of us.

After tools came music. And cables too, he liked cables, connecting leads and all that stuff. It came in handy. It meant too if ye saw an auld computer or hi-fi separate, like an actual auld-style deck or whatever, just whatever. Ye never knew until ye found something then saw what it was for.

In the auld days down the Barrows Robert aye started at the first close past Pearson's corner. Until they knocked down the building. But there was another close he liked, that one round the lane and across the wee backcourt. Dragon Pass the auld folk called it except it wasnay 'dragon' it was 'dragoon', from when the King's dragoon guard came to quell the weavers – quell or kill, the bastards, they fucking shot them dead, ordinary working-class guys. On the first floor they had the deli where they done a nice breakfast. The dealers all used it so ye knew it was cheap. One time him and Tracy were in for a coffee and some cunt tried to sell them a rabbit. No for a pet for a pot of fucking soup. Make a stew out it, the guy says, just haud its ears. I'll haud your fucking ears, says Tracy.

Up the stair and roundabout, up the stair and roundabout. Then up ye went and roundabout again till that was you. All sorts of stuff. This was where she found the boy the Christmas train set whenever the hell that was, thirty year ago. A fucking beauty it was. All the bits and pieces: levers, signal boxes, split rails and wee bridges; farmyard animals, wee cows and sheep. It must have came from a rich house, there was hardly a scratch on it. Wealthy cunts, they dont play with the toys. They get the Manservant to do it for them. Play with the train-set, there's a good fellow. Attennnshun.

Tools, music, stamps and watches, plus militaria; medals and Nazi helmets. What ye call a male preserve, for the ones that didnay know any better. It was a smack in the mouth these cunts needed. Soldiers meant fuck all to them; it was only their medals, what was their medals? was it scarce? the DSM and Iron Crosses, Victoria Crosses? Whose medals were they? Oh a guy that got killed. Oh was it an Officer? Naw, just a guy. Aw that's a shame. Did they gie him a medal for gallantry? Naw, just for all the campaigns he did; North Africa, Borneo, Iraq and Afghanistan, window of the world, join the army and ye might see through it.

One stall was especially good for vinyl. Except their fucking prices man. Jesus christ: ye would have thought it was platinum gold discs they were selling. Charlie Pride and Kitty Wells, Loretta Lynn, George Jones and that auld cowboy bloke everybody looks for whose name Robert could never remember. Everybody wants them but ten quid an album! Who dreamt up these prices? Did they ever sell a record? Sometimes ye wonder. After the CDs came in ye would have thought vinyl sales would plummet but they didnay. Then when CDs were on their way out back came the vinyl, with a fucking vengeance. Folk get sick of downloading. They need to hold something. You go to secondhand shops nowadays, they're full of fucking teenagers. Oh look at that the Everly Brothers! Is that a Beatles original! Oh who is that Elvis? Naw, Hank Williams. Pardon? Ha ha. So that bumped up the price. Fifteen quid a pop, are ye fucking kidding?

Although just now was quiet. Robert was the only one there. It was a joke Tracy made. The stalls he liked, naybody else used except him; he was the only one. But it wasnay true. He wished it was. He flipped fast through the spines of the album covers and found a Jerry Lee Lewis from the rock and roll days. Very unusual. But the price for fuck sake. Twelve quid. Ye kidding! He lifted it out the sleeve. No bad condition. But twelve quid was a take-on. He wouldnay have bothered even looking except he didnay recognise a couple of numbers. The vinyl surface was covered in smudges, whatever it was, auld fucking snotters man it was disgusting. He stuck it back in the sleeve.

The lassie behind the stall looked like she was texting but she wasnay, she was watching Robert. She was, she was staring at him. What did she think he was goni drap the fucking record? Or knock it? That was it! She thought he was trying to knock the record! He took his time reading the cover just to annoy her. Because she was annoying him. She fucking was, she was watching him. Nay question about that.

He shoved the record back in the sleeve, stuck it back in the pile. If she didnay want a customer he wasnay goni burden her. She was young too. No even forty, at a guess. A crabbit bastard but ye could tell it by looking. They said it was auld folk were crabbit but it wasnay it was the fucking young yins. Grow up hen: ye felt like saying it to her, except what would she have done? sent for the polis. She had probably took a picture of him. So what, he was back flipping through the records then there it was, Ernest Tubb *Alive at Billy Bobs*. He grabbed at it nearly dropping the damn thing trying to dig out the record. He slowed down.

Alive at Billy Bobs.

He lifted out the record. It wasnay Ernest Tubb it was Mario Lanza. Mario Lanza. The lassie was hovering. It's Mario Lanza, he said, look! And he showed her the record. She hardly looked at it. What's wrong? she said.

I'm showing ye what's wrong, the bloody record is wrong.

She stared at him like it was his fault. What else did he expect inside these auld album sleeves anyway? How come he was buying such shite in the first place? It was obvious she had nay respect for what she was selling except it made money. He pointed at the price sticker: Eight quid!

The lassie shrugged.

I mean okay Ernest Tubb but no Mario Lanza. Mario Lanza's an opera singer.

So?

So it's a mistake. It's in the wrong record sleeve. He showed her the record label then the record sleeve which had a drawing of Ernest Tubb wearing a white stetson hat and one of these Texas suits with the curved pockets, the wee string tie and the leather boots. She looked at it as if she had never seen anything like it in her life before. Robert frowned. Okay if it wasnay cool but the guy's singing was good and he had a brilliant band, aye the best musicians, and cheery as fuck man waltzing across Texas, cheery stuff, good stuff, walking the floor over you. That's who should be singing on the actual record, he said, Ernest Tubb. No Mario Lanza. Know what I mean, O Sole Mio, Show me the road to old Sorrento! Robert smiled, showing her the record cover.

Well if ye dont want to buy it dont buy it.

Pardon?

Dont buy it, said the lassie, folding her arms and raising her eyebrows.

I'm just saying it's the wrong record for this record sleeve.

Huhhhh. Give me it ower.

Robert paused a moment. He held the record out to her and she near grabbed it out his hand. She looked to the side then up in the air. What was she doing that for? Drawing attention to Robert for the benefit of the guy that owned the stall. Robert saw him now, he was sitting with his back to the wall reading the Sunday Mail. Probably her da. Robert hadnay been for several months but he recognised him.

So ye dont want it? she said.

Robert shrugged. See for yerself. The record is opera and the cover says country. One's opera one's opry.

She didnay hear him, she didnay listen, she didnay bother to read the fucking labels, the notes on the record, the record sleeve, fuck all, she just bent below the table to stick it away someplace. When she straightened up the phone was back in her hand and she was scrolling, and she did this wee double-take like surprised to see him. Who's kidding who. What was the problem but? He felt like asking, he didnay. Obviously she had taken a dislike to him. That happens and there isnay a thing ye can do about it. People hate yer guts and they dont even know ye. Miss Girny was like that. Unless she just hated everybody. Probably she did. Probably she thought he was a time-waster. Mair browsing than buying. If she had asked the energetic cunt on the chair he would have told her different. Fair enough he was a browser but so what? Maist people are the same. Tell ye what, he said, I'll carry on looking through the albums. Maybe I can find the Mario Lanza cover and the Ernest Tubb record will be inside the sleeve.

Beg pardon?

What I mean, if I find them. I'll look for them, if I find them I can swop them round.

She didnay know what he was talking about. It was just stupid, she didnay know. She didnay care, she just didnay fucking care. She just stared at him. Imagine Tracy, Tracy would have slapped her face. She didnay even listen. Ye telt her stuff and she didnay listen. Opera was history. Who listened to it nowadays? Yer maw. Yer granny. Robert might have bought it for his granny. She played the piano and was good at it. All the auld songs. He would have been her cup of tea, Mario Lanza. Oh he is lovely-looking. That would have been the auld yin. Oh he's a fine figure of a man. A matinee-idol type of guy till he put on the weight. All that spaghetti. O Sole Mio right enough. Ye felt sorry for him, auld Mario, he died young. Probably they had opera at the Grand Ole Opry, back when they first built it. Cowboys and the wild west. It made sense. Probably in the auld days that was how it started, opera came first then opry. People all went to hear it. That was what they did for enjoyment, and ye've got to have some of that. Otherwise it's an Alfie situation, what's it all about?

Miss Girny was standing farther along now. Out of earshot. In case he asked her a question. Next time she would send for the polis. Once upon a time folk would have been helpful. Naw they wouldnay. That was sentimental shite. Whoever took a pride in their job? Nay cunt. What was there to take a pride in? Probably she hated the job. Maist people did. Ye were just exploited. Working a fucking Sunday too ye couldnay blame her. She wasnay that auld either. Take away the girny face and she wasnay a bad-looking lassie; lovely pair of tits, what ye would say attractive. Ye just had to watch it with her da there, the fat cunt on the chair, if ye were a young guy and ye fancied her. Ye looked the wrong way and he would be there in a flash. Big bastard. Lazy but, reading the paper with his cup of tea, ye would dance rings round him, just fucking pick him off, jab jab bump ya cunt; sitting there and his lassie doing the work.

Robert had a boy. A lassie would have been nice. He had one now anyway, a granddaughter. That was the best, she was good; aye keeping Robert right, telling him stuff. She took after Tracy. Kids were great; they cheered ye up. It was just what's out there, that was the worry. That was always the worry. Any lassie at all.

Boys too. Is there anything sickens ye mair, a child killer? Murdering evil bastards. It's just yer luck too because what can ye do? Ye cannay keep them in the house day after day and ye cannay go out and watch them. Every week there was a story about some kid getting taken away and then they find them in a field. A fucking nightmare. Robert would have cut off their fucking tadger man no fucking danger and some of them would have been grateful, paedophile bastards, it wasnay me it was my sex-drive. It doesnay even itself out either, if it happens to ye. People say it does but it doesnay. Some things are beyond the pale. Murders and killings in yer family. Who gets over that? Nay cunt. Afflictions too, ye can be born with afflictions, major ones. What is fair about that? There is nothing fair about that. Ye feel sorry for folk but there is nothing ye can do. There's nay balance, nay rhyme nay fucking reason. Fuck religion, who gives a fuck about that. It's just how it is for folk. Naybody escapes. Even the lassie there, ye felt like gieing her a cuddle. Except she would have belted ye one. Miss Girny, well named.

Another guy had appeared and was thumbing through the CDs. How long had he been here? Cunts flit in and out. Near where he stood was the place they stacked the orange and green. Name yer poison. Sectarian shite. Nowadays they called it 'specialist' and tried to lump it in with country, blues and jazz. The lassie hovered about. It was him she was interested in, this other guy. A few years younger than Robert by the looks of it. She thought it would be him spending the dough. She thought wrong. He was flipping too fast through the CDs. Naybody could read information that quick. Two minutes it would take him to reach the vinyl; instead of half an hour. He would never even see the vinyl, no at that speed, the state of the actual records. Some of them were scratched to fuck, covered in grease. Mind you a good wipe would do it; for some of them anyway, that was all ye needed. Eh excuse me, called Robert. Can I see that record again?

She turned to him.

The one I was looking at!

She stepped a pace and reached under the table, drew the record out the sleeve and held it to him. The actual record! By itself. The actual fucking vinyl, Mario Lanza, and she was waiting for the fucking money! What was she expecting him to take the record without a record sleeve? Fucking unbelievable. He pointed at the £8 sticker. Eight quid! he said. And it's no got a sleeve. Mario Lanza. It's no even Mario Lanza I want. Eight quid jesus christ a record without a sleeve!

Pardon?

It's no even got a sleeve!

Sleeve?

The thing you put the record in.

Ye mean the cover?

I dont mean the cover I mean the sleeve; ye call it a sleeve. It's a record sleeve. Robert shrugged. Okay a cover, call it a cover.

The big guy on the chair was looking ower at him. Robert called to him: Ye cannay charge me for an album cover if it's no got one.

It has got one, called the lassie. He said he didnay want it.

Robert sighed. Because it's the wrong one. It's the wrong one, the bloody thingwi, what-dye-call-it, Ernest Tubb, that is the name on the cover, that is like . . . Then ye look inside, ye see the record christ almighty it's a different one; Mario Lanza, I mean . . . !

The way the lassie was staring at him.

How come even he was talking to her! And her fingers, ye saw her fingers, the way she was holding the record. It was just fucking, it was just, ye couldnay believe it! Not by the tips or the edges, no even trying to keep the thing clean. Not even making the effort, she wasnay. Her actual fingers were right on the fucking grooves and whatever was on her fingers, that make-up she was wearing and what not, mascara. That stuff leaves a sticky residue. Her fingers would have been full of it so then wedging into the grooves on the record like fucking superglue and then the needle itself, the actual needle, it would damage the actual fucking needle. That was obvious! Without fail it would damage the needle. When ye think about the cost of needles. Ye have to order them online too, fucking Amazon then from America or some fucking place, Germany or Hong Kong. Robert's boy ordered the last couple for him and when the package came the label was someplace else. Her nails too jesus christ her nails, ye couldnay believe her nails. Unbelievable. She shouldnay have been allowed to handle vinyl records at all. Once she had her mitts on them, ye would have been as well scraping the surface with a cast-iron chisel.

Do you want it or no? she said.

Robert gazed at her. The big guy on the chair was kidding on he was reading his paper but he was all ears for the answer. She held the record out to him. Robert gestured at the boxes under the table. Why dont ye check for a Mario Lanza record sleeve; ye'll probably find it's got the Ernest Tubb record inside, so then ye can switch them.

Look, do ye want it?

I do want it I'm only – what I'm saying

Then she shut her eyes, she shut her eyes and shut up Robert; that was him. Her doing that stopped him. He was talking and she came in and stopped him. It was amazing she would do that. All he did was ask a question, he only just

It didnay matter. It didnay matter. What did it matter, it didnay.

JAMES KELMAN

The other customer was watching, him browsing the CDs, taking it all in. Kidding on he wasnay but he was, he fucking heard everything, he fucking made sure he did.

She was about to put the record away again. Robert said, I want that. I just eh . . . He sniffed. Eight pound but know what I mean, it isnay a fair price, no if it's no got a sleeve.

Robert glanced at the big guy. I'm goni take it, he said, I just feel like I should get a record sleeve with it. He pointed at the Ernest Tubb album cover lying at the edge of the table. I'll just take that one there.

But that's the wrong one ye says it was the wrong one!

Robert sniffed. I'll take it but, it's better than nothing.

The lassie frowned at Robert, she lifted the Ernest Tubb album cover and raised it up to read the liner notes.

He said: I'm only wanting it to protect the record. But I mean eight quid . . . !

She stopped reading the notes. The big guy on the chair had gied her a wave. She handed him the record and the album cover. He looked them over then looked at Robert, he sniffed. He read the sleeve notes and looked at Robert again. Seven, he said.

Robert shrugged and passed the lassie a tenner. She had these snappy blonde curls. Robert aye liked them. He had a girlfriend once, if ye put yer finger in them, twisting, it was kind of nice. Miss Girny had them. She was no a bad-looking lassie at all. It was just the way she acted, it put ye off.

Opera with nay sleeve and Ernest Tubb with nay record. Seven quid. Dick Turpin didnay have a look in. He checked the vinyl for scratches. It wasnay bad considering. Mario Lanza. Tracy would like it. Take me back to old Sorrento. No so much opera as Italian traditional. Country music didnay interest her. Except if it was religious, she quite liked that, the auld hymns.

Yer change!

Thanks dear.

The 'dear' was sarcasm. She missed it but, it was too deep for her.

What touched her? That is what ye wondered. What touches you hen? Did she even have a guy? Just a young woman too, it made ye sad.

Look twice at a woman. What do ye see? It didnay matter how tough they were, a man would batter her. A tough lassie like her, so what? Maist any guy. Maybe no any guy but maist. Probably she wondered about him. She would know his clothes; he wasnay just some stupid auld cunt. So what he was aulder? He was fit, he took care of himself. He liked a beer, so what? a couple wasnay a problem. Okay he liked a smoke but a half ounce lasted him. She would see that if she looked. Some folk didnay, they looked at ye but no properly. They saw the auld guy but no beneath the surface.

She was waiting for him to take the £3 change. The coins chinked when she put them into his hand. Her fingers were cold; and white, awful white. Sometimes ye see fingers like that, so so white. Where does the blood go? That was Robert's feet. He went for a walk and came hame and his feet were freezing. When he took off his socks to see them they were pure white. Nay fucking blood, the blood had vamoosed; where was the blood? gone. What if it went white all the way up? And yer fingers too, white all the way down; frae yer shoodirs, yer neck. Ye would be fucking deid! Nay blood in yer body, how could ye live! Ye couldnay.

Robert smiled. Never mind, he had the cover. It was the cover he wanted and he had fucking got it. *Alive at Billy Bobs*. What a brilliant title. He had never seen it before. Never even heard of it! Maybe it was a one-off. That happened. Live shows at some wee venue in Holland or Denmark and some mad fan taped it, then it was never remastered. Probably worth a fortune on eBay. Except no without the record, if ye didnay have the record. Ach well. Although even without the record it was a snip. One of these days he could find it. Who knows? Ye browse the secondhand record stalls long enough and ye might, then too with charity shops and boot sales.

He should have said to Miss Girny how if she kept an eye open for the Mario Lanza cover she might find the Ernie Tubb record inside. He should have said it but he didnay. Even talking to her was a problem. It was. Any woman at all, just about. Tracy! fucking hell man scratch yer eyes out soon as look at ye! Saying hullo to a lassie man it was a fucking nightmare. That was a question for the granddaughter. How come us auld cunts are the problem?

Then ye looked twice at the lassie. She might have been tough but she was just a skinny wee thing. She reminded Robert of ones he saw in Spain, local women; they were all wee and skinny; good-looking lassies but just so wee, so wee. Robert done a bit of training there once. Him and five other boys. The trainer took them for a week, auld Andra, a great auld guy, fucking great auld guy. Malaga, running up and down the beach, using the local gym. That was brilliant, putting on a show for the locals, sparring a round, just boys, fucking brilliant man, the big breakfasts! Spanish – what was that? sausages, all spicy and bacon; blood puddings, eggs, piles of toast. Piles of this, piles of that. Then steaks; steaks and steaks. Fucking feed! Ho! Then ye turned a corner and saw the locals, skinny wee people. That was the politics. That side of it. The auld guys went on about it, the Civil War and all that, the fascists and Britain supporting them. I'm only goni train mister no support Franco. His da was as bad, when Robert joined up – the fucking army! Jesus christ!

The big guy on the chair glanced ower at him on his way

out. Robert was going to say something but didnt. He felt like a smoke. He felt like a seat too. He saw one but it was beside the military medal stall. A few guys hung about there chatting. There was a market for war memorabilia. It wasnay Robert's cup of tea. Ye want my medals? Here, stick them up yer fucking arse. That was Robert. He took out the polybag and shoved in the album.

Outside on the landing he saw another flight up. He had forgot there was another floor. Now he saw it he remembered Joe McColl. Was Joe still around? Joe done the driving up here. It would have been nice saying hullo. He helped Robert back in the days he had a transit van and survived doing small removals. Joe was mates with Robert's young brother and got Robert a couple of wee jobs through his contacts. At the same time he owed Robert. No that that mattered, a couple of quid. It wasnay a lot of dough. Ye dont break the connection for that. Joe had a problem, him and Robert's young brother, and it rhymes with ramble.

On his way up the twisting staircase to the top storey he heard some funny sounds. It was doos, the way they gurgled in their throats – mair 'gargle' than 'gurgle'.

It was a nuisance carrying the polybag; it banged into yer fucking knee.

Never mind. Pech pech. Fuck. Just the wheezing, the usual. Robert felt it in the lungs and stopped for a minute.

Ye laugh at yerself but nay wonder the morbid stuff sets in. All the what ifs. What if ye dropped dead, what if ye had a stroke, couldnay talk, couldnay walk, what if, what if. Pech pech. Ye laugh at yerself. But what about Tracy? if something did happen. What would happen to her? That was the fucking worry, if he wasnay here to look eftir her. A fucking cabbage or some-fucking thing. Better aff deid. Better for her. What would she do? She would still get out right enough. She had her ayn pals. Mair than him. She did. She enjoyed life. Church and these wee events they put on: jumble sales and fetes and the rest of it; wee days here and there, excursions. She loved all that. Country dancing. Heel for heel and toe for toe.

All he done was the pub and the fucking bookie. He didnay even watch the fitba: he had stopped the fucking fitba! How come? Tracy said it to him too: Away and meet yer pals. Dont just come out with me, go to a game.

Go to a game. Maybe he would. He used to watch the boy, he liked watching the boy.

Robert got to the top. Oh for fuck sake man when ye saw the place it was just depressing, so depressing. Bare stalls and empty pitches. Decrepit was the word. It was fucking decrepit! A couple of places were open but the folk that ran them were too desperate. Ye recognised that, how they tried no to look at ye in case they put ye off. Car-boot sales had changed everything. Folk said it was eBay and fucking gumshoe or whatever ye call it but here it was the car-boots. At one time this entire building was stowed out. A real hustle and bustle. Sundays especially. Fucking teeming with folk; and Saturdays werenay bad either. That was the real Barrows, the way it used to be. The way things were gon it would wind up dead and buried, selled out to whoever, some gangster cunt, second cousin of the Party Leader's sister-in-law's uncle's fucking da's wee brother; the usual party politics shite. Robert would have shot the bent bastards. They didnay care about working-class people at all; Byres Road and fucking Bearsden; all the middle-class cunts. It made ye angry.

Nay wonder.

In through the nose, breathe;

fucking hernia, the belly, breathe out. Lungs, bla bla.

Amazing how it affects ye. Nay wonder ye got angry but. So

did Tracy. She got angry at him, for getting angry at them. It's you gets the heart attack.

True.

Time for a smoke. Nay Joe McColl. Maybe he was here and hiding. He saw Robert before Robert saw him. Nah, no Joe, Joe wasnay like that. It was only a few quid anyway, who gives a fuck. Fucking dough man problems, aye fucking problems. Coming down from the top stair he had the lid off the tobacco tin and was extracting a ricepaper from the packet, the polybag handle over his left wrist. What-if scenarios! Somebody comes up the stairs and doesnay see ye and bangs yer elbow, there it goes, tobacco all over the stairs! Disaster, call the cops!

He was wary but with the tin open and the tobacco spread along the paper. Rolling the fag was a one-handed operation: two fingers and thumb, a very delicate manoeuvre, ye felt like a surgeon, and if yer elbow got bumped it was all up in the air; tobacco and cigarette paper, the entire tin, all ower the stone paving. And it was soaking wet too. The fucking dampness in this place was atrocious. Then if ye fell down the fucking stair, that was another thing, the polybag man fumbling the record and it falls out the sleeve, smash; in the name of fuck.

Somebody turned the corner coming up, somebody coming up. Robert moved sideways to make space. It was the guy from the record stall. The other customer. Him browsing the CDs. He looked straight at Robert. A hard look. For whatever reason. Then he says, Heh bud, ye spare a fag?

A fag, aye, okay. Robert sniffed. The guy had brought out his ayn tobacco tin, a wee auld-looking thing, and he prised off the lid. It was empty inside. Not a fucking shred.

Robert had less than half an ounce himself. He split it and gave the guy haufers. The guy nodded. He didnay say thanks, he concentrated on the tobacco. Probably he would have done the same. That was how Robert read it. He gave the guy a few papers. Another time another place, the boot on the other foot, we've all been there, bla bla bla. Some might have read it different. Fair enough. At that moment but it was Robert and how he read it. Nothing to do with any other cunt. There must have been threequarters of a half ounce in the tin so what he gave him was the equivalent of eight fags, depending how thick ye rolled them. The guy was rolling one already, it would be thin; the guy would roll them thin. An educated guess, from the school of life. Robert didnay like them too thin himself but he knew the guy would; where he came from, wherever that was. Robert could have guessed about that too. He carried on down the stairs. What he had noticed was how when the guy spoke it was out the corner of his mouth, watching what he was saying and who was listening. Nay question the guy had done time, that was for fucking definite. Public spaces, watching yer back. His eyes too. What was it about his eyes? What the fuck was it? Robert couldnay think. Except the creeps, the fucking heebie-jeebies, but it wasnay as bad as that. Eyes gieing ye the heebie-jeebies. Gie us a break. How can eyes gie ye the heebie-jeebies? If ye are a grown man? Gieing ye the heebie-jeebies means ye get scared. So he was scared! What of? That guy? Ye fucking kidding?

Robert didnay know what it was, except it wasnay that. Maybe it had to do with the close; this actual building. How long had this place been on the go? What kind of things happened in here. Some horrible stuff, ye can put yer money on that. There again but why blame the building? It wasnay the building's fault. That was bricks and mortar. It isnay the close but the people up the close. Jesus christ, even the thought! Just stupid, stupid.

Down the stairs and out the close. He went fast, fast. Almost like scared, he wasnay scared: he wasnay scared. Fucking hell man he had been up and down this stair for years. All round-about here. He wasnay a Calton boy but he had jumped about the place all his life. The Barrows was the Calton. The Calton had a history; a fucking real one. Good stuff happened here. Bad too, all the way back; weans getting snatched from their families and stuck on a boat ower the sea; these churches doing the dirty work. Cheap labour for capitalist cunts in Australia or wherever, fucking Canada. Fucking place, nay wonder it gave ye the creeps. The guy was a throw-back. What did he actually say? Ye spare a fag, ye got a fag, ye got a smoke, ye spare a smoke, a wee dod of yer tobacco?

Nayn of that at all, it was just how he looked. What is it eyes do? Eyes do something. Eyes gie ye the creeps. How come? What is it they do? They have to do something. What can eyes do? A pair of eyes. They look. They hypnotise. Eyes hypnotise. If ye let them. It is all about will. Do ye want to be hypnotised? If so ye shall be hypnotised. Okay him up the close, he wasnay smarmy but at the same time – what is the opposite of 'smarmy'? That guy was the fucking exact opposite of 'smarmy'. He didnay give a fuck. Robert gied him haufers because if he hadnay

Because if he hadnay.

Robert was smoking by this time, and he needed it. There was a wee café along the street. He bypassed it, glad to be walking in the fresh air, daylight, sun and blue sky. Thank fuck.

Seriously but what was he doing rooting about secondhand record stalls! That LP summed it up. Mario Lanza by christ! He should never have bought the damn thing. How come he bought it? Fucking stupidity. Tracy – she never listened much to music anyway. No properly. It was aye just background for her like if she was doing the ironing or something: ye switched it off and she didnay notice.

A coffee was required. Better still a pint.

He would gie her the album exactly the way it was. She would see Ernest Tubb in the stetson hat and think it was a joke. Well it was a joke. In a way. At the same time

Up ahead was a commotion. What was it? A wee crowd had gathered. Somebody caught thieving. A boy about thirteen or fourteen. A stallholder had a grip of him and was slapping him about the shoodirs and the back of the heid. It was a liberty. The boy went down on the ground yelling, feet in the air trying to shield himself. A couple of folk had the phones out taking pictures. Viral in the morning, the boy fuckt, it was a shame.

Fucking farcical too, the stallholder, some man he was. Ye felt like shouting it to him: Some hero you ya cunt, battering a boy.

Fucking boo ya bastard. That was what Robert was thinking. These guys think they can fight. Cowardly cunts, knocking a boy about.

When he stopped hitting him the boy got up off the ground, rubbing his neck then doing some funny wriggling thing with his arms, like he was fixing them back in the joints. He was making funny wee noises and rubbing at his ribs. He knew people were watching, maybe wondering if somebody else was goni take a swipe at him.

Robert headed back to the Gallowgate, along up by the auld railway track, took a left and another left, wound up back at the Barrows again. He was away in a sort of fog, a fucking haze, a mental haze. How to say it? The world wasnay breaking in. He knew he was walking but where to? Where was he walking and what was he thinking about? Nay idea. Hypnotists or some fucking thing. Where did that come from, hypnotists? How come he was thinking about hypnotists? He wasnay thinking about them, it was just in his head, the idea of it, hypnotists and eyes, eyes looking. Usually his head was full of all sorts; worries about his ayn boy and how life was for him, if his marriage was falling apart, sometimes it looked that way and then what would happen? The wee granddaughter, worries about her. What if she went with her mother's side of the family? The marriage broke up and the boy's missis took the lassie. She would. Mothers got the wean. That was what happened. So she wouldnay come to visit. So him and Tracy wouldnay see her. If that happened man, that would be fucking horrible. Tracy doted on that wee lassie. What would happen then? if she didnay come visiting! Fuck.

That was life but. Ye couldnay do nothing either. That son of his, Robert couldnay talk to him. Ye saw him make mistakes and ye couldnay tell him. He was just a worry. How could ye relax ye couldnay. Robert couldnay, this that and the next fucking thing, these cunts, fucking bastards man just worries everywhere, fucking politics, people getting shafted by that bunch of fucking rightwing fucking horrible fucking fascist bastards, the fucking British so-called fucking government, gie Robert a bomb man fucking Guy Fawkes ye kidding! Robert would blow the bastards up, he would sit on the fucking roof and light a fire in below his fucking arse man fuck these cunts, he would blow them to fucking smithereens man, fucking bastards.

Robert stopped at the corner, the corner of the street. A wallpaper shop. Where had that come from? He didnay remember it. He looked in the window. An excuse to stop walking. He couldnay fucking be bothered. The walk should have been clearing his heid but it wasnay. It should have been getting fresh air into his lungs, but it wasnay. He needed his lungs to be clear and full of fresh oxygen. These strange fucking weird feelings ye get sometimes. Robert was getting one now. Another part of his brain was thinking Tracy Tracy what if, what if – and the what if here was a fucking heart attack. Whose? His! Obviously fucking his man who else's? No Tracy's, she was built like a fucking –

whatever man, a rolls royce, a fucking bulldozer. Yer brain does mair than think, it goes to work with yer body. If yer brain isnay working yer body isnay either. Two guys passed; one had a phone in his hand and was talking into it. The other one glared at Robert. What for? What was he glaring at Robert for? Robert didnay know him from Adam and he stepped back the way but it was Micky jesus christ – Micky!

Where's your heid! said Micky, grinning.

Fuck sake Micky!

Calm down. How ye doing man?

I'm doing alright, aye.

Good. How's Tracy?

Aye fine, aye. Audrey, how's Audrey?

Aye good, she's good. What is that? Micky pointed at the album in the polybag.

A book, said Robert.

Micky chuckled, glancing at his mate. Robert took out the LP and showed them it. Never judge a book by the covers, he said, about to relate the tale of the vinyl and Missis Girnygub but before he could say anything the guy with Micky asked, Who's the cowboy? And he pointed at the hat Ernest Tubb was wearing in the picture. It's a stetson, said Robert. People wear them in America, it doesnay mean they're cowboys.

Ye like cowboys?

Robert glanced at Micky. The guy was peering at the album cover. Robert held it so it was easier to read. The guy said, Billy Bobs . . . ?

That's the name of the album *Alive at Billy Bobs*. Ernest Tubb is the singer, said Robert. Billy Bobs is a venue. It's no cowboys, know what I mean, it's country music.

Micky's mate grinned. Never mind the cowboys, what about the indians!

Robert looked at him. He felt like laughing too but no at the stupid joke, if that was what it was.

Micky said, It's what's inside that counts. Eh Robert?

Mair like who's inside, said his mate.

Micky laughed. His mate said, I could tell ye a few stories.

We could all tell stories, said Robert, but some of us cannay.

Micky didnt say anything. His mate smiled. Robert stared at him. Even if we want to we cannay, he said. Know what I mean, we do things for people and that's that. We're no all selfish bastards. Ye meet somebody out the game, what do ye do, ye help him along, that's what ye fucking do, that's life, that separates us from the fucking animals, the ruling-class man know what I'm talking about? A guy's in the grubber ye help him out. Robert sniffed. He shifted and spat into the gutter. We've all been there, he said. I have anyway, I dont know about you. Robert glanced at Micky. Actions speak louder than words Micky know what I'm saying?

Micky smiled.

Robert shrugged. It's no a big deal, he said. Ye just appreciate it when somebody does ye a turn.

How's the Missis? asked Micky.

Aye ye said that, said Robert, she's doing fine.

Was she no ill?

I'm meeting her the now, said Robert.

Tell her I was asking for her anyway.

Will do.

Micky gave him a wave. Robert nodded. He should have said the same back to him about his wife – Audrey. A good-looking woman, a bit on the heavy side for Robert, no that that mattered. He used to know her quite well too. There was an auld lady called Mabel was a friend of his mother. Mabel! Ye didnay get Mabels nowadays. A lot of these other names too. Audrey, a nice-looking woman. That was life but how things changed. Everything did. Robert crossed the road into one of the covered market areas. Two stalls next to each other were selling mobile phones and the one next to that was selling covers for mobile phones and calling them blankets. Phone blankets. In the name of fuck.

Robert carried straight through and out the other side. A pint would have been nice but he couldnay go for one, in case it was two. Twenty minutes to rendezvous. That would be that if Tracy arrived and he wasnay there to meet her. She wouldnay stand on her ayn. Women get pestered.

Ah fuck it, he went for a pint. Life drives ye to drink and here he was. He ordered a Guinness and a packet of strong mints. Some pubs keep them in stock. They disguise the smell of booze. That was what ye hoped. Probably they didnay.

He watched the barman pour the pint. His wasnay the first thank christ. Ye have to watch it on a Sunday morning, first out the barrel's a barrel of laughs. Once he near choked, swallied a mouthful and thought he was goni spew, a mixture of Irn-Bru and fuck knows what else, the entire dregs' tray.

He was feeling better already. Relaxed is the word. It is all ye ask for, a seat and a sip of beer. He had been tense. He realised that.

The sun was shining in the window, revealing the dust. It was shocking what ye breathed in. The worst was wee hairs. What else? Ye didnay want to think about it.

Robert left with five minutes to go, sucked a mint going along London Road when who should he see but Tracy in among a crowd round a crockery stall. That was good, he hadnay expected it.

He touched her elbow. She was engrossed in the proceedings, and almost smiled. The stallholder was a whizz at the job. Next thing he was tossing a pile of dinner plates up in the air. He flipped them, and caught them as they fell. What a clatter! How would they survive? Surely they had to at least crack? But naw. The guy was a juggler supreme, calling out how good a purchase it was, dear at half the price and the same auld patter.

Then Tracy was holding her hand up! Oh for christ sake and the guy flung a set at her. An entire set of fucking dinner plates man he fucking flung them! Oh but no at her thank christ. A guy standing next to her in the crowd, he caught them instead, he was one of the stallholder's helpers. He shovelled them into a big cardboard box, and was about to heave it onto Tracy. She waved it onto Robert instead while she paid the guy the money. While she was doing that Robert thought to check the plates to make sure they were okay. Except they were crammed so tight it was hard to see. It wasnay the right box man it was too fucking tight how they were wedged in. It was just fucking a joke, it was a joke! The way the guy flung them too, it was a wonder they werenay all smashed. Ye pay good money and who takes care? Nay cunt.

Be careful, said Tracy.

I am, he said, I was wanting to check them out.

Doesnay matter, she said.

Christ hen we're entitled to check!

It'll be okay. It will, it'll be okay.

Robert nodded. Probably ye could have bought the same stuff in Argyle Street for half the price. But he didnay mention that.

There's still curtains to get, she added.

Nay bother. We'll have a bite to eat after.

If we dont get them the day when will we?

Will we what?

Get the curtains?

Naw I know hen I'm just saying once ye've got them we'll go for a bite to eat.

Ye cannay keep putting things off.

I'm no trying to put anything off. We'll get the curtains right now.

If we can find them.

Aye well if ye dont ye might find other stuff.

Tracy sighed. Is that sarcasm?

Not at all.

It sounded like it to me.

Well it wasnay.

I thought ye were going up to look at the tools?

I did but that was a while ago. I bought an LP . . . Robert indicated the polybag wrapped round his wrist, then gestured at the bags Tracy was carrying. Want me to carry them?

No.

Ye sure?

Give me yours.

It's okay.

Robert, give me it. The dinner service is enough.

Ye sure?

Just give me it. Tracy unfankled the bag from his wrist. She smelled his breath. Did you go for a pint?

Just the one.

She nodded. Robert shrugged. He had to step out the way for a young woman with a roll of linoleum over her shoulder who was shoving a pram at the same time and had a wee girl clinging onto her wrist. How the hell did she manage it! And where was her husband? Probably in the fucking boozer. Unless he was working. Nowadays ye had to. Weekends went for nothing. Nay overtime and nay days off in lieu. It was like the whole world had changed. The older generation wouldnay have recognised it. Then politics. Nay politics. A young woman like that too, she shouldnay have been carrying a roll of linoleum. It was an offcut too, the price of linoleum these days, fucking extortionate. She was heading into one of the big covered areas, going quite quickly, and the way the wee girl clung onto the pram ye hoped she wouldnay fall. Wee kids werenay always quick, if they took a tumble and banged their chin or something, one time it happened to Robert's young brother and his teeth came right through the lip, and the blood jesus christ beyond crying, he was in fucking agony. Robert helped him hame and Maw had to rush him up to the Sick Children's Hospital. Robert went too. That was the young brother. When did they last have a pint the gether? Fucking months ago.

He followed Tracy along. This corner of the street was busy. It was awkward with the box. It had to be on his forearms; he couldnay get the shoodirs into it; no properly. So where was the power there? The same like throwing a punch if ye couldnay get some force behind it, it wasnay even a punch, if ye couldnay get yer shoodirs into it, that was basic man that was the whole fucking thing.

The box of crockery balanced in his arms. Something about it made him smile. Except the sun! Where was the sun? Clouds. The sun was there and now it wasnay. How come? It was supposed to be sunny all day then it wasnay. Imagine a downpour!

The cardboard box would get soaked. The plates would be fine, just a wash. Probably they needed a wash, so if the rain did come . . . It wasnay that bad anyhow. White clouds passing, that wasnay rain.

Anyway if it did ye just got on with it. That was life. Get on with it. People said that: Get on with it!

The curtain place was half a street away and ye could see the bloke there gieing his spiel. Behind there was another stall, a weer one selling some kind of contraption – a gadget. Some kind of thing. A new invention. Labour-saving. So they said. They aye said. Two women were there watching. Ages with him. Quite nice-looking too; one especially, and smiling, that smile. It was a nice smile. A lot of women had it. What was that smile? Women just smiled. The stallholder guy was in with the patter. Aw aye missis, I know, ye've already got a labour-saving device, yer man; he's the one wears the trousers, unless it's you wears the trousers. Ha ha ha.

Aw jesus christ embarrassing, that was a showing up. Stupid auld fucking jokes. The women laughing too. How come? That wasnay funny in the slightest. It was bloody sexist man it was shite. Robert didnay like that kind of thing. That was yer 'nay politics'. Everywhere ye looked, 'nay politics' here, 'nay politics' there. Fucking tadger politicians man. Naybody knew what ye were talking about. Politics, I'm talking about politics! Robert shook his head.

The stallholder guy took something out a bag that looked like a hi-fi separate with two ends attached. Nay wires that ye could see. It maybe worked off wi-fi. Currents through the air. A funny-shaped thing aw the gether. It had wee feet, like castors, but not for moving, the opposite: for gripping! What would that be for? A slidey surface maybe. Some kind of biggish peeler or chopper with a strong vibration so if it didnay have the feet it would skite about the table. Robert wasnay that good with mechanical stuff. No bad, but no great.

Other women were there too. The stallholder was about to start the demonstration. Robert shuffled a bit nearer. The first thing he saw was a load of dirt spread across the stall table. Ye couldnay avoid seeing it. A right load of it there on the surface. What was that about? The guy with his stupid fucking contraption. Start with the basics for fuck sake. Clean tools, know what I'm talking about, a dirty worker man. Gie the table a wipe, he said.

The guy looked at him.

Gie the table a wipe. Robert snorted and glanced at the women.

The young guy winked at somebody. He's my straight man!

Fucking straight man . . . Robert turned his head.

The guy stopped with the contraption and peered at Robert. What are ye interested in buying? he asked.

Robert held his gaze.

The guy said, Eh?

The women were watching. Robert said, Naw son.

How no?

Because I dont need it.

Need what? said the guy and he winked, he winked at the women.

So that was him and there was Robert the fucking daftie. Well well. Little cunt, nay idea, just nay idea. Robert smiled. That? he said, pointing at the thing. I dont even know what it is.

Then how come ye dont need it? if ye dont know what it is?

Robert smiled.

The guy kept looking at him, kidding on it was a serious question. Quite a cheeky thing to do; really, when ye thought about it. The women were waiting on Robert to say something. Another two women as well, they were there too, but they werent smiling. They would have seen the cheeky wee bastard for what he was worth. A good fucking smack on the jaw he needed. Nay wonder the stall was quiet. The guy wasnay smiling now. He said to Robert, Ye might surprise yerself and buy it.

Ye kidding!

I thought ye wanted to buy it. Eh, I thought ye wanted to buy it?

Robert smiled. Ye're being cheeky now.

The young guy stopped and looked like he was taken by

surprise. Who me? like it was the very last thing he wanted to be was cheeky.

What do ye think I'm a fucking idiot? said Robert.

What? said the guy. What ye talking about?

I cannay fight! Ye think I cannay fight? I'll fucking batter you son any day of the week. I'm no some wee boy, ye want to take me on ye take me on, and I'll take ye round that fucking corner and fucking . . . fucking batter fucking lumps ya little cunt, fucking lumps out ye. Robert gripped the cardboard box, stopping himself, stopping himself from going any further he would be across that fucking stall and grabbing the cunt and flinging bloody – jesus christ. People think ye're a fucking nutter. Robert stared at the guy. The guy was watching Robert. Robert knew what he was doing. Some people watch and it doesnay count but this one was different. He was waiting for his chance and he was like, Who are you ya cunt, that was how he was acting. Who are you! Robert. Who was Robert? Ha ha. Fucking bastard man after the life he had had? A little prick like that, no knowing fuck all but acting like everything, just everything. And he stood there no moving an inch, this young guy, stall-holder bastard, he wasnay moving an inch: till that wee sideways look. Robert saw it! And knew what it was. It was a signal to his fucking mates! If any of his mates were there, that was that. Fucking team-handed, that was how they would come at him. Ha ha fucking ha.

Robert smiled. Ye had to laugh at these bastards. Naybody was there anyway. Eh? he said to the guy. Where's yer mates? They goni come and gie me a doing, eh, is that what it is? fucking little fucking, hoh! Robert shook his head, fucking chib the cunt man is that it, fucking chib me ya fucking halfwit bammy bastard, fucking life I've had ya fucking – stallholder cunts man all sticking the gether if one of ye gets a doing yez are all into it the gether, take on one ye take on the fleet, ya cunts ye, you and the fucking polis, fucking bastards.

Tracy was there, at his side, tugging his sleeve. Worried about him. Goni be a heart attack, what, a stroke. Nay stroke, he said, dont worry.

For Heaven sake, she said.

The young guy was standing there shaking his head. Take him away for christ sake, he said.

What? Robert smiled. Take me away?

The guy turned his back. There were other people there, just punters, just watching. That was Robert, it was him. Thinking there was goni be a fight. Nay fight. Ye dont fight cunts like that ye fucking batter them. Robert glanced at Tracy. Forget it, he said.

Tracy didnt respond here but just made sure Robert knew he was to come away and not get any further involved. Of course. Robert knew that. She was stating the obvious. Of course he wasnay getting involved. Nay need worrying about that. That was women just like worrying worrying, women worrying, how come they worry? worrying about shite, as if Robert was goni let a cunt like that, a young fucking stupid fucking idiot man a fucking numbskull fucking whippersnapper bastard.

Tracy said, Robert for God sake.

Robert shook his head, took the polybag from her, the vinyl album.

Robert!

I'll go back there and batter fuck out him, he said, if he thinks I'm goni just like take shite — what, off him? I'll take shite off him! Fucking kidding! Robert stopped walking, set to return any moment, any moment. Tracy. Tracy staring at him, she had stopped too, he saw her face.

Oh Robert . . .

Dont worry, he said.

Where's the dinner service?

He frowned, looked about, then returned to the stall immediately. A few people were there, the guy demonstrating the contraption. Robert moved in without looking at him, not even glancing in his direction, just nothing, just bending to lift the big cardboard box off the ground under the table, from where he had laid it, he had laid it; this was where, out the road; just making it safe. He had forgot. Nay wonder.

The guy was watching him, had paused in the spiel. The wee smile. Who cares, the cunt. Robert ignored him but was awkward with the big cardboard box, still with the polybag, pulling the two ends ower his left wrist – nowadays his strongest. Another what-if scenario, ye fumble one and drop the other one trying to catch it. What if, what if – she had gied him her bags to carry? What if she had? He would have been struggling. He couldnay have managed it, and if he had left them under the stall they would have been fucking away. Some cunt would have lifted them. They would have been fucking gone and Tracy would have been up to high doh: what a nightmare. It was all mad. Everything. That was him but what a fool, just a fucking daftie. Tracy knew that. She caught him in time. If it wasnay for her. She stopped him. She stopped the process. It was a process and she halted it, she put the blocks on. She laughed about it too, she wasnay letting her man, something happen to her man, she wasnay letting that happen, nothing was goni happen to him.

It isnay that he was looking for gratitude off that guy. He had fuck all and Robert gave him haufers. He didnay regret it. Why should he?

It was just something in how the guy looked. Ye think of 'gloating'. Just fucking gloating. Because Robert gave him the tobacco. Like maybe he had won, like it was a fucking fight or some damn stupid thing, he was out to screw Robert and there ye are he had done it, a fucking knockout man, kay-oh you nine ten fucking out, hauf a wad ya fucking dumpling.

What did he think Robert had never done time? Fucking halfwit fucking bastard. Never done time! Ha fucking ha. Robert would have battered the cunt.

Talk about survival. That's the fittest. Robert was aye fit, the greatest athletes of all, that was boxers, better than any cunt; runners, fucking weightlifters man fitba players dont talk about fitba players, their fucking ham and eggs thingwi, the way they go about jack the fucking lad right enough, Robert would have whacked the bastards, any fucking one of them, ye're a boxer man that's a weapon, yer fists are weapons. That was auld Andra drumming it into them, get yer balance son yer balance, look at that, I'll push ye ower, one pinky, ye're off balance, wherrs yer shoodirs punch with yer shoodirs, ye were just proud, Robert was proud, ye were a fucking boxer and ye were fucking proud man and ye try telling these cunts, ye cannay, ye cannay fucking tell them. He knew Robert's granda too, auld Andra knew him, Oh aye son, he said and he laughed because like granda, say hello to the General. Granda I'm only going to train, it isnay Franco.

It annoyed him but. Nay wonder. Making it a big deal, it wasnay a big deal. That was Micky too, him and his stupid fucking mate fucking doughball cunt making it a big deal. It wasnay a big deal. Just a guy down on his luck and ye gied him haufers. Ye're in the grubber man that's the story, we've all been there. In this day and age especially.

Micky had nay politics. Who did but these days? Nay cunt. Fucking nationalists and fucking what have ye, rightwing cunts. Fighting the good fight. Who fought that? No nowadays. That aulder generation man they were the goodies. No Robert. Fuck Robert. Robert wasnay. He just wasnay. He fucking knew he wasnay man fucking bastards, fuck that. He kept walking, holding onto the stuff, boxes and fucking fuck knows what. He was going along London Road and he could just have kept on walking. That was the wey he felt. Sun shining. Fuck the lot of them. Except he had to go back. He fancied a seat. He was bloody tired. All the stupidities, just stupidities. She would keep him right. That was Tracy. She knew these things. Woman do, they know, what is it they know? They know something. Or dont. A guy like Robert. Having to fight. He had to fight. He didnay fucking fight but how come? How come? He didnay batter that cunt, how come? He needed a battering. Robert was the boy would do it. Fucking taking shite off him! What is that a joke? Fucking comic cuts man ha ha ha. The guy took the tobacco and rolled a fag and never even looked at him. Not even a look. A stupit fucking look! He didnay even do that. Never mind a 'thanks mate'. Nothing. Sure it rankled. It rankled. Somebody gies ye something be good enough to say thanks, it isnay much to ask. Fucking bastard man what did he think, Robert was auld? Aye he was auld but he wasnay too auld.

The kind of cunt that buys military medals and Nazi helmets, one of these cunts, fucking Nazi hero-worshippers, racist bastards fucking fuckpigs. Memorabilia. Soldiers dying meant nothing to them. It did to Robert. He might no believe in the patriotic shite but yer comrades dying was a different story. Okay ye're opposed to the war and opposed to the army. Okay. Fine, the fucking capitalist enemy, we all know about that. But that was the auld days. Auld days is auld days.

People tell ye stuff and ye believe them. Boys believe stuff. Robert was a boy. Battalion champion man the age of eighteen. That was proud, attenshun ya fucking bastards. See if the enemy's over the hill, there's a good fellow.

His maw and da said fuck all. It was up to them and they

said fuck all. So then if ye do join up whose fault is that?

Aye and it does rankle, ye go wrong and he gies ye a look. That was Da. That look he gied. People gie ye looks. Just their eyes. Do they even know they're doing it? Maybe they dont. And ye were just doing yer best. That was being a boy, ye just done yer best and ye got shat upon, time after time after time, the boy getting a doing, that stallholder cunt, ye were doing yer best, what happened? they gied ye a kicking. Behind the Naafi club, these cunts, ha ha, fucking three of them man that was what it took, two lance corporals and fucking fuckpig whatever the fuck he was who gives a fuck. Robert got sick of it, the fucking lot of them. Military fucking medals. Any auld shite and they sold it. Except honesty. Ye got fuck all for that. Other people, if ye thought about them, that was that. He wasnay ashamed of it. Fuck gratitude, these cunts, fuck them. The likes of the older generation, ye think of them, all it takes is once. Just once. Conned and cheated and ripped off. Except if ye started thinking about it ye would never leave the house. Except what happens in the house? The fucking washing machine goes on the blink. The fucking telly. Ye break a plate, doing the fucking dishes, there goes another tumbler and ye've cut yer wrist again, oh Robert that's a deep one. Deep one fuck all. She didnay even know what a cut was. Robert bled. He wasnay a bleeder but he bled. Some guys are bleeders. Great fighters. One tap on the nose man that's them. The outside aerial, he was going up to fix that. What if ye fall off? What if what if. But ye've got to go up because who else? No yer boy, he's got his ayn fucking life, all his worries, worry worry. Only you. Get up there! The fucking roof too, a windy day man know what I'm talking about, night-time. Okay ye do it. Okay backwards. That was auld Andra, lose yer balance son and kay-oh aff ye go, it is windy, ye have to balance, ye just balance. Ssshh, quiet, the weans are sleeping.